The Devotion of Suspect X

Keigo Higashino

TRANSLATED BY ALEXANDER O. SMITH
WITH ELYE J. ALEXANDER

W F HOWES LTD

This large print edition published in 2011 by
W F Howes Ltd
Unit 4, Rearsby Business Park, Gaddesby Lane,
Rearsby, Leicester LE7 4YH

1 3 5 7 9 10 8 6 4 2

First published in the United Kingdom in 2011
by Little, Brown

A CIP catalogue record for this book is available
from the British Library

ISBN 978 140748 590 4

Typeset by Palimpsest Book Production Limited,
Falkirk, Stirlingshire
Printed and bound in Great Britain
by MPG Books Ltd, Bodmin, Cornwall

CHAPTER 1

At 7:35 A.M. Ishigami left his apartment as he did every weekday morning. Just before stepping out onto the street, he glanced at the mostly full bicycle lot, noting the absence of the green bicycle. Though it was already March, the wind was bitingly cold. He walked with his head down, burying his chin in his scarf. A short way to the south, about twenty yards, ran Shin-Ohashi Road. From that intersection the road ran east into the Edogawa district, west towards Nihonbashi. Just before Nihonbashi, it crossed the Sumida River at the Shin-Ohashi Bridge.

The quickest route from Ishigami's apartment to his workplace was due south. It was only a quarter mile or so to Seicho Garden Park. He worked at the private high school just before the park. He was a teacher. He taught maths.

Ishigami walked south to the red light at the intersection, then he turned right, towards Shin-Ohashi Bridge. The wind blew in his face, making his coat flap around him. He thrust his hands deep into his pockets and hunched over, quickening his pace.

A thick layer of clouds covered the sky, their

1

grey reflection making the Sumida River look even murkier than usual. A small boat was making its way upstream. Ishigami noted its progress as he crossed the bridge.

On the other side, he took a set of stairs that led from the foot of the bridge down to the Sumida. Passing beneath the iron struts of the bridge, he began to walk along the river. Pedestrian walkways were built into the moulded concrete riverbanks on both sides of the water. Further down, near Kiyosu Bridge, families and couples often strolled along the river, but such people seldom visited the riverbanks this far up. The long row of cardboard shanties covered in blue vinyl sheets kept them away. This was where the homeless lived, in the shadow of an expressway overpass that ran along the west side of the river. Ishigami figured the looming overpass must have provided some shelter from the wind and rain. The fact that not a single shack stood on the other side of the river gave weight to this hypothesis, though it was possible the first squatters had settled there by accident and the others had simply followed them, preferring the safety of their community, such as it was, to solitude across the water.

He made his way down the row of shanties, glancing briefly at them as he walked. Most were barely tall enough for a man to stand up inside, and some of the structures only rose as high as his waist. They were more boxes than shacks. Maybe it was enough to have a place to sleep.

Plastic laundry hangers had been rigged up near the boxes, signs of domestic life. A man was leaning up against the railing that ran between the walkway and the water, brushing his teeth. Ishigami had seen him around. He was past sixty, and his greyish white hair was bound in a long ponytail. He had probably given up on work. If it was physical labour he wanted, he wouldn't have been hanging around now. Those jobs were filled in the early morning hours. He wouldn't be going to the unemployment office, either. Even if they did find a job suitable for him, with that long hair of his he'd never make it as far as the interview. The chances of anyone wanting him for a job at his age were close to zero anyway.

Another man stood near his sleeping box, crushing a row of empty cans under his foot. Ishigami had witnessed this scene several times before, and he had secretly named this fellow the Can Man. The Can Man looked to be around fifty. He had good clothes and even a bicycle. Ishigami figured that his can-collecting trips kept him more active and alert than the others. He lived at the edge of the community, deep under the bridge, which must have been a position of privilege. The Can Man was a village elder, then – an old-timer, even in this crowd – or so Ishigami saw him.

A little way on from where the line of cardboard shanties petered out, another man was sitting on a bench. His coat must have once been beige, but now it was scuffed and grey. He was wearing a suit jacket underneath it, though, and beneath that a white work shirt. Ishigami guessed that he had a necktie stashed away in his coat pocket. Ishigami had labelled him the Engineer a few days earlier, after spotting him reading an industrial trade magazine. He kept his hair cropped short, and he shaved. Maybe he hoped he'd be going back to work soon. He would be off to the unemployment office today, but he probably wouldn't find a job. He would have to lose his pride before that happened. Ishigami had first seen the Engineer about ten days ago. He wasn't used to life along the river yet, still drawing an imaginary line between himself and the blue vinyl sheets. Yet here he stayed, not knowing how to live on his own without a home.

Ishigami continued walking along the river. Just before Kiyosu Bridge, he came upon an elderly woman taking three dogs for a walk. The dogs were miniature dachshunds, each with a different coloured collar: one red, one blue, and one pink. As he approached, the woman seemed to notice him. She smiled and nodded. He nodded in reply.

'Good morning,' he offered.

'Good morning. Cold, isn't it?'

'Quite,' he replied, grimacing for effect.

The old woman bade him a good day as she passed by, and he gave her a final nod.

Some days before, Ishigami had seen the woman carrying a plastic convenience store bag with

4

something like sandwiches in it – probably her breakfast. He surmised from this that she lived alone. Her home wouldn't be far from here. She was wearing flip-flops, and she wouldn't be able to drive a car in those. She had probably lost her husband years before and now lived in a nearby apartment with her three dogs. A big place, if she was keeping three dogs there. No doubt her pets had kept her from moving to a smaller room somewhere. Maybe she had already paid off the mortgage, but there would still be maintenance fees, so she had to scrimp and save. She hadn't been to the beauty salon once this winter. Her hair showed its natural colour, free from dye.

At the foot of Kiyosu Bridge, Ishigami climbed the stairs back up to the road. The school was across the bridge from here, but he turned and walked in the opposite direction.

A sign facing the road read 'Benten-tei'. Beneath it was a small shop that made boxed lunches. Ishigami slid open the aluminium-framed glass door.

'Good morning! Come in, come in,' came the call. It was a familiar greeting and a familiar voice, but it somehow always managed to put a spring in his step. Yasuko Hanaoka smiled at him from behind the counter. She was wearing a white hat.

Ishigami felt another thrill as he realized that there were no other customers in the shop. They were alone.

'I'll take the special.'

'One special, coming up,' she replied brightly. Ishigami couldn't see her expression as he was staring into his wallet, unable to look her in the face. Given that they lived next door to each other, Ishigami felt like he should have something to talk about other than his boxed lunch order, but nothing came to mind.

When he finally came up with 'Cold today, isn't it', he mumbled the words, and they were lost in the sound of another customer opening the sliding glass door behind him. Yasuko's attention had turned to the new arrival.

Boxed lunch in hand, Ishigami walked out of the store. This time, he headed straight for Kiyosu Bridge, his detour to Benten-tei finished.

After the morning rush, things slowed down at Benten-tei, at least as far as customers were concerned. In the back, however, there were lunches to be made. Several local companies had the shop deliver meals for all their employees by twelve o'clock. So, when the customers stopped coming, Yasuko would go back into the kitchen to lend a hand.

There were four employees at Benten-tei. Yonazawa was the manager, assisted by his wife Sayoko. Kaneko, a part-timer, was responsible for making deliveries, while Yasuko dealt with all the in-shop customers.

Before her current job, Yasuko had worked in a nightclub in Kinshicho. Yonazawa had been a

regular there and Sayoko had been the club's
mama – though Yasuko hadn't known they were
married until just before Sayoko quit.

'She wants to go from being the *mama* at a bar
to the good wife at a lunch shop,' Yonazawa had
told her. 'Can you believe it? Some people never
fail to surprise me.' Rumours had begun to fly at
the club, but according to Sayoko, it had been the
couple's long-held dream to run a place of their
own. She had only been working at the club to
save up for that.

After Benten-tei opened, Yasuko had made a
habit of dropping in now and then to see how the
two were doing. Business was apparently good –
good enough that, a year later, they asked her if
she'd be interested in helping out. It had become
too much for the two of them to handle on their
own.

'You can't go on in that shady business forever,
Yasuko,' Sayoko had told her. 'Besides, Misato's
getting bigger. You wouldn't want her developing
a complex because her mum's a nightclub hostess.
Of course,' she'd added, 'it's none of my business.'

Misato was Yasuko's only daughter. There was
no father in her life after Yasuko's last divorce, five
years ago. Yasuko hadn't needed Sayoko to tell her
she couldn't go on as she was. Besides
her daughter's welfare, there was her own age to
consider. It was far from clear how long she could
have kept her job even if she wanted it.

It only took her a day to come to a decision,

and the club didn't even try to hold on to her. They had just wished her well, and that was all. Apparently she hadn't been the only one concerned about her future there.

She had moved into her current apartment in the spring a year ago, which coincided with Misato entering junior high school. Her old place was too far from her new job. And, unlike the club, getting to her new work on time meant getting up by six and being on her bicycle by six thirty. Her green bicycle.

'That high school teacher come again today?' Sayoko asked her during a break.

'Doesn't he come every day?' Yasuko replied, catching Sayoko sharing a grin with her husband. 'What? What's that for?'

'Oh nothing, nothing. We were just saying the other day how we thought he might fancy you.'

'Whaaat?' Yasuko leaned back from the table, a cup of tea in her hand.

'You were off yesterday, weren't you? Well, guess what? He didn't come in yesterday. Don't you think it's strange that he should come every day, except for the days when you're not here?'

'I think it's a coincidence.'

'Well, we think maybe it's not.' Sayoko glanced again at her husband.

Yonazawa nodded, still grinning. 'It's been going on for a while now,' he said with a nod at his wife. 'Every day that Yasuko's out, he doesn't come here for his lunch,' she says. 'I'd wondered about it

8

myself, to tell the truth, and when he didn't show yesterday, that kind of confirmed it for me.'

'But I don't have any set vacations, other than the days the whole shop is closed. It's not like I'm out every Monday or something obvious like that.'

'Which makes it even more suspicious!' Sayoko concluded, a twinkle in her eye. 'He lives next door to you, doesn't he? He must see you leave for work. That's how he knows.'

Yasuko shook her head. 'But I've never met him on my way out, not even once.'

'Maybe he's watching you from someplace. A window, maybe?'

'I don't think he can see my door from his window.'

'In any case, if he is interested, he'll say something sooner or later,' Yonazawa said. 'As far as we're concerned, we have a regular customer thanks to you, so it's good news for us. Looks like your training in Kinshicho paid off.'

Yasuko gave a wry smile and drank down the rest of her tea, thinking about the high school teacher.

His name was Ishigami. She had gone to his apartment the night she moved in to introduce herself. That's when she'd learned he was a teacher. He was a heavyset man, with a big, round face that made his small eyes look thin as threads. His hair was thinning and cut short, making him look nearly fifty, though he might easily have been much younger. He wasn't particularly fashion

9

conscious, always wearing the same sort of clothes. This winter, when he came in to buy his lunch, he was wearing the same coat over a brown sweater. Still, he did do his laundry, as was evidenced by the occasional presence of a drying rack on the small balcony of his apartment. He was single and, Yasuko guessed, not a divorcé or widower.

She thought back, trying to remember something that might have clued her in to his interest, but came up with nothing. He was like the thin crack in her apartment wall. She knew it was there, but she had never paid it that much attention. It just wasn't worth paying attention to.

They exchanged greetings whenever they met and had even discussed the management at their apartment building once. Yet Yasuko found she knew very little about the man himself. She had only recently learned that he taught maths, when she happened to notice outside his apartment door a bundle of old maths textbooks, wrapped in string and awaiting disposal.

Yasuko hoped he wouldn't ask her out on a date. Then she smiled to herself, trying and failing to imagine the dour-looking man's face as he asked the question.

As on every other day, the midday rush at Benten-tei began right before lunchtime, peaking just after noon. Things didn't really quiet down again until after one o'clock.

Yasuko was sorting the bills in the register when

the sliding glass door opened and someone walked in. 'Hello,' she chimed automatically, looking up. Then she froze. Her eyes opened wide and her voice caught in her throat.

'You look well,' said the man who was standing there. He was smiling, but his eyes were darkly clouded.

'You . . . how did you find me here?'

'Is it so surprising? I can find out where my ex-wife works if I have a mind to.' The man looked around the shop, both hands thrust into the pockets of his dark navy windbreaker, like a prospective customer trying to figure out what he should buy.

'But why? Why now?' Yasuko asked, her voice sharp but low. She glowered at him, inwardly praying that the Yonazawas in the back wouldn't hear them talking.

'Don't look so frightening. How long has it been since I saw you last? And you can't even manage a polite smile?' He grinned.

Yasuko shivered. 'If you're here to chitchat, you can save yourself the trouble and turn around right now.'

'Actually, I came for a reason. I have a favour to ask. Think you can get out for a bit?'

'Don't be an idiot. Can't you see I'm working?' Yasuko said, then immediately regretted it. *That makes it sound like I would talk with him if I wasn't at work.*

The man licked his lips. 'What time do you get off?'

11

'It doesn't matter. I don't want to talk to you. Please, just leave and don't come back.'

'Ouch. Cold.'

'What did you expect?'

Yasuko glanced outside, hoping that a customer would walk in, but the street was empty.

'Well, if this is how you're going to act, guess I'll try someone else,' the man said, scratching his head.

Warning bells went off in Yasuko's head. 'What do you mean by that?'

'I mean if my wife won't listen to me, maybe her daughter will. Her school's near here, right?'

'Don't you dare.'

'Okay, then maybe you *can* help. Either way's fine by me.'

Yasuko sighed. She just wanted him to leave. 'I'm on till six.'

'Early morning to six o'clock? That's some long hours they got you working.'

'It's none of your concern.'

'Okay, I'll come back at six, then.'

'No, not here. Take a right outside, and walk down the street until you come to a large inter-section. There's a family restaurant on the near corner. Be there at six thirty.'

'Great. And, try to make sure you're there. Because if you don't show up—'

'I'll be there. Just leave. Now.'

'Fine, fine. Kick me out on the street.' The man took another look around the shop before walking out, closing the sliding door behind him a little too hard.

Yasuko put her hand to her forehead. A headache was coming on, and she felt nauseated. A weight of hopelessness began to spread inside her chest.

It was eight years since she married Shinji Togashi. Now the whole sordid story replayed in her mind . . .

When she met him, Yasuko was working as a hostess in a club in Akasaka. Togashi was a regular.

He was a foreign-car salesman. He lived large, and he had included her in his high-flying lifestyle. He gave her expensive gifts, took her to pricey restaurants. When he proposed, she felt like Julia Roberts in *Pretty Woman*. She was tired of working long hours to support her daughter after a failed first marriage.

In the beginning, they were happy. Togashi had a steady income, so Yasuko could wash her hands of the nightclub scene. He was great with Misato, too, and for her part, Misato seemed to try hard to think of him as 'Daddy'.

When things fell apart, it happened suddenly. Togashi was fired from his job when his employers discovered that he had been embezzling company funds for years. The only reason they didn't press charges was that they wanted to cover the whole thing up, afraid their own judgment and oversight would be called into question. So there it was: all the money he had been spending in Akasaka had been dirty.

After that, Togashi changed. Or maybe it was just that the real person he had always been finally came to the surface. The days he didn't go out gambling he spent lying about at home. When Yasuko complained, he became violent. He started drinking more, too, until it seemed as though he was always bleary-eyed drunk and looking for a fight.

Yasuko had no choice but to go back to work. But all the money she made, Togashi took from her by force. When she tried hiding it, he started turning up at the club on payday and taking the money before she could stash it away.

Misato learned to be terrified of her stepfather. She didn't like being left alone with him at home. At times she even came to the club where Yasuko worked just to avoid him.

Yasuko asked Togashi for a divorce, but he wouldn't hear of it. When she pressed harder, he started hitting her. Finally after months of anguish she turned to a lawyer recommended by one of her customers. The lawyer was able to get a reluctant Togashi to sign the divorce papers. Evidently, her husband realized that he had no chance of winning in court and that unless he agreed to go quietly, he might even end up having to pay alimony.

Yet divorce alone did not solve the problem. In the months that followed, Togashi had made a habit of dropping in on Yasuko and her daughter. His affairs were all settled, he told her; he was

14

devoting himself to his work. Wouldn't she consider mending things between them? When Yasuko tried to avoid him, he started approaching Misato, sometimes even waiting outside her school.

When he came to Yasuko literally on his knees, she couldn't help but feel pity, even though she knew the whole thing was a performance. Perhaps a little bit of the affection she had once felt for him remained. She gave him a little money.

It was a mistake. Once Togashi got a taste, he started coming more frequently – always with the same grovelling demeanour, yet growing increasingly shameless in his requests.

Eventually Yasuko switched clubs and moved to a new apartment. Even though she hated to do it, she also changed Misato's school. And Togashi stopped appearing. Then a year ago she moved again and took the job at Benten-tei. She had wholly believed she had rid herself of that walking catastrophe for good.

She couldn't let the Yonazawas hear about her ex-husband and his reappearance. She didn't want to worry them. Misato couldn't know about it either. She had to make sure, on her own, that he never came back to see her again. Yasuko glanced at the clock on the wall and gritted her teeth.

Just before six thirty, she left the shop and made her way to the restaurant. She found Togashi sitting near the window, smoking. There was a coffee cup on the table in front of him. Yasuko sat

15

down, ordering hot cocoa from the waitress. She usually went for the soft drinks because of the free refills, but today she didn't intend to stay that long.

'Why?' she asked with a glare.

Togashi's mouth softened. 'You're sure in a hurry.'

'I've got a lot to do, so if you really have a good reason for coming here, out with it.'

'Yasuko—' Togashi reached out for her hand where it lay on the table. She drew it back quickly. His lip curled. 'You're in a bad mood.'

'Why shouldn't I be? You better have a good reason for stalking me like this.'

'So antagonistic! I know I might not look it, but I'm serious about this.'

'Serious about what?'

The waitress brought her cocoa. Yasuko picked it up and took a scalding sip. She wanted to drink it as fast as she could and get out of there.

'You're living by yourself, right?' Togashi asked, staring at her from under lowered brows.

'So? What business is it of yours?'

'Hard for a woman living by herself to raise a kid. She's just going to cost more and more, you know. What do they pay you at that lunch shop, anyway? You can't guarantee her future on that. Look, I want you to reconsider. Reconsider *us*. I've changed. I'm not like I was before.'

'What's changed? You working?'

'I will. I've already found a job.'

16

'But you're not working yet, are you.'

'I said I got a job. I'm supposed to start next month. It's a new company, but once things get rolling, hey, you and your daughter could live the easy life.'

'Thanks, but no thanks. If you're making all that money, I'm sure you won't have any problem finding someone else to share it with. Just, please, *leave us be.*'

'Yasuko, I need you.'

Togashi reached out again, trying to touch her hand where she held the cup. 'Don't touch me!' She recoiled from his grasp; a little bit of the cocoa spilled as she moved, dripping on Togashi's fingers. 'Ow!' He jerked back his hand. When next he looked at her there was malice in his eyes.

Yasuko glared back. 'You can't just come here and give me the same old lines, not after what's happened. How do you expect me to believe you? Like I said before, I haven't the slightest desire ever to be with you again, not the slightest. So just give it up. Okay?'

Yasuko stood. Togashi watched her in silence. Ignoring his gaze, she put the money for her cocoa down on the table and headed for the door.

As soon as she was outside the restaurant, she retrieved her bicycle from its parking spot and began to pedal away. She pictured Togashi running after her, snivelling, and it made her pedal faster. She went straight down Kiyosubashi Road, turning left after Kiyosu Bridge.

She had said everything there was to say, but she was sure she hadn't seen the last of him. He would show up at the shop again before long. He would stalk her, become a nuisance, maybe even make a scene. He might even show up at Misato's school. He would wait for Yasuko to give in, figuring that when she did, she would give him money.

Back at her apartment, Yasuko began making dinner. Dinner wasn't much more than warmed-up leftovers she had brought back from the shop, but even so, tonight cooking seemed like a difficult chore; every few moments her hands fell still as some horrible thought occurred to her, some scene played out in her mind.

Misato would be home soon. She was in the badminton club at school and usually spent time after practice talking with the other girls. She usually made it back around seven o'clock.

The doorbell rang. Yasuko frowned and went to the door. It wouldn't be Misato. She had her own key.

'Yes?' Yasuko called without opening the door. 'Who is it?'

There was a brief pause, and then, 'It's me.'

Yasuko didn't answer. Her vision dimmed. A terrible feeling crept up inside her. Togashi had already found their apartment. He had probably followed her from Benten-tei one night.

Togashi began knocking on the door. 'Oi!'

She shook her head and undid the lock, leaving the door chain fastened.

The door opened about four inches, revealing Togashi's face right on the other side. He grinned. His teeth were yellow.

'Why are you here? Go away.'

'I wasn't finished talking. Boy, short-tempered as always, aren't you?'

'I told you, we're done. Finished. Never again.'

'You can at least listen to what I have to say. Just let me in.'

'I won't. Go away.'

'Hey, if you won't let me in I'll just wait here. Misato should be getting home anytime now. If I can't talk to you, I'll just have to talk to her.'

'She's got nothing to do with this.'

'So let me in.'

'I'll call the police.'

'Go ahead. What's wrong with a man coming to visit his ex-wife? The police will take my side. *You could at least let him in, ma'am*, they'd say.'

Yasuko bit her lip. She hated to admit it, but he was probably right. She had called the police before, and they had never done the slightest thing to help her. That, and she didn't want to make a scene. Most tenants had a guarantor backing up their rent, but she had moved in here without one. One troubling rumour and she could be kicked out onto the street.

'Okay. But you have to leave right away.'

'Sure, of course,' Togashi said, a light of victory in his eyes.

Yasuko undid the chain and opened the door.

19

Togashi stepped in, taking off his shoes as he glanced around the room. It was a small apartment, just a kitchen and two other rooms. The room closest to the door was done in the Japanese style and was wide enough for six tatami mats on the floor, with a doorway on the right side leading into the kitchen. There was an even smaller Japanese-style room towards the back, and beyond that, a sliding door opened onto a small balcony.

'Little small, little old, but not a bad place,' Togashi commented as he sat down, tucking his legs underneath the low, heated kotatsu table in the middle of the room. 'Hey, your kotatsu's off,' he grumbled, fumbling around for the cord and switching it on.

'I know why you're here.' Yasuko stood, looking down at him. 'You can say whatever you like, but in the end, it's all about money.'

'What's that supposed to mean?' Togashi frowned, pulling a pack of Seven Stars from his jacket pocket. He lit one with a disposable lighter and started looking around more deliberately, noticing the lack of an ashtray for the first time. Getting up, he fished an empty can out of the rubbish and set it on the table. Sitting back down, he flicked his ashes into it.

'It means you're only here to get money out of me. I'm right, aren't I?'

'Well, if that's how you want it to be, then I'm fine with that.'

'You won't get a single yen out of me.'

He snorted. 'That so?'

'Leave. And don't come back.'

Just then, the door to the apartment flew open and Misato came in, still dressed in her school uniform. She stopped for moment when she saw the extra pair of shoes in the doorway. Then she saw who was there and a look of abject fear came over her face. The badminton racket dropped from her hand and clattered on the floor.

'Hello, Misato. It's been a while. You've grown,' Togashi said, his voice casual as could be.

Misato glanced at her mother, slipped out of her sneakers, and walked in without saying a word. She made a beeline for the room in the back and closed the sliding door behind her tightly.

Togashi waited a moment before speaking again. 'I don't know what you think this is all about, but all I want to do is make things good between us again. I don't see what's wrong in asking that.'

'Like I said, I'm not interested. Surely you didn't think I would really say yes? You're just using that as an excuse to bother me.'

That had to have hit the mark. But Togashi didn't respond. Picking up the remote, he turned on the television. It was a cartoon show.

Yasuko sighed and went into the kitchen. She reached into the drawer by the sink and pulled out her wallet. Opening it, she took out two ten-thousand yen bills.

'Take it and leave,' she said, putting the money on top of the kotatsu.

'What's this? I thought you weren't giving me any money.'

'This is it. No more.'

'Well, I don't need it.'

'You won't leave until you get something. I'm sure you want more, but things aren't easy for us either.'

Togashi looked at the bills, then up at Yasuko's face. 'Fine, I'll leave. And I really didn't come here for money. This was your idea.'

Togashi took the bills and shoved them into his pocket. Then he pushed the rest of his cigarette butt inside the can and slid out from under the kotatsu. Rising, he turned, not towards the front door, but towards the back room. Moving quickly, he threw open the sliding door. Yasuko could hear Misato's yelp from the other side.

'What the hell do you think you're doing?' Yasuko shouted at his back.

'I can say hello to my stepdaughter, can't I?'

'She's no daughter or anything else of yours any more.'

'Give me a break. Fine. See you later, Misato,' Togashi said, still peering into the room. The way he was standing blocked Misato from Yasuko's view, so she couldn't see how her daughter was reacting.

Finally, he turned back towards the front door. 'She'll make a fine woman someday. I'm looking forward to it.'

'What nonsense are you talking about?'

'It's not nonsense. She'll be making good money in three years. Anybody would hire her.'

'I want you to leave now.'

'I'm going, I'm going. For today, at least.'

'Don't you dare come back.'

'Oh? Don't think I can promise that.'

'You'd better not—'

'Listen, Yasuko,' Togashi said without turning around. 'You'll never get rid of me. You know why? Because you'll give in before I will, every time.' He chuckled quietly, and then leaned over to put on his shoes.

Yasuko, stunned into silence, heard something behind her. She turned to see Misato, still in her uniform, rushing past her. Holding something above her head, Misato came up behind Togashi. Yasuko, frozen in place, couldn't move to stop her, or even to cry out. She could only watch, horrified, as Misato brought the object down, striking Togashi on the back of his head. All she heard was a dull thud, and then she saw Togashi collapse on the floor.

CHAPTER 2

Then something fell from Misato's hand. It was a copper flower vase – a thank-you gift the Yonazawas had handed out to customers when Benten-tei opened for business.

'Misato!' Yasuko screamed, finally finding her voice. She went over to her daughter.

Misato's face was blank. She had become a statue; for one long moment she stood unmoving. Then her eyes jerked open wide. She was looking past Yasuko – over her shoulder.

Yasuko whirled around to see Togashi staggering to his feet. He was grimacing, one hand pressed to the back of his head.

'Son of a . . .' Togashi grunted, his face red with hate. His eyes were fixed on Misato. He stumbled again, then took a lunging step towards her.

Yasuko kept herself between them. 'No, stop!'

'Out of my way!' Togashi grabbed her arm and roughly shoved her aside. Yasuko reeled, hitting the wall hard and falling to her knees.

Misato turned to run, but Togashi grabbed her by the shoulders and brought all his weight to bear, pushing the girl down to the floor. Then he leapt astride her, grabbing her long hair and striking the side of her face with his right hand. 'I'm gonna kill you, you little bitch!' he roared.

He is going to kill her, Yasuko thought. *He really is going to kill her—*

Still on her knees, Yasuko looked around frantically. The electrical cord snaking out from beneath the kotatsu caught her eye. She reached over, grabbed it, and yanked it out of the wall socket. The other end was still attached to a corner of the kotatsu top. She stood, making a loop out of the cord in her hand.

She stepped behind Togashi where he sat atop her daughter, hitting her repeatedly, howling in blind anger. She slipped the loop over his head and pulled with all her strength.

Togashi gave a strangled yelp and fell over on his back. Realizing what was happening, he tried to work his fingers under the cord, but Yasuko kept pulling. This man was a curse on her and her daughter. She had to get him off her daughter. She had to be rid of him. If she let go now she might never get another chance.

But Yasuko had only a fraction of her ex-husband's physical strength. The cord slipped in her hands as they struggled. Meanwhile, Misato had scrambled out from beneath the man when he toppled over. Now she joined in the fight, clawing at Togashi's fingers, pulling them away from the cord around his neck. She straddled his chest, pinning him to the floor.

25

'Quick, mum! Quick!' Misato shouted.

There was no time for hesitation. Yasuko screwed her eyes shut and pulled as hard as she could. Her heart pounded in her chest. She could hear the blood surge inside her as she drew the garrote tighter and tighter.

She could not have said how long she stood like that, straining blindly, desperately. Finally, a faint voice calling *'Mum, Mum,'* began to penetrate her mental fog and brought her back to her senses.

Slowly Yasuko opened her eyes, the cord still tightly gripped in her hands.

Togashi was right in front of her face. His open eyes were blank, the colour of slate, glaring out into nothingness. His face was a sullen blue, suffused with blood. The cord had left a dark line across his neck.

Togashi wasn't moving. A line of drool hung from his lips. His nose ran. Yasuko yelped and dropped the cord from her hands. Togashi's head hit the tatami with a thud. He still showed no sign of life. Misato gingerly slid off him and onto the floor. The skirt of her school uniform was a wrinkled mess. She leaned back against the wall. For a moment mother and daughter sat in silence, their eyes glued to the unmoving man. The buzzing of the fluorescent light in the kitchen sounded loud in Yasuko's ears.

'What do we do?' Yasuko said, her voice barely a whimper. Her mind was blank. 'I killed him.'

'Mum . . .'

Yasuko looked up at her daughter. Misato's face was white, but her eyes were red, and dried tear tracks ran down her cheeks. She must've been crying, though Yasuko couldn't imagine when she'd had the time.

She looked again at Togashi. She was torn, half wanting him to spring back to life and half wanting him to stay dead. Not that it mattered what she wanted. From the looks of him, he wasn't coming back.

'*He* did this. It was *his* fault.' Misato drew up her legs, hugging her knees to her chest. She buried her face between them and began to whimper.

'What do we do . . . ?' Yasuko began. Then the doorbell rang, and her whole body jerked with surprise.

Misato looked up, her cheeks glistening. Their eyes met, asking each other, *Who could it be?*

Then there was a knock on the door, and a man's voice. 'Ms Hanaoka?'

It was a voice she'd heard before, though she couldn't for the life of her place it. Yasuko was fixed to the spot, paralyzed. She and Misato simply stared at each other.

Knock, knock.

'Ms Hanaoka. Ms Hanaoka?'

Whoever was outside knew they were home. One of them would have to respond. But how could they open the door when inside was . . . this?

'Go to the back room. Close the door, and don't

27

come out,' Yasuko ordered Misato in a hushed voice. Her brain was slowly regaining its function.

Another knock at the door.

Yasuko took a deep breath. *Nothing happened. Just another ordinary evening.* 'Yes?' she called, acting the part she knew she had to play. The part of a woman who hadn't just strangled her ex-husband to death on the living room floor. 'Who is it?'

'Oh – it's me, Ishigami. From next door.'

Yasuko started. Who knew what kind of noise they'd been making? Of course their neighbours would have ample cause for suspicion. Ishigami was checking in on them.

'Just a moment please,' Yasuko called back, trying to sound calm, and entirely unsure of her success.

Yasuko looked around the room. Misato had retreated to her room and closed the sliding door. Yasuko then looked at Togashi's body. She would have to do something about that.

The kotatsu table was at an angle to the wall, pulled out of its usual place. She dragged the table a few more feet until it just covered the body; the thick quilt hanging down from its sides hid Togashi from sight. It was an odd placement for a kotatsu, but there was nothing she could do about that now.

Yasuko checked to see that her clothes were in order and stepped down into the entranceway. Then she noticed Togashi's scuffed shoes lying there. She shoved them out of sight.

Then, careful not to make any noise, she gently slid off the door chain. The door was unlocked. She patted her chest to stop her heart from fluttering.

Opening the door at last, she found Ishigami's large round face hovering just outside. His narrow eyes stared in at Yasuko. There was no discernable expression on his face; it gave Yasuko the chills.

'Um, er, can I help you?' Yasuko said, managing a smile, even as she felt the muscles in her forehead twitch.

'I heard some noise,' Ishigami said, his face still impossible to read. 'Did something happen?'

'Oh, no, nothing,' she replied, shaking her head vigorously. 'S . . . Sorry to have bothered you.'

'Well, if you're sure it's nothing,' Ishigami replied, his eyes wandering towards the room behind her.

Yasuko's skin was on fire. She said the first thing that came to mind. 'It was a bug. A cockroach.'

'A cockroach?'

'Yes. A cockroach on the wall, and I – my daughter and I were trying to get it. I'm afraid we made quite a ruckus . . .'

'Did you kill it?'

Yasuko's face hardened. 'What?'

'The cockroach. Did you kill it?'

'Yes . . . yes, we did,' Yasuko said, bowing her head with each word. 'Killed it good. Everything's fine. Thanks.'

'I see. Well, if there's ever anything I can help with, don't hesitate to ask.'

'Thank you very much. I'm sorry. Really sorry. For all the noise.' Yasuko bowed her head deeply and shut the door. Then she locked it. Only when she'd heard Ishigami return to his own apartment and shut the door behind him did she allow herself a deep breath. Then she crouched down, putting her hands to the floor to keep from toppling over.

She heard the sliding door open behind her. 'Mum?'

After a long moment Yasuko stood shakily. She glanced at the bulge in the kotatsu cover and a new wave of despair came crashing down on her. 'We didn't have a choice,' she said at last.

'What are we going to do?' Misato asked, looking up at her mother.

'What can we do but call the police?'

'You're going to turn yourself in?'

'You have a better idea? He's dead. I killed him.'

'But what'll happen to you?'

'I don't know.' Yasuko pulled back her dishevelled hair. She realized that she must have looked frightful. She wondered what the mathematician next door had thought. Not that it mattered.

'Will you go to jail?' Misato asked.

'Well, I suppose so, yes.' Yasuko's lips shaped a smile. She could already feel herself giving up. 'I did kill him, after all.'

Misato shook her head violently. 'But that's not fair!'

'Why not?'

'It's not your fault. It was all *his* fault. He was

gone, history! But he kept coming back, tormenting you, and me . . . me . . . You shouldn't have to go to jail for him.'

'Murder is murder. Everything else is just details.'

Oddly enough, Yasuko could feel her own feelings coming under control as she explained the situation to Misato. She could almost be cool-headed about the whole affair. And as soon as she began to calm down, she started wondering if it was really true that she had no other option. She hadn't wanted Misato to grow up the daughter of a nightclub hostess. A murderer's daughter had to be worse. But she couldn't think of a way out. Still, even if there was no getting around the fact of what had happened, at least she could try to make both of them look as good as possible in the public eye.

Yasuko saw the cordless phone where it lay in a corner of the room. She went over and picked it up.

'Mum, no!' Misato darted across the room, trying to take the receiver from her mother's hand.

'Let go!'

'No, you can't!' Misato shouted, grabbing Yasuko's wrist. She had a strong grip, probably from those hours of badminton practice after school.

'Let go of me, *please.*'

'No, Mum, I won't let you do it. I'd rather turn myself in.'

'Nonsense! What are you talking about?'

Misato shot her mother a defiant look. '*I* hit him first. You were just trying to save me from him. And even after it all started, I helped. I killed him, too.'

Yasuko's body stiffened, and her grip on the phone weakened. Misato snatched it from her hand. Hugging it to herself she went to the far corner of the room, turning her back on her mother.

Yasuko thought furiously. What would the police do? Would they believe her if she said she'd killed Togashi by herself? Would they just take her word for it?

No, the police would make a thorough investigation. She had seen enough police dramas on television to know that they would want evidence – and they would use every means at their disposal to get it. They would question the neighbours, there would be a forensics team, and then—

Yasuko's vision dimmed. The police could threaten her all they wanted, she would never tell them what Misato had done, she was sure of that. But what if their investigation revealed the truth anyway? It would all be over.

She wondered if there was some way she could make it look like she had killed him by herself, but she soon discarded the idea. If she tried anything of the sort, they'd see right through her amateurish efforts.

I have to protect Misato. The girl had had it so tough,

growing up with a mother like her. Yasuko would gladly give her own life if it meant Misato would not have to suffer any more.

So what should I do? Is there anything I can do?

A curious sound shook Yasuko out of her thoughts. Gradually, she realized it was the phone, ringing as Misato clutched it. Misato's eyes went wide and she looked at her mother.

Yasuko quietly extended her hand. Misato bit her lip, then slowly handed over the phone.

Yasuko steadied her breath, then lifted the receiver to her ear and pressed the talk button. 'Yes? Hello? Hanaoka speaking.'

'*Um, hi. It's Ishigami, from next door.*'

Yasuko stared stupidly at the phone. *It's that teacher again. What could he possibly want this time?* 'Yes? Can I help you?'

'*Erm, well, actually, I was wondering what you were going to do.*'

Yasuko had no idea what he meant. 'I'm sorry, about what?'

'*Just, well—*' Ishigami paused before continuing. '*If you were going to call the police, well that's fine, I'll say nothing about it. But if you weren't, then I was thinking there might be something I could do to help.*'

'What?' Yasuko's mouth hung open. What the hell was he saying?

'*How about I come over there now,*' Ishigami said, his voice hushed over the phone. '*Would that be okay?*'

'What? No, I don't think – no, that would not be okay.' Yasuko stammered, her body breaking out in a cold sweat.

'*Ms Hanaoka,*' Ishigami went on. '*It's very difficult to dispose of a body. A woman can't do it by herself.*'

Yasuko was speechless.

He must have overheard. He must've been able to hear her talking with Misato. Maybe he had been listening to everything – her argument with Togashi, the struggle, everything.

It's over, she thought, lowering her head. There was no escape now. She would have to turn herself in. She would just have to try to make sure that Misato's involvement never came to light.

'*Ms Hanaoka, are you listening to me?*'

'Um, yes. I'm listening.'

'*Can I come over then?*'

'But I just told you—' Yasuko stopped and looked at her daughter. Misato stared back at her, fear and confusion on her face. *She must really be wondering who I'm talking to.*

If Ishigami had been listening to everything from the neighbouring apartment, then he knew Misato was involved in the murder. And if he were to tell the police what he knew . . .

Yasuko swallowed. 'Right. Okay. There is something I wanted to ask your help with anyway. Please do come over.'

'*Be right there,*' came Ishigami's reply.

34

'Who was it?' Misato asked as soon as Yasuko had hung up.

'The teacher from next door. Mr Ishigami.'

'Why? How did he—'

'I'll explain later. You go to your room, and close the door. Quickly!'

Still looking confused, Misato went into the back room again. At almost the same instant that the girl shut her door, Yasuko heard Ishigami step out of his apartment.

A few moments later, the doorbell rang. Yasuko went to the entryway, unlocked the door, and removed the chain.

Ishigami was waiting there with a curious expression on his face. For some reason, he had put on a dark navy jacket. *He wasn't wearing that a moment ago.*

'Come in.'

Ishigami nodded and stepped inside.

While Yasuko locked the door behind him, the teacher stepped into the room and without the slightest hesitation pulled back the cover on the kotatsu. He went down on one knee to get a closer look at Togashi's corpse. From his expression he seemed to be deep in thought. For the first time, Yasuko noticed that he was wearing gloves.

Hesitantly, Yasuko joined him where he knelt. All the life had drained from Togashi's face. Spittle, or something else – it was hard to say – had run down from his lips and dried on his skin.

'You heard us, didn't you?' Yasuko asked.

'Heard? Heard what?'

'Through the wall. You could hear us. That's why you called.'

Ishigami turned to Yasuko, his face blank. 'I couldn't hear you talking, if that's what you mean. For all its faults, this building's quite soundproof. That was one of the reasons why I moved here, actually.'

'Then how did you—'

'Realize what happened?'

Yasuko nodded.

Ishigami pointed to a corner of the room. An empty can lay there on its side. Some ash had spilled from it onto the floor.

'When I knocked on your door a few minutes ago, I smelled cigarette smoke. Figuring you had a guest, I looked for shoes by the door, but I couldn't see any. I glanced into the room, and noticed it looked like someone was under your kotatsu, and the cord was pulled. But if someone wanted to hide, they could've just gone into the back room. Which meant that the person under the kotatsu wasn't hiding there, they *had been hidden there*. When I put that together with the thumping noises I'd heard, and the fact that your hair was unusually dishevelled, it wasn't hard to imagine what had happened. Oh, and one more thing: there aren't any cockroaches in this building. I've lived here several years now and never seen one.'

36

Yasuko stared at Ishigami's mouth as he talked. His voice was calm, never rising, his expression never changing. *I'll bet that's exactly how he talks when he's giving a lesson to his students,* thought Yasuko, her mind wandering nervously.

Then she realized she was staring at him, and she averted her eyes. She felt that he had been watching her, too.

He's terribly levelheaded, and smart, she thought. How else could he have accurately reconstructed such an elaborate scenario after only a glance through her front door? At the same time, Yasuko felt relieved. If he hadn't heard her conversations, he didn't know the details of what had happened.

'He was my ex-husband,' she said. 'We've been divorced for several years, but he kept coming around. He wouldn't leave unless I gave him money . . . that's what he came for today, too. I couldn't take it any more, and I guess I just snapped . . .' Yasuko lowered her eyes. She wasn't going to tell him everything that had happened. She had to keep Misato's involvement out of this.

'Are you going to turn yourself in?'

'I think that's the only way. I hate to do this to Misato, though. She doesn't deserve this.' She would have said more, but she heard the sliding door of the back room fly open. Misato, furious, stepped into the room.

'No, Mum, you can't! I won't let you.'

'Misato, be quiet!'

37

'I won't. I said I won't. Listen, Mr Ishigami? I'll tell you who killed that man—'

'Misato!' Yasuko raised her voice.

Misato's mouth snapped shut and she glared daggers at her mother. Her eyes were completely red.

'Ms Hanaoka,' Ishigami said evenly, 'you don't have to hide it from me.'

'I'm not hiding anything—'

'I know you didn't kill him by yourself. Your daughter must have helped you.'

Yasuko shook her head. 'No, that's not true. I did do it myself. She only just came home – she came home right after I killed him. She had nothing to do with it.'

It was clear Ishigami wasn't believing a thing she said. He sighed and looked at Misato. 'I think hiding it is only making it harder on your daughter.'

'I'm not lying. You have to believe me!' Yasuko laid her hand on Ishigami's knee.

Ishigami stared at her hand for a moment, then looked back at the corpse. Then he tilted his head. 'What matters is how the police see things. I'm afraid they'll not be fooled so easily.'

'Why not?' Yasuko asked, before realizing that she had as good as admitted her lie.

Ishigami pointed to the corpse's right hand. 'There's bruising on the wrist and the back of his hand. I think I can even make out finger marks. I'm guessing he was strangled from behind, and

38

naturally tried to protect his throat. These marks came from someone stopping him from doing so. The evidence is plain to see.'

'It was me,' Yasuko insisted. 'I did that, too.'

'Ms Hanaoka, that's impossible.'

'Why?'

'You strangled him from behind, right? How could you pull his hands forward at the same time? It's impossible. You'd need four arms.'

Yasuko had nothing more to say. She felt trapped in a tunnel from which there was no exit. She lowered her head, her shoulders sagging. If Ishigami could tell all this with just a glance, the police would surely see even more.

'I just don't want to get Misato involved. I have to help her . . .'

'I don't want you to go to prison, either, Mum,' Misato said, her voice choked with tears.

Yasuko covered her face with her hands. 'I just don't know what to do.'

She felt the air growing heavier around her. It felt like she would be crushed where she sat.

'Mister,' Misato spoke. 'You came here to tell Mum she should turn herself in, right?'

There was a beat before Ishigami replied. 'I called thinking I could help you and your mother in some way. If you want to turn yourselves in, that's fine, I won't argue with you. But, if you weren't going to turn yourselves in, I thought it might be hard managing with just the two of you.'

Yasuko let her hands fall away from her face.

She remembered something odd Ishigami had said over the phone. How a woman couldn't dispose of a body by herself—

'Is there some way we *don't* have to turn ourselves in?' Misato asked.

Yasuko looked up. Ishigami tilted his head, thinking. His face betrayed no emotion.

'It seems to me that you have two options: hide the fact that anything happened, or hide the fact that you had anything to do with it. Either way, you have to get rid of the body.'

'Can we?'

'Misato,' Yasuko said sternly. 'We're not doing anything of the sort.'

'Please, Mum.' She turned back to Ishigami. 'You really think we can?'

'It will be difficult, but not impossible,' Ishigami replied, his voice calmly mechanical. To Yasuko, this lack of emotion made everything he said sound somehow more logical than her own rattled thoughts.

'Mum,' Misato was saying, 'let's let him help us. It's the only way!'

'But I couldn't—' Yasuko looked at Ishigami.

His narrow eyes were fixed on the floor. He was waiting for them to decide.

Yasuko remembered what Sayoko had told her, that the maths teacher had a crush on her. That he only came to buy lunch at the shop when she was there.

Now she was glad Sayoko had said so, or she

would have seriously doubted Ishigami's sanity. Why else would someone go so far out of his way to help a neighbour to whom he had barely even spoken? He had already risked arrest just by coming into the room.

'Wouldn't somebody find the body? If we hid it, that is,' Yasuko asked.

'We haven't decided whether we will hide the body yet or not,' Ishigami replied. 'Sometimes it's best not to conceal anything. We'll decide what to do with the body once we have all the information at hand. The only thing we know now for certain is that we can't leave him lying here like this.'

'What information?'

'Information about this man,' Ishigami explained, looking down at the corpse. 'About his life. I need to know his full name, address, age, occupation. The reason he came here. Where he was planning to go afterwards. Does he have family? Please tell me all that you know.'

'Well, I—'

'No, actually,' Ishigami cut her off, 'before that, let's move the body. We should clean up this room as quickly as possible. I'm sure there are mountains of evidence here as it is now.' Before he had even finished talking, Ishigami set about lifting the head and torso of the corpse.

'Move it? To where?'

'To my place,' Ishigami said, with a look that indicated this was the obvious choice; and he

41

hoisted the body over his shoulder. He was surprisingly strong. Yasuko noticed the words *Judo club* embroidered in white thread on his navy windbreaker. Stepping out the door, Ishigami quickly made his way into the neighbouring apartment, with Yasuko and Misato anxiously following. The teacher's apartment was a mess, with piles of mathematics books and journals scattered about the front room. Still carrying the body, Ishigami kicked a few piles aside to clear a space on the tatami mats. Then he casually lowered his burden to the floor. The body fell in a heap, and the dead man's eyes, frozen open, stared into the room.

Ishigami turned back to the mother and daughter, who stood at the open apartment door. 'Ms Hanaoka, I want you to stay here. Your daughter should go next door and start cleaning. Use the vacuum, and get it as clean as possible.'

Misato nodded, her face pale, and after a quick glance at her mother she vanished from the entryway.

'Close the door,' Ishigami said to Yasuko.

'Oh . . . okay.' Yasuko did as she was told, then stood in hesitation.

'You might as well come in. It's not as clean as your place, I'm afraid.'

Ishigami pulled a small cushion off a chair and placed it on the floor next to the body. Yasuko stepped into the room, but she did not sit on the cushion. Instead, she sat with her back against one wall, turning her face away from the body. Ishigami belatedly realized she was afraid of it.

'Er, sorry about that.' He picked up the cushion and offered it to her. 'Please, use this.'

'No, it's all right,' she said, looking down, with a light shake of her head.

Ishigami returned the cushion to the chair and then sat next to the body.

A reddish-black welt had risen around the corpse's neck.

'The electrical cord, was it?'

'What?'

'When you strangled him. You used an electrical cord?'

'Yes – that's right. The kotatsu cord.'

'Of course, the kotatsu,' Ishigami said, recalling the pattern of the kotatsu quilt. 'You might consider getting rid of that. Actually, never mind, I'll handle that myself later. Incidentally—' Ishigami looked back to the corpse. 'Had you planned on meeting him today?'

Yasuko shook her head. 'No, not at all. He just walked into the shop around noon, unexpectedly. Then in the evening, I met him at a family restaurant nearby. It was the only way I could get him to leave the shop. After that, I thought I'd gotten away from him. Then he showed up at my apartment.'

'A family restaurant, huh?'

That rules out the possibility of there being no witnesses, Ishigami thought. He put his hand into the corpse's jacket pocket. A rolled-up ten-thousand-yen bill came out, then another.

'That's the money I—'

'You gave him this?'

She nodded, and Ishigami offered her the money. Yasuko didn't reach for it.

Ishigami went to where his suit hung on the wall nearby and pulled his wallet from the pocket. Removing twenty thousand yen he replaced it with the bills from the dead man's jacket.

'I can appreciate why you wouldn't want his,' Ishigami said, handing the money he had taken from his own wallet to Yasuko.

She made a show of hesitating for moment, then took the money with a quiet 'Thank you.'

'Well then,' Ishigami said, searching the corpse's pockets again. He found Togashi's wallet. There was a little money inside, a driver's licence, and a few receipts.

'Shinji Togashi . . . West Shinjuku, Shinjuku Ward. Do you think that's where he was living now?' he asked Yasuko, after looking at the licence.

She frowned and shook her head. 'I'm not sure, but I don't think so. I know he lived in Nishi-Shinjuku a while back, but he said something – it sounded like he'd gotten thrown out because he couldn't pay the rent.'

'It looks like the driver's licence was renewed a year ago, which means he must have kept the papers for his old location while finding another place to actually live.'

'I'm pretty sure he moved around a lot. He

didn't have a steady job, so he wouldn't have been able to rent anything long-term.'

'That would seem to be the case,' Ishigami remarked, his eyes falling on one of the receipts.

It read 'Rental Room Ogiya'. The price had been ¥5,880 for two nights, paid up front, it seemed. Ishigami calculated the tax in his head and came up with a price of ¥2,800 per night.

He showed the receipts to Yasuko. 'I think this is where he was staying now. And if he doesn't check out, someone there will empty out his room. If he left anything behind, they might wonder, and call the police. Of course, they might not want the trouble and just do nothing at all. They probably have people skip out on them all the time, which is why they make them pay up front. Still, it's unwise to be too optimistic.'

Ishigami resumed searching the corpse's pockets. He found the key. There was a round tag on it with the number 305.

In a daze, Yasuko looked at the key. She looked like she didn't have the faintest idea what she should do.

The muffled sound of a vacuum cleaner bumping against the walls came from next door. Misato was in there, cleaning every nook and cranny with the desperation of someone who doesn't know what she should do, and so pours everything into doing what little she can.

I have to protect them, thought Ishigami. He would never be this close to so beautiful a woman

45

ever again in his life. He was sure of that. He had to summon every last bit of his strength and knowledge to prevent any calamity from happening to her.

Ishigami looked at the face of the dead man. Whatever expression he'd been wearing had already faded. He looked more like a lump of clay than a person. Still, it was possible to see that this man had been a real looker in his youth. Though he had clearly gained a little bit of weight in recent years, his was the kind of face women found easy to like.

And Yasuko fell in love with him. When Ishigami thought this, it was like a little bubble popped inside him and envy spread through his chest. He shook his head, embarrassed at his own capacity to have such feelings at a time like this.

'Is there anyone he kept in contact with, anyone close that you know of?' Ishigami resumed his questions.

'I don't know. I haven't seen him for years.'

'Did you hear what he was planning to do tomorrow? Did he say if he was going to meet anyone?'

'No,' Yasuko said, her head sagging. 'He didn't tell me anything like that. I'm sorry. I know I'm not much help.'

'No, I just had to ask. Of course you wouldn't know any of those things. Please don't worry about it.' Ishigami reached out with a gloved hand and pushed open the dead man's lips, looking inside his mouth. He could see a gold crown on one of the molars. 'He'll have dental records, then.'

'He went to the dentist regularly when we were married.'

'How long ago was that?'

'We were divorced five years ago.'

'Five years?' That was too recent for any reasonable hope that they had thrown out his charts. 'Does he have a criminal record?'

'I don't think so. Of course, I don't know what he's been doing since we broke up.'

'So it's a possibility, then.'

'I suppose . . .'

Even if the man hadn't committed any major crimes, he could easily have been fingerprinted for some minor traffic violation. Ishigami didn't know whether police forensics bothered comparing fingerprints with traffic records, but it wouldn't hurt to consider the possibility.

So, no matter how they disposed of the body, its identity would eventually come to light if it was found. They would have to resign themselves to that. Still, they needed time. Leaving fingerprints or teeth behind could hurt their chances.

Yasuko sighed. To Ishigami it sounded sexual, almost like a moan, and his heart fluttered. *I won't let you down*, he thought, steeling his resolve anew.

The situation wasn't easy, for sure. Once they discovered the identity of the body, the police would almost surely come calling on Yasuko. Ishigami wasn't sure she or her daughter would be able to withstand tough questioning from the city detectives. Preparing a weak cover story wouldn't be enough. As soon as the detectives found an inconsistency, the whole thing would fall apart, and the Hanaokas would likely just blurt out the truth.

What they needed was a perfect defence based on perfect logic.

Whatever you do, don't panic, he told himself. Panicking wouldn't help them reach a solution. And he was sure their problem had a solution. Every problem had one.

Ishigami closed his eyes. It was a habit he had developed when confronting particularly ornery mathematical challenges – all he had to do was shut out all information from the outside world, and the formulas would begin to take shape. Except this time, it wasn't formulas that filled his head.

After a time, he opened his eyes. First, he looked at the alarm clock sitting on the table. It was eight thirty. Next he looked at Yasuko. She swallowed and drew back.

'Help me undress him.'

Yasuko blinked. 'What?'

'We have to take off his clothes. Not just his jacket, but his sweater and pants, too. And we'd better do it quick, before rigor mortis sets in.' Ishigami reached for the man's jacket while he talked.

'Yes, right,' Yasuko said. She leaned forward to help, but her fingers trembled with revulsion.

Ishigami paused. 'Actually, never mind. I'll do this. You go help your daughter.'

'I'm sorry,' Yasuko said, nodding, then stood slowly.

'Ms Hanaoka,' Ishigami called to her turned back. She looked around. 'You'll need an alibi.'

'An alibi? But I don't have an alibi.'

'That's why we have to create one,' Ishigami said. He put on the jacket he had just taken from the body. 'Trust me. Logical thinking will get us through this.'

CHAPTER 3

'**I**f this is what you call "logical thinking", I'd enjoy analyzing your brain functions one of these days.'

Manabu Yukawa, his cheek propped up on one hand, gave an exaggerated yawn. He'd taken off his smallish wire-frame glasses some time ago and set them aside, as if to say, *I won't be needing these.*

Which was probably true. Kusanagi had been sitting across from him, staring at the chessboard, for over twenty minutes now, unable to think of a way to break out of his predicament. There was nowhere for his king to run; he couldn't even play the cornered rat and take out a piece or two of his opponent's on his way down. He had considered every possible move by now, and each led straight to certain defeat.

'You know, chess really isn't my kind of game,' Kusanagi muttered.

Yukawa rolled his eyes. 'Here he goes again.'

'First of all, what's all this about taking your opponent's pieces and not being able to use them? They're the spoils of war! Why can't I add them to my army?'

'Don't go blaming the rules of the game. Besides, the fact of the matter is your opponent's pieces aren't spoils, they're soldiers. When you take them off the board, you're killing them. Not much use for dead soldiers.'

'But you can use them in shogi!'

'Well, credit the man who thought up shogi for being so flexible. I suppose that when you capture pieces in shogi you're making them surrender, not killing them. That's why you get to use them again.'

'Chess should be the same way.'

'I don't think going turncoat sits well with the spirit of knighthood. Look, stop making lame excuses, and look at the situation *logically*. You can only move one piece on your turn. And you have only a few pieces that actually can move, and none of those moves will do the slightest thing to stop me. Whatever you do, on my next move I will advance my knight, and – checkmate.'

'I give up.' Kusanagi slumped in his chair. 'Chess is boring.'

'With you, yes.' Yukawa glanced at the clock on the wall. 'Forty-two minutes. And most of that was you thinking. I wonder how it is that a man such as yourself has so much time to waste here. Won't that hardheaded supervisor of yours chew you out?'

'Nah, I just cleaned up this stalker murder case. Gotta take it easy a bit *sometimes*.' Kusanagi reached for his darkstained mug. The instant

51

coffee Yukawa had offered him when he arrived had gone completely cold.

At the moment, Yukawa and Kusanagi were the only ones in Lab 13 of the Imperial University physics department. The students had all stepped out for classes, which was precisely why Kusanagi had chosen this time to drop in.

Kusanagi's mobile phone rang in his pocket. Yukawa put on his white lab coat and grinned. 'See, they're onto you already.'

Kusanagi frowned as he looked at the incoming call display. It seemed Yukawa was right. The call was from a junior detective in his department.

The crime scene was on the Tokyo side of the Old Edogawa River, not far from a sewage treatment facility. Just across the water, on the river's other bank, was Chiba Prefecture. *Why couldn't they have dumped it on the other side?* Kusanagi wondered as he lifted up the collar of his coat against the cold.

The body had been left on the side of the sloping embankment, wrapped in a blue plastic tarp of the kind often used in factory yards.

An elderly man out for a jog along the river had called it in. He'd seen something that looked like a foot protruding from the tarp and had lifted the plastic for a peek.

'How old was the guy who found it, seventy-five? He sure picked a frigid day to go for a run. Poor guy probably didn't expect to see something like this around here. My heart goes out to him.'

The junior detective, Kishitani, had arrived at the scene first; he'd explained the circumstances to Kusanagi. Now the older man frowned. The trailing edge of his long coat fluttered in the wind.

'So, Kishi, you see the body?'

'I did,' Kishitani said with a grimace. 'The chief wanted me to take a good long look at it.'

'That's because he doesn't want to look at it himself.'

'You want to peek, Kusanagi?'

'Nope. I'll take your word for it on this one.'

According to Kishitani's report, the body had been left in a sorry state. It had been stripped of clothes, shoes, even socks. The face had been smashed – like a split melon, the young detective had said, which was more than enough to make Kusanagi queasy. The fingers had been burned, too, completely destroying any fingerprints.

The corpse was male. Marks around the neck indicated he had been strangled. There were no other wounds apparent on the rest of the body.

'I hope forensics finds something,' Kusanagi said, pacing in a circle. With people watching, he thought it best to make a show of looking for clues – some lucky hint, something that might have belonged to the killer. The truth of the matter was that he left most of the crime-scene examination to the specialists. He was unlikely to find anything of much importance himself.

'There was a bicycle nearby. Some people from the local station in Edogawa already came to pick it up.'

'A bicycle? Probably junk somebody threw out.'

'It was a little new for that. And both of the tires were flat. Someone put a hole in them with a nail or something.'

'Hmph. The victim's, then?'

'Hard to say. It had a registration number on it, so we might be able to find out who owned it.'

'Well, I hope it was the victim's,' Kusanagi said. 'Or else this is going to be a real tricky one. Heaven or hell.'

'How's that?'

'This your first John Doe, Kishi?'

Kishitani nodded.

'Think about it. The face and fingerprints were destroyed, which means that the killer didn't want anyone to know who the victim was. Of course, that also means, if we find out who the victim was, it should be easy to identify the killer. The question is how long it'll take us to figure out the poor bastard's identity. That right there's what determines our fate.'

Just then, Kishitani's mobile phone rang. He took the call, talked briefly, then turned to Kusanagi. 'They want us down at the Edogawa station.'

'Well, then, things are looking up,' Kusanagi said. He stretched and straightened, massaging his lower back with clenched fists.

★　★　★

54

When they reached the Edogawa police station, Mamiya was standing by the heater, warming his hands. Mamiya was their division chief in criminal affairs. Several men – probably local homicide – were scurrying around him, prepping the room to serve as investigation headquarters.

'You come in your own car today?' Mamiya asked when he saw Kusanagi walk in.

'Sure did. Train station's too far away.'

'You familiar with this part of town, then?'

'I wouldn't say familiar, but I've been here a few times.'

'So you don't need a guide. Good. Take Kishitani with you and go – here.' He held out a piece of paper.

It was a memo with an address in Shinozaki, Edogawa Ward, beneath which was written a woman's name: Yoko Yamabe.

'Who's this?' Kusanagi asked.

'You tell him about the bicycle?' Mamiya asked Kishitani.

'Yes, sir.'

'You mean the bicycle they found near the body?' Kusanagi inquired, peering into the chief's rugged face.

'That's the one. We checked it out, and found a stolen bicycle report. The registration numbers match. That Ms Yamabe's the owner. I had someone give her a ring to make sure she's home. I want you to go over there, get her to identify the bike and hear what she has to say.'

'You get any fingerprints from the bicycle?'

'Don't you worry about that for now. Just get going,' Mamiya growled, his voice pushing them out the door.

'Great, the bike was stolen. I figured it was something like that.' Kusanagi clicked his tongue as he guided his car out into the street. He was driving a black Skyline, the same car he'd had for almost eight years now.

'You think the killer took the bicycle and left it there?'

'Maybe. But asking the owner's not going to do us much good. It's not like she knows who stole her bike. Though we might get a glimpse of the path the killer took that day, which is something.'

Following the memo and a map, Kusanagi drove around Shinozaki, the two detectives hunting for the address. Finally they found it: a modern-looking place with white walls. A nameplate by the door read 'Yamabe'.

Yoko Yamabe was a housewife in her mid-forties. Her makeup looked newly applied; she'd probably put it on when she heard that detectives would be coming.

'No doubt about it, that's my bicycle,' she announced crisply when Kusanagi showed her a photograph he'd gotten from forensics.

'I was hoping you could come down to the station and identify it in person.'

'I'd be happy to – I'm getting it back, right?'

'Of course. However, our colleagues at the

station are still looking into a few things, so you might have to wait until they're done.'

'Oh, but I need it back right now! It's almost impossible going shopping without it,' she said, her brow furrowing with disappointment. The tone of her voice made it sound as if she blamed the police for her bicycle having been stolen in the first place.

Kusanagi sighed inwardly. He knew the type. He could just see her down at the station, demanding that they pay to fix her punctured tires. For a fleeting moment he considered telling her that the bicycle had been used in connection with a murder, just to see how quickly she lost interest in ever riding the thing again.

According to her, the bike had been stolen the day before – in other words, on March tenth – sometime between eleven A.M. and ten P.M. She had gone out to meet a friend in Ginza, gone shopping and had dinner, and by the time she'd returned to Shinozaki Station, it was already past ten o'clock at night. She had taken the bus home.

'Did you leave the bicycle in the lot?'

'No, along the pavement.'

'And it was locked?'

'Of course. I attached it to the guardrail with a chain.'

Kusanagi hadn't heard anyone mention finding a chain lock at the scene.

He gave Ms Yamabe a ride down to Shinozaki

Station to see the spot where the bicycle had been stolen.

'It was right around here,' she said, indicating a section of pavement about twenty yards from the small supermarket in front of the station. There were a few bicycles lined up there now.

Kusanagi looked around. There was a bank branch office nearby, and a bookstore. There probably would have been quite a bit of pedestrian traffic during the day and early evening. Someone crafty enough could have cut the chain quickly during that time and taken the bike as though it were their own, but it was far more likely that the deed had been done later, after the streets had cleared somewhat.

Next, the detectives brought Ms Yamabe down to the Edogawa police station to identify the bicycle.

'I think I'm just unlucky, you know,' Kusanagi heard her saying from the backseat. 'I only bought that bicycle last month. I was so mad when I realized it had been stolen that I went and filed a report at the police box by the station before I even got on the bus.'

'And you knew the registration number? That's impressive.'

'Well, I'd only just bought the thing. I still had the receipt at my house. I called and had my daughter tell me the number.'

'I see. Good thinking.'

'I was wondering – just what sort of case is this?

The man on the phone didn't give any details. But I have to admit all this has me very curious.'

'Well, we're not even sure there really is a case just yet, ma'am. I'm afraid we don't have the details.'

'What? Really?' She snorted. 'I didn't know you police types were so tight-lipped about these things.'

In the passenger seat, Kishitani was trying to keep from laughing. Kusanagi was glad he had gone to visit the woman today and not later. If the murder had already become public knowledge, he would have had to suffer through a deluge of questions.

Ms Yamabe took one look at the bicycle down in the evidence room at Edogawa station and ID'd it on the spot. Then she turned to Kusanagi and asked who was going to pay for repairing her tires.

The forensics team got several fingerprints off the bicycle's handlebars, frame, and seat. They had found other evidence as well. What they thought to be the victim's clothes had turned up, stuffed into a five-gallon oil can, several hundred yards from the place where the body was found.

The clothes were partially burned. There was a jacket, a sweater, pants, socks, and underwear. Forensics guessed that the killer had set fire to the clothes and then left. But the fire had gone out before finishing the job, and they hadn't burned as well as he had hoped.

There was nothing special about the style or manufacture of the clothes. All of them were standard designs, common throughout the country. A police artist had used the clothing and the shape of the victim's body to draw an approximation of how he had looked before he was killed. Some policemen had already been to Shinozaki Station, illustration in hand, to ask around. However, without anything distinctive about either the person or the clothes, they had gathered no information of any worth.

A picture of the illustration went up on the nightly news that evening, and a mountain of calls came in, but none of them offered any positive link to the body from beside the Old Edogawa.

Meanwhile, the police had compared everything they knew about the victim to the missing persons list, but they were unable to find even the thinnest thread connecting anyone to their John Doe. Only a survey of hotels and hostels in the Edogawa area, checking to see if any single men had abruptly disappeared, turned up something of merit.

A customer staying at a place in Kamedo called Rental Room Ogiya had gone missing on March 11, the day the body was found. When he hadn't shown up at the desk at checkout time, one of the staff had gone to check the room and had found it empty, save for a few of the man's personal belongings. The manager hadn't bothered to inform the police because the customer had already paid in advance.

Forensics descended on the place immediately, picking up every fingerprint and loose piece of hair. Finally they struck gold. One of the hairs was a perfect match with those on the body. There were also fingerprints on the walls and belongings that matched those from the stolen bicycle.

The missing man had signed his name in the rental room's guestbook: Shinji Togashi. His address was listed as being in West Shinjuku, Shinjuku Ward.

CHAPTER 4

They walked from the subway station towards Shin-Ohashi Bridge, taking a right onto the narrow road just before the river. The neighbourhood they had entered was mainly residential, though there were a few small shops here and there, all of which felt like they had been around for years – real mom-and-pop establishments. Most other parts of town had long since been overrun with supermarkets and chain stores, but this area was different. *This is the old downtown district, Shitamachi,* thought Kusanagi. *Maybe that's what makes it feel different.*

It was already past eight P.M. An old woman carrying a washbasin ambled past them along the pavement. *There must be a public bath nearby,* Kusanagi conjectured.

'Close to the station, lots of shopping . . . not a bad place to live,' Kishitani remarked quietly.

'Your point?'

'Nothing, really. I was just thinking this isn't a terrible place for a single mother to raise her daughter.'

Kusanagi grunted. The junior detective's comment

62

would have seemed a little odd if they weren't now on their way to meet a single mother and her daughter. That, and Kusanagi knew that Kishitani himself had been raised by a single mum.

Kusanagi walked steadily, occasionally glancing at the small address plates on the telephone poles, comparing them to the address written on the memo in his hand. They should be arriving at the apartment building soon. The memo gave a name, too: Yasuko Hanaoka.

At the time of his death, Shinji Togashi had still been a registered occupant at the address he'd left in the guest-book at the rental room. It just wasn't where he had actually been living.

Once they'd identified the body, the police had put out a bulletin on the television and in the newspapers, asking for anyone who knew anything about the dead man to contact their local law enforcement. That had turned up nothing. But the real estate agent who had rented Togashi the old apartment in Shinjuku knew where he used to work: a used-car place. He hadn't been there long, though, quitting before his first year was up.

Still, the lead had been enough to give the investigation some legs. It turned out that the victim had once been an import luxury car salesman, and he'd been fired when he was caught skimming from the till. He hadn't been charged, however. The detectives had found out about it when they went to the car dealership to do some questioning. The importer was still doing business, but no one on staff there now knew much about Togashi – or at least, no one who was willing to talk.

The investigators did learn that, at the time that he was working there, Togashi had been married. And according to someone who knew him after the divorce, he had made a habit of visiting his ex-wife, and the ex-wife had a child from a former marriage.

It wasn't hard for the detectives to trace their movements. Pretty soon, they had an address for Yasuko and Misato Hanaoka: the apartment they were heading for now, here in the Morishita district of Eto Ward.

'Well, I sure pulled the short straw on this one,' Kishitani said, sighing.

'What? Doing footwork with me is the short straw?'

'No, it's not that. I just don't enjoy the idea of bothering this poor lady and her daughter.'

'If they had nothing to do with the crime, what's the bother?'

'Well, from the sound of it, this Togashi wasn't the best husband, or the best father. Who'd want to have to remember all that?'

'Well, if that's the case, you'd think they'd welcome us. After all, we're here to tell them the big bad man is dead. Just try not to look so glum, okay? You're making me depressed just looking at you. Ah, here we are.' Kusanagi stopped in front of an old apartment building.

The building was a dirty grey colour, with several marks on the walls where repairs had been made. It was two storeys high with four units on each floor. Only half of the windows were lit.

'Room 204, which means we go upstairs.' Kusanagi put a hand on the concrete railing and started up. Kishitani followed.

Room 204 was the unit furthest from the stairwell. Light spilled from the apartment window, and Kusanagi breathed a quick sigh of relief. They hadn't called in advance; if Ms Hanaoka had been out, the detectives would have had to come back.

He rang the doorbell. Immediately, he heard someone moving inside. The door was unlocked; it swung open a crack, the door chain still attached. *Not unusual*, Kusanagi thought, *considering a single mother and her daughter live here alone. They're right to be cautious.*

A woman looked out through the opening, peering suspiciously at the two detectives. She had a small face with strikingly dark eyes. In the dim light, she looked as if she could have been in her late twenties, but the hand on the door was not a young woman's hand.

'Sorry for dropping in like this, but are you Ms Yasuko Hanaoka?' Kusanagi asked as gently as he could.

'I am,' the woman replied. She seemed ill at ease.

'We're from the police department. Actually, I have some bad news.' Kusanagi pulled out his badge, flashing his ID. Beside him, Kishitani did the same.

'The police?' Yasuko's eyes widened. A ripple passed through the pools of black.

'Can we come inside?'

'Oh yes, please, come in.' Yasuko shut the door, undid the chain, and opened the door again. 'May I ask what this is all about?'

Kusanagi stepped into the apartment. Kishitani followed behind.

'Ma'am, do you know a Mr Shinji Togashi?'

Kusanagi noticed Yasuko's face tighten in response, and he chalked it up to surprise.

'Yes, he's my ex-husband . . . has he done something?'

So she didn't know he'd been killed. She probably hadn't seen it on the news or read it in the papers. The story hadn't garnered too much attention from the press, after all.

'Actually,' Kusanagi began, and his eyes wandered back into the room behind her. The sliding doors towards the rear were closed tightly. 'Is there someone else home?' he asked.

'My daughter, yes.'

'Ah, right.' He noticed the sneakers by the door. Kusanagi lowered his voice. 'I'm afraid Mr Togashi is dead.'

Yasuko's expression seemed to freeze while her lips made an open circle. 'He – he died? Why? How? Was there an accident?'

'His body was found on an embankment by the

Old Edogawa. We don't know for sure, but there is suspicion of murder,' Kusanagi said. He figured that breaking the news to her straight would make it easier to ask questions afterwards.

For the first time, a look of shock passed over Yasuko's face. She shook her head. 'Him? But why would anyone do that to him?'

'That's what we're investigating now. Mr Togashi didn't have any other family, so we thought you might know something. I'm sorry to drop in so late.' Kusanagi bowed stiffly.

'No, of course, I had no idea—' Yasuko put a hand to her mouth and lowered her eyes.

Kusanagi's gaze shifted again to the sliding doors at the rear of the room. Was Ms Hanaoka's daughter behind there, listening in on their conversation? If so, how would she take the news of her former stepfather's death?

'We did a little looking through the records. You divorced Mr Togashi five years ago, is that correct? Have you seen him since then?'

Yasuko shook her head. 'I've hardly seen him at all since we separated.'

Which meant they *had* met. Kusanagi asked when.

'I think the last time I saw him was over a year ago . . .'

'And you've received no contact from him since? A phone call, or letter?'

'Nothing,' Yasuko said, firmly shaking her head.

Kusanagi nodded, glancing casually around the

room. It was a small apartment, done in the Japanese style with tatami mats on the floor. The unit was old, but the woman kept it clean and orderly. A bowl of mandarin oranges sat on the low kotatsu table in the middle of the room. The badminton racket leaning against one wall brought back memories for the detective; he had played the game in college.

'We've determined that Mr Togashi died on the evening of March 10,' Kusanagi told her. 'Does that date or the embankment on the Old Edogawa mean anything to you? Even the slightest connection could help our investigation.'

'I'm sorry, but I can't think of anything. There's nothing special about that date, and I really don't know what he's been up to.'

'I see.'

The woman was clearly getting annoyed. But then, few people cared to talk about their ex-husbands. This was getting nowhere fast.

Might as well leave it here for now, he thought. There was just one last thing he needed to check.

'By the way,' he asked, trying to sound as casual as possible, 'were you home on the tenth?'

Yasuko's eyes narrowed. She was clearly uncomfortable. 'Do I need to know exactly where I was that day?'

Kusanagi laughed. 'Please, don't take this the wrong way. Of course, the more precise you can be, the more it will help us.'

'Well, can you wait a moment?' Yasuko glanced

at a wall Kusanagi couldn't see from where he stood. He guessed there was a calendar hanging there. He would have liked to look at her schedule, but he decided to refrain for now.

'I had work in the morning that day, and . . . that's right, I went out afterwards with my daughter,' Yasuko replied.

'Where'd you go out to?'

'We went to see a movie. At a place called the Rakutenchi in Kinshicho.'

'Around what time did you leave? Just a general idea is fine. And if you remember which movie it was . . . ?'

'Oh, we left around six thirty . . .'

She went on to describe the movie they'd seen. It was one Kusanagi had heard of; the third installment in some popular series out of Hollywood.

'Did you go home right after that?'

'No, we ate at a ramen shop in the same building, and then we went out to karaoke.'

'Karaoke? Like, at a karaoke box?'

'That's right. My daughter wanted me to go.'

Kusanagi chuckled. 'Do the two of you do that often?'

'Only once every month or two.'

'How long were you there for?'

'We usually only go for about an hour and a half. Any longer and we get home too late.'

'So you saw a movie, ate dinner, then went to karaoke . . . which puts you home at?'

'It was after eleven o'clock, I think. I don't remember the time exactly.'

Kusanagi nodded. There was something about the story that didn't sit right, but it wasn't anything he could put his finger on. It might be nothing at all.

They asked the name of the karaoke box, bid Ms Hanaoka goodnight, and left.

'I don't think she had anything to do with it,' Kishitani said in a low voice as the two detectives walked away from apartment 204.

'Hard to say.'

'I think that's great that they go out to karaoke together. It's not often you have a mother and daughter who get along so well.' It was clear from his tone that Kishitani did not consider Yasuko Hanaoka a suspect.

As they walked down the hall they became aware of a man coming up the stairs towards them. He was middle-aged and heavyset. The two detectives stopped and let him pass. The man continued on to apartment 203, unlocked the door, and went inside.

Kusanagi and Kishitani glanced at each other, then turned around.

The plate next to the door of 203 read 'Ishigami'. They rang the doorbell, and the man they had just seen opened the door. He had taken off his coat, revealing a sweater and slacks beneath.

The man's face was a blank as he looked at Kusanagi and Kishitani. In Kusanagi's experience, almost everyone viewed him with suspicion at first, if not alarm, but this man's face revealed absolutely nothing.

'Sorry to disturb you this late. I was wondering if you could help us,' Kusanagi said with a friendly smile, showing the man his police badge.

Still, the man's face didn't twitch a muscle. Kusanagi took a step forward. 'It'll only take a few minutes. We'd like to ask you some questions.' Thinking that perhaps the man hadn't been able to see his badge, he held it out closer.

'What's this about?' the man asked without even glancing at the badge in Kusanagi's hand. He seemed to know already that they were detectives.

Kusanagi took a photograph from his jacket pocket. It was a picture of Togashi from when he had been a used-car salesman.

'This is photo from a few years ago, but – have you seen anyone resembling this man around here recently?'

The man stared intently at the photograph for a moment, then looked up at Kusanagi. 'Can't say I know him.'

'Right, I'm sure you don't. But, I was wondering if you had seen anyone who looked like him?'

'Where?'

'Well, for example, somewhere in the local area?'

The man squinted again at the photograph. *This is a dead end*, thought Kusanagi.

'Sorry, never seen him,' the man said. 'I don't really remember the faces of people I pass on the street, anyway.'

'Yes, of course,' Kusanagi said, already regretting having come back to question the man. But, since he was here, he might as well be thorough about it. 'Might I ask, do you always come home at this time?'

'I suppose it depends on the day. Sometimes I'm late with the team.'

'Team?'

'I supervise a judo club. I'm responsible for closing up the dojo at the end of the day.'

'Oh, you're a schoolteacher, then?'

'Yes, high school,' the man replied, and he told them the name of the school where he worked.

'I see. Well, then, I'm sorry to have bothered you. You must have had a long day,' Kusanagi apologized, lowering his head.

It was then that he noticed the mathematics textbooks piled up in the entranceway. *Oh, great*, he thought, a lump growing in his stomach, *a maths teacher*. Maths had been Kusanagi's worst subject in school.

'Ah, I was wondering—' he said, trying to shake off the feeling. 'Your name here on the plate by the door . . . do these characters read "Ishigami"?'

'That's right, I'm Ishigami.'

'Mr Ishigami, I was wondering if you remember what time you came home on the tenth of March?'

'The tenth of March? Why, did something happen?'

'No, nothing to do with you, sir. We're just gathering what information we can about events in the local area that day.'

'I see, well, March 10, huh?' Ishigami stared briefly into the distance before returning his gaze to Kusanagi. 'I'm pretty sure I came home directly that day. I would say around seven o'clock.'

'Anything unusual happen next door that evening?'

'Next door?'

'Yes, um, Ms Hanaoka's place?' Kusanagi asked, lowering his voice.

'Did something happen to Ms Hanaoka?'

'No, nothing. We're just gathering information.'

A curious look crept over Ishigami's face. He was probably starting to imagine what could possibly have happened to the mother and daughter living next door. From the look of his apartment, Mr Ishigami was single.

'I don't recall anything unusual, no,' Ishigami replied.

'No loud noises, or talking?'

'Hmm.' Ishigami scratched his neck. 'Sorry, nothing comes to mind.'

'I see. Are you friends with Ms Hanaoka by any chance?'

'Well, she lives next door, so we meet each other now and then and say hello. But that's about all.'

'I see. Thanks, and we're sorry to have bothered you.'

'Not at all,' Ishigami said, nodding and reaching for the door. Kusanagi saw that he was lifting his mail from the box that hung on the inside of the door. The detective's eyes went wide for moment when he saw the words 'Imperial University' written on one of the letters.

'Erm,' Kusanagi said hesitantly. 'Did you graduate from Imperial University?'

'Huh?' Ishigami started, his eyes opening a little wider. Then he, too, noticed the address on the letter in his hand. 'Oh, this? Must be an alumni letter. Does whatever you're investigating have anything to do with the university?'

'No, I had a friend from there is all.'

'Oh, yes, I see.'

'Er, sorry for the trouble.' Kusanagi bowed curtly, turned, and departed.

When the detectives had left the apartment building behind, Kishitani spoke up suddenly. 'Wait, sir – didn't you go to Imperial University? Why didn't you tell that guy?'

'No reason, really. Just didn't want to start anything, is all. I'm sure he was from the science department, and frankly, my bunch didn't get along with the fellows over there.'

'You have a thing about the sciences, don't you?' Kishitani said, grinning. 'Do I detect an inferiority complex?'

'I'd be fine if someone didn't keep rubbing my face in it,' Kusanagi muttered, the image of Manabu Yukawa – the friend he half-jokingly called 'Detective Galileo' – rising in his mind.

After the detectives had been gone a good ten minutes, Ishigami stepped out into the hallway outside his apartment. He glanced next door. The light was on. He turned and went down the stairs.

It was quite a walk to the nearest public phone where he had a reasonable chance of not being observed. He didn't own a mobile phone, and he couldn't use the landline in his own apartment.

As he walked, he went back over the details of his conversation with the police. He was sure he hadn't given them a single reason to suspect he was involved in any way. But there was always a chance, however slight. If the police suspected Yasuko, they would have to figure that a man had been involved in disposing of the body. They might start looking for someone connected to the Hanaokas, a man who would be willing to dirty his hands for them. They might even consider investigating the mathematics teacher who lived next door.

Ishigami knew he had to avoid going to their apartment, of course. He had been avoiding any direct contact. That was why he didn't call from his own house. The investigators might see from the phone records that he had made frequent calls to Yasuko Hanaoka and find it suspicious.

But what about Benten-tei?

He still hadn't made up his mind about that. All things being equal, he should probably avoid the place for a while. But the police might come around asking questions. The owners might tell them about how the mathematician who lived next to Yasuko came by there every day to buy lunch.

75

Wouldn't they find it odd if he stopped coming right after the day of the murder? Shouldn't he keep going there as usual so as not to raise suspicions?

Ishigami didn't trust his own capacity to come up with a logical answer to this question, because he knew that, in his heart, he wanted to keep going to Benten-tei. That lunchbox shop was his connection to Yasuko. If he didn't go there, he would never see her at all.

He arrived at the public phone and inserted a telephone card. The card had been a gift from another teacher – the front showed a picture of the teacher's newborn baby.

The number he dialled was for Yasuko's mobile phone. They might have put a tap on her home phone, after all. The police claimed they didn't wiretap citizens, but he didn't trust that one bit.

'Yes?' came Yasuko's voice over the line. She would have already guessed that it was he, because of the public number. He had told her he would contact her this way.

'It's me, Ishigami.'

'Oh, yes.'

'The police came to my apartment a few minutes ago. I'm guessing they dropped by your place as well.'

'Yes, a little while ago.'

'What did they want to know?'

Ishigami listened to every word Yasuko said, organized it in his head, analyzed it, and committed it to memory. It seemed that, for the time being, the police didn't directly suspect Yasuko. They had probably just been following procedure when they asked after her whereabouts. They might have someone check out her story, but it probably wouldn't be a high priority.

But if they found out that Togashi had visited on the tenth, that he had come to see Yasuko, they wouldn't be so friendly the next time they turned up. And the first thing they were bound to check out would be her statement that she hadn't seen Togashi recently. Luckily, he had already prepared her for that eventuality.

'Did the detectives see your daughter?'

'No, Misato was in the back room.'

'I see. Still, they will probably want to question her before long. You know what to do if that happens, right?'

'Yes, you were very clear. I think she'll be okay.'

'I don't mean to repeat myself, but remember, there's no need to make an act of it. She just needs to answer the questions they ask as mechanically as possible.'

'Yes, I told her that.'

'Did you show the police your ticket stubs?'

'No, I didn't. You told me I didn't have to show them unless they asked for them specifically.'

'Then that's fine. By the way, where did you put the stubs?'

'In a kitchen drawer.'

'Put them inside the cinema pamphlet. Nobody

goes out of their way to store ticket stubs. They might suspect something if you have them in your drawer.'

'Okay, I'll take them out.'

'By the way . . .' Ishigami swallowed. He tightened his grip on the receiver. 'The owners at Benten-tei . . . do they know about me going there to buy my lunch?'

'What . . . ?' Yasuko asked, momentarily taken aback.

'What I'm asking is, do the people who run the store where you work know that your neighbour comes there frequently to buy lunches? This is rather important, so please be honest.'

'Well, yes, actually. The owners were saying they were happy you were such a reliable regular.'

'And they know that I'm your neighbour?'

'Yes . . . is that bad?'

'No, I'll worry about that. You just do as we discussed. All right?'

'Yes.'

'Right,' Ishigami said, turning to set down the receiver.

'Oh, um, Mr Ishigami?' Yasuko's voice came softly.

'Yes?'

'Thank you. Thank you for everything. We're in your debt.'

'No . . .' Ishigami paused. 'Don't mention it,' he said, and he hung up the phone.

When Yasuko said 'Thank you', he had felt a tingle rush through his body. Now his face was flushed, and he welcomed the night breeze on his skin. He was even sweating a little.

Ishigami headed home, elated. But his high didn't last long when he remembered what she had said about Benten-tei.

He realized that he had made a mistake when talking to the detectives. When they asked how well he knew Yasuko, he had only told them that they said hello when they chanced to meet. He should also have told them about the lunchbox shop.

'Did you confirm Yasuko Hanaoka's alibi?'

Mamiya had called Kusanagi and Kishitani over to his desk. He was clipping his nails.

'The karaoke box checked out,' Kusanagi reported. 'The person at the desk there knew her face. And they were in the book, from nine forty for an hour and a half.'

'What about before that?'

'Considering the time, they probably caught the seven o'clock show at the cinema. It ended at nine ten. If they went to eat ramen after that, their story holds,' Kusanagi said, looking over his notes.

'I didn't ask if their story held, I asked if you checked it out.'

Kusanagi closed his notebook. His shoulders sagged. 'Just the karaoke box.'

'You call that doing your job, Detective?' Mamiya asked, glaring up at him.

'C'mon, Chief. You know it's almost impossible to check out alibis in cinemas and ramen shops.'

One ear listening to Kusanagi, Mamiya pulled out a business card and threw it on the desk. The card read 'Club Marian'. It gave an address in Kinshicho.

'What's that?'

'The place where Ms Yasuko used to work. Togashi dropped in there on the fifth of March.'

'Five days before he was murdered.'

'Apparently, he was asking about Yasuko. Anyway, I think that's more than enough for even you to figure out what I'm getting at.' Mamiya pointed to the door behind the two detectives. 'I want you to go and check out that alibi, every bit of it. If anything doesn't fit, I want you to go back and talk to this Yasuko again.'

CHAPTER 5

A small pole about thirty centimetres long stuck up from a square box on the lab table. There was a ring, only a few centimetres across, encircling the base of the pole. The strange item would have looked a bit like a carnival ring-toss game were it not for the cord snaking out of the side of the box and the single toggle switch on top.

'What the heck's this?' Kusanagi muttered, bending down to stare at the device.

'I wouldn't touch that if I were you,' warned Kishitani beside him.

'Nah, I'm sure it's fine. If this thing were dangerous, he never would've left it lying out here like this.' Kusanagi flicked the switch. The moment he did so, the ring around the pole began to float upward.

Kusanagi gaped. The ring was hovering in mid-air, wobbling slightly.

'Try pushing the ring down,' came a voice from behind him.

Kusanagi looked around as Yukawa walked into the room, a file folder cradled in his arms.

81

'Welcome back. Class?' Kusanagi asked as he turned back to the floating ring. Reaching out gingerly, he tried to push it down with his fingertips. A second later he yanked back his hand. 'Yowch! That thing's hot!'

'It's true, I'm not in the habit of leaving dangerous objects lying about. I do, however, assume a basic knowledge of physics.' Yukawa strolled over to the table and flicked off the switch. 'This device is only high school-level physics, as a matter of fact.'

'Well, I didn't take physics in high school,' Kusanagi said, blowing on his fingertips. Kishitani laughed immoderately.

'Who's your friend?' Yukawa asked with a raised eyebrow.

The smile vanished from Kishitani's face and he bowed curtly. 'Kishitani. I work with Detective Kusanagi. I've heard a lot about you, Professor. You've helped us out with a lot of cases, haven't you? They call you Detective Galileo down at the station.'

Yukawa frowned and waved his hand. 'Don't call me that. I don't help out because I enjoy it, you know. I just couldn't bear listening to Detective Kusanagi's faulty attempts at reasoning on a certain occasion, and I made the mistake of correcting him. I'd be wary of spending too much time with him, if I were you. You might catch whatever he has that's hardened his brain into a rock.'

Kishitani guffawed, earning him a glare from his superior.

'You laugh too much,' Kusanagi grumbled. 'Besides,' he said, turning to Yukawa, 'you know you enjoy trying to solve our cases.'

'What's there to enjoy? Do you know how much valuable research time I've squandered on your account? I certainly hope you haven't brought me another of your annoying, so-called "unsolvable" puzzles today?'

'No, you're off the hook for now. We just happened to be in the area, so we dropped in.'

'Ah, that's a relief.' Yukawa walked over to a nearby sink, filled a kettle with water, and set it on a gas burner – the start of his usual instant coffee ritual. 'So, did you resolve the murder along the Old Edogawa River?' he asked, measuring coffee powder into a cup.

'How did you know we were working on that case?'

'Simple deduction. It was on the news the same night you took a call while in my lab. And from the look on your face, I would further deduce that the investigation isn't going so well.'

Kusanagi gestured dismissively. 'Oh, I wouldn't say it's going all that badly. We have a few suspects now. It's just getting started.'

'Oh? Suspects?' Yukawa asked over his shoulder, not sounding particularly interested.

'Actually,' Kishitani chipped in, 'I don't think we're heading in the right direction, myself.'

Yukawa lifted an eyebrow at him. 'You object to the direction the investigation is taking?'

'Well, I wouldn't call it an objection . . .'

'I'd prefer you didn't call it anything,' Kusanagi said with a scowl.

'Sorry, sir.'

'Why apologize?' Yukawa asked, clearly starting to enjoy himself. 'You follow orders, yet you have your own opinion – sounds perfectly reasonable to me. Proper, even. Without people to question the status quo, how can we ever hope to arrive at truly rational decisions?'

'Nah, that's not why he's against the investigation,' Kusanagi said with a sigh. 'He just wants to be a knight in shining armor.'

'What? That's not why—' Kishitani began.

'It's okay, you can admit it. You sympathize with the single mother and her daughter. Truth be told, I wish they weren't suspects myself.'

'Sounds complicated,' Yukawa said, smirking as watched the two detectives' faces.

'Nothing complicated about it. The man who was killed used to be married, and apparently he'd been searching for his ex-wife just before it happened. So, we had to check out her alibi, that's all.'

'And she has an alibi?'

'That's the rub.' Kusanagi scratched his head.

'Oh? You're not sounding so sure yourself, any more,' Yukawa laughed as he headed for the kettle. Steam was rising from its spout. 'Can I interest you gentlemen in some coffee?'

84

'Please,' Kishitani said, nodding eagerly.

'I'll pass,' Kusanagi frowned. 'See, there's something about the alibi that doesn't feel right.'

'Well, *I* don't think they're lying.'

'On the basis of what? We haven't finished checking out their story yet.'

'But didn't you just tell the chief that it was impossible to confirm alibis at ramen shops and cinemas?'

'I didn't say it was impossible. I just said it was *almost* impossible.'

'Ah,' Yukawa joined in as he arrived with two coffees in hand. 'So these women, the suspects, claim they were seeing a movie at the time of the crime?' He handed one of the cups to Kishitani.

'Thanks,' Kishitani said, nodding. Then his eyes went wide as he noticed the layers of grime on the cup's rim. Kusanagi stifled a laugh.

'If the movie's their alibi, that would seem hard to corroborate.' Yukawa seated himself in a chair.

'But they went out to karaoke afterwards. And we have an affidavit from one of the staff there,' Kishitani said, a bit too stridently.

'Which doesn't mean we can just ignore the cinema. They could have committed the crime and then gone out for karaoke,' Kusanagi pointed out.

'But the Hanaokas went to the movies at seven or eight o'clock. I can't imagine any place so deserted at that time of night that they could have just killed someone there. And they didn't just kill him, they stripped him bare.'

'I agree, but you have to consider all the possibilities before you go writing them off as innocent.' *Not to mention you have to satisfy that stickler Mamiya,* Kusanagi added to himself.

'So, I gather from your discussion that you were able to ascertain the time of the murder?' Yukawa asked.

'The autopsy put the estimated time of death after six P.M. on the tenth,' Kishitani said.

'Great. Why not go ahead and divulge every last detail about the case?' Kusanagi grumbled.

'But I thought Professor Yukawa was assisting the department?'

'Only when there's some bizarre mystery in need of unravelling. There's no need to go outside our people for help with this case.'

'I am a mere civilian, yes. But please don't forget my ongoing contribution to the effort. I provide you with a place to shoot the breeze.' Yukawa took a long sip of his instant coffee.

'I hear you. You want us to leave.' Kusanagi stood up from his chair.

'No, wait,' Yukawa said. 'About these suspects . . . Could they *prove* they had been to the movies?'

'They seemed to know the story well enough. Of course, that doesn't tell us when they went.'

'Did they have ticket stubs?'

Kusanagi looked back at Yukawa. Their eyes met. 'They did.'

'Oh? And where were these stubs?' The rims of

Yukawa's glasses sparkled in the sunlight coming through the window.

Kusanagi snorted. 'I know what you're getting at. Who holds onto ticket stubs, right? Believe me, even I would have found it suspicious if Yasuko Hanaoka had pulled them out of her kitchen drawer and produced them immediately.'

'So they weren't someplace in particular, then?'

'At first she said she'd thrown them away. But when she pulled out the movie programme she'd bought at the cinema, the stubs were inside.'

'Ah, the movie programme to the rescue. It's believable enough.' Yukawa crossed his arms. 'And the date on the tickets matched the date of the murder?'

'Of course. But that doesn't necessarily mean anything. They could have bought tickets but never gone inside, or fished those stubs out of the rubbish.'

'Regardless, it means that the suspects went to the cinema – or near it, at least.'

'We had the same thought. So we've been canvassing the area since this morning, looking for someone who might have seen them. Unfortunately the girl who was taking tickets that night had today off, so we had to go all the way to her house to interview her. Which was near here, so I decided to visit.'

'And the ticket girl told you absolutely nothing of value, I see,' Yukawa said with a chuckle, noting the dour look on Kusanagi's face.

'The tenth was a few days ago, and she can't be expected to remember the faces of everyone who comes to the cinema. Not that I'm disappointed. I didn't expect anything to come of it in the first place. And I see we've taken up enough of the *assistant* professor's time. We'll be on our way.' Kusanagi clapped Kishitani on the back, making him cough up a swig of coffee, and headed for the door.

'Hang in there, Detective,' Yukawa called after Kusanagi. 'If this suspect of yours is the true killer, you could be in for a rough time.'

Kusanagi turned around again. 'What's that supposed to mean?'

'Like I just said, a common criminal wouldn't think to put ticket stubs procured for an alibi in such a credible place. If we assume that the tickets really were bought to establish an alibi, that she put them in the pamphlet expecting you to come and ask her for them, I'd say that makes her an adversary to be feared.' The smile died from Yukawa's eyes as he spoke.

Kusanagi nodded, mulling over the warning. 'Yeah, I'll keep that in mind.' He said goodbye and once more started to leave. But just before he put his hand on the doorknob, he remembered something and turned around a third time. 'You know, one of your classmates lives next door to the suspect. He would have been an upperclassman when you were starting out.'

'Upperclassman?' Yukawa echoed, lifting an eyebrow.

'Guy by the name of Ishigami. Teaches high school maths. He graduated from Imperial University. Probably from your department, too.'

'Ishigami . . .' Yukawa muttered to himself, then his eyes went wide behind his glasses. 'Ishigami the Buddha!'

'The Buddha? Huh?'

Yukawa held up a hand, motioning for them to wait, then disappeared into the next room. Kusanagi and Kishitani exchanged curious glances.

The professor returned a moment later. He was carrying a black university folder in his hand. He opened it and pointed to a page. 'This Ishigami?'

There were several photographs on the page, all of them young students. At the top of the page was the heading, 'Masters of Science Received in the 38th Term.'

Yukawa was pointing to the picture of a chubby-faced graduate student. Unlike the students in the other photos, this fellow wasn't smiling; his thin eyes merely stared straight ahead impassively. The name beneath the photo read 'Tetsuya Ishigami'.

'Hey, that's him,' Kishitani said. 'He's a lot younger here, but there's no mistaking that look.'

Kusanagi covered the top of the man's head with one finger and nodded. 'Yeah. That's the guy. Didn't recognize him at first with all that hair. You know him?'

'Yes, but he wasn't an upperclassman. We were the same year. The science department in those

89

days split us up by major after the second year. I was in physics, and Ishigami was in maths.' Yukawa closed the file.

'So that guy's the same age as us, then? Hmph.'

'He always looked old for his years, even back then.' Yukawa grinned. Then a look of surprise came over his face. 'A teacher? You said he teaches high school maths?'

'Yeah, at a school near where he lives. And he coaches the judo club there.'

'That's right. I'd heard he did judo from an early age. I think his grandfather ran a dojo, or something like that. At any rate, you're sure he teaches at a high school?'

'Yeah, I'm sure.'

'That's unexpected, but I'll take your word for it. I hadn't heard anything, so I assumed he was buried in research at a private university somewhere . . . Huh. Ishigami teaching maths in high school . . .' Yukawa's voice trailed off as he gazed into his memory.

'So he was a hotshot in school, then?' Kishitani asked.

Yukawa sighed. 'I don't use the word *genius* lightly, but it fits him well. One of our professors said he was the kind of student you only see once every fifty or a hundred years. Even though we were in separate departments, stories about him made the rounds. He didn't care for computers, so he would lock himself in the school lab, working out problems with paper and pencil all night.

When you saw him, it was usually from the back while he sat hunched over a desk – that's how he got the nickname "the Buddha". A term of respect, of course.'

Kusanagi nodded. It was odd to hear Yukawa talk about someone even more brilliant than himself. The detective had always thought of his friend as the genius, but he supposed that even when you were at the top, there was always something higher.

'But wouldn't someone that gifted automatically get snatched up by a university?' Kishitani asked.

'Well, it takes all types, even at a university,' Yukawa mumbled, sounding uncharacteristically perplexed. Kusanagi didn't imagine his friend had wasted much time worrying about how old acquaintances were faring in the world.

As if on cue, Yukawa asked, 'How is he doing? Did he seem well?'

'I can't say. He didn't seem ill, at least. We talked to him for a bit, but he was hard to get a handle on. Maybe he just wasn't very personable . . .'

'No man can know the mind of the Buddha,' Yukawa said with a wry chuckle.

'That's just it. Normally, when detectives come calling, you expect people to be surprised, or a little flustered, or give some reaction at least, but it was as if he was carved out of stone. It was like he couldn't be bothered to react to anything external.'

'He's not interested in anything but maths. Not

that he's without any charms, of course. He was a nice enough guy in his own way. Listen, could you tell me his address? I'd love to drop in on him when I get a slow day.'

'You, paying a social call? Now that's unusual.'

Kusanagi took out his notebook and gave Yukawa the address of the apartment building where Yasuko Hanaoka lived. Yukawa wrote it down, seeming pleased at the unexpected connection. He didn't mention the murder again.

At 6:28 P.M., Yasuko Hanaoka arrived home on her bicycle. Ishigami saw her from his apartment window. The desk in front of him was covered with a mountain of paper, each sheet filled with mathematical formulas. It was his custom to do battle with his formulas every evening after his return from school. He'd gotten out early today – no judo practice – but even so, he wasn't making much progress. In fact, he hadn't made much progress for several days now. He just sat in his room, listening for sounds next door, wondering when the detectives would come back.

They had come again the night before – the same two who had visited Ishigami's apartment. He remembered the name Kusanagi from reading it off the senior officer's badge.

Yasuko had told him they'd come to check her alibi at the cinema, as expected. They'd asked if anything memorable had happened. If she had met anyone she knew on the way in, or way out, or even during the movie. Did she have the ticket stubs, by any chance? Did she buy anything in the cinema? Did she have receipts? What had the movie been about, who had been the lead actor—?

As they hadn't asked anything about the karaoke box, he assumed they'd called on that establishment already. Of course that part of the alibi checked out. Ishigami had chosen the place because he knew it would.

Yasuko said she had shown the detectives the ticket stubs, the receipt for the programme, just as Ishigami had instructed. Other than describing the plot of the movie, she'd told the police nothing. She hadn't seen anyone, and nothing memorable or out of the ordinary had occurred. Ishigami had told her to say all of this, too.

The detectives had left, seemingly satisfied, but he didn't think for a moment that they had given up yet. The fact that they had come back to check on the cinema alibi meant they had enough data to make them suspicious of Yasuko. Ishigami wondered just what those data were.

He stood and picked up his jacket. Telephone card, wallet, and room key in hand, he stepped out of his the apartment.

He was just on the stairs when he heard footsteps coming up from below. He slowed his pace and lowered his eyes.

It was Yasuko. She didn't seem to notice who he was right away. Just before they passed, her feet stopped. She had seen him. Even looking down at his feet, Ishigami could tell she wanted to say something.

Ishigami spoke first. 'Good evening.'

He tried to say it like he would say it to anyone he happened to meet, his tone relaxed, his voice low. He didn't make eye contact or slow his pace. Passing Yasuko, he continued on down the stairs in silence.

There was no telling when the police might be watching, so whenever they did meet, they had to act like neighbours and nothing more. Another of Ishigami's own instructions. Yasuko had paused for a moment in her ascent, but then – perhaps remembering what he had told her – replied, 'Good evening' in a small voice, then continued up the stairs without another word.

Reaching the park, Ishigami quickly strode over to the phone, picked up the receiver, and put in his telephone card. There was a small convenience store about thirty metres away. The owner was closing up shop for the night. Other than that, no one else was around.

'Yes, it's me,' Yasuko said, picking up the phone immediately. She sounded like she knew the call was coming from Ishigami. Somehow, that made him happy.

'Anything unusual to report?'

'Um, yes. That detective came to the store today.'

'To Benten-tei?'

'Yes.'

'What did he ask this time?'

'He was asking whether Togashi had come to the shop at all.'

'What did you tell him?'

'I said no, he hadn't, of course. The detective said that maybe he had been there when I wasn't in, and he went back to talk to the owners. The owner told me that the detective showed him a picture of Togashi, and asked about him. You know, I think the detective suspects me.'

'That's nothing we didn't expect. There's nothing to be afraid of. Is that the only thing the detective asked?'

'No, he also asked about the club I used to work at – the bar in Kinshicho. He wanted to know if I'd been in contact with the people there. I told him no, just like you said. Then I asked him why he wanted to know where I used to work, and he told me Togashi had been there recently.'

'Ah yes. Of course.' Ishigami nodded, the receiver pressed to his ear. 'So Togashi was at your old workplace, asking after you.'

'It seems so. That must be where he heard about Benten-tei. The detective said that since it sounded like Togashi had been looking for me, it would have made sense for him to drop in at Benten-tei next. And I told him, "Well, I suppose that's true, but he didn't, so I can't help you."'

Ishigami called to mind the detective named Kusanagi. He seemed like a personable man. Soft-spoken, not too imposing. But if he was a detective in Homicide, that meant he had the requisite

95

information-gathering skills. He wasn't the kind to scare a witness into revealing something, but the sort who casually drew the truth out of them. He had noticed the letter from Imperial University in Ishigami's mail, too, which meant he was observant. And all of this made Kusanagi someone who required caution.

'Did you ask him about anything else?'

'That was the only thing I asked. But Misato . . .'

Ishigami's grip tightened on the receiver. 'They went to her school?'

'Yes, I only just heard about it myself. They caught up with her on the way home after classes. I think it was the same two detectives that came here.'

'Is Misato there now?'

'Yes, hold on.'

Misato was on the phone immediately. She must have been standing right next to her mother. 'Hello?'

'What did the detectives ask you?'

'They showed me his picture, asked if he'd been by the apartment . . .'

'Togashi. You told them he hadn't, right?'

'Yeah.'

'What else did they want to know?'

'They wanted to know about the movie. If I'd really gone on the tenth or not. They thought maybe we'd got the date wrong. I told them I knew it was then, absolutely.'

'What did the detectives say then?'

'They wanted to know if I'd told any of my friends about the movie, or texted them.'

'And?'

'I told them I didn't text anybody, but I did tell a friend. Then they wanted to know who my friends were.'

'Did you tell them?'

'I only gave them Mika's name.'

'Mika's the girl you told about the movie on the twelfth, correct?'

'Yeah, that's right.'

'Good. You did good. Did the detectives want to know anything else?'

'Nothing big. They wanted to know if I was enjoying school, how badminton practice was, that kind of stuff. I wonder how they knew I was on the badminton team? I didn't have my racquet with me.'

Ishigami surmised that Kusanagi had seen her racquet when he visited the Hanaokas' apartment. This detective was turning out to be formidable.

Yasuko got back on the phone and asked, 'Well, what should we do?' Her voice sounded faint on the other end of the line.

'Nothing, for now. This isn't a problem,' Ishigami said with conviction. He wanted to put her at ease. 'Everything is going according to my calculations. I should expect that the detectives will be back again soon. Just follow my instructions and everything will be all right.'

'Thank you, Mr Ishigami . . . you know I don't have anyone to turn to but you.'

'That's all right. Good luck. This will soon be over. I'll speak with you again tomorrow.'

Ishigami hung up the phone and took out his phone card, already slightly regretting his final words. He shouldn't have told her it would be over soon. Just how long was 'soon'? He shouldn't be saying things that couldn't be quantified like that.

However, it was true that events were developing according to plan. He had known they would find out eventually that Togashi had been looking for Yasuko – that was why Ishigami had made the effort to establish an alibi. He had also expected the police to question that alibi.

And he had expected that the police would try to make contact with Misato. They must have hoped she would be the weak link in the chain, a way to take apart the alibi in the absence of any witnesses. Ishigami had taken several steps to prevent that from happening, but he thought now that it would behoove him to check once more and make sure he hadn't overlooked anything.

Ishigami returned to his apartment, his mind racing, only to find a man standing in front of his door – a tall fellow, unfamiliar, wearing a thin, black jacket. He must have heard Ishigami coming up the steps, for he was facing towards him. His wire-rim glasses glittered.

At first, Ishigami thought it was another detective. But then he realized that no, that was wrong. The man's shoes were in perfect condition, as good as brand-new.

He approached, warily, and the man spoke. 'Ishigami?'

Ishigami looked up at the stranger's face. The man was smiling. It was a smile he remembered.

Ishigami took a deep breath, and his eyes went wide as the memories came vividly back to him from a twenty-year distance.

'Manabu Yukawa.'

CHAPTER 6

The classroom felt deserted that day, as always. The room was large enough to seat a hundred students, but there were only twenty or so there now. Most of them were in the back row so that they could slip out after attendance had been taken or work on some project of their own during the lecture.

Very few undergraduates wanted to be mathematicians. In fact, Ishigami was probably the only one in his entire class. And this course, with its lectures on the historical background of applied physics, was not a popular one.

Even Ishigami wasn't all that interested in the lectures, but he sat in the second chair from the left edge in the front row. He always sat there, or in the closest available position, in every room, at every lecture. He avoided sitting in the middle because he thought it would help him maintain objectivity. Even the most brilliant professor could sometimes err and say something inaccurate, after all.

It was usually lonely at the front of the classroom, but on this particular day someone was sitting in the seat directly behind him. Ishigami wasn't paying his visitor any attention. He had important things to do before the lecturer arrived. He took out his notebook and began scribbling formulas.

'Ah, an adherent of Erdös, I see,' said a voice from behind.

At first, Ishigami didn't realize the comment was directed at him. But after a moment the words sank in and his attention lifted from his work – not because he wanted to start a conversation, but out of excitement at hearing someone other than himself mention the name 'Erdös'. He looked around.

It was a fellow student, a young man with shoulder-length hair, cheek propped up on one hand, his shirt hanging open at the neck. Ishigami had seen him around. He was a physics major, but beyond that, Ishigami knew nothing about him.

Surely he *can't be the one who spoke*, Ishigami was thinking, when the long-haired student, still propping up one cheek, remarked, 'I'm afraid you're going to hit your limits working with just a pencil and paper – of course, you're welcome to try. Might get something out of it.'

Ishigami was surprised that his voice was the same one he'd heard a moment earlier. 'You know what I'm doing?'

'Sorry – I just happened to glance over your shoulder. I didn't mean to pry,' the other replied, pointing at Ishigami's desk.

Ishigami's eyes went back to his notebook. He had written out some formulas, but it was only a part of the whole, the beginnings of a solution. If this guy knew what he was doing just from this, then he must have worked on the problem himself.

'You've worked on this, too?' Ishigami asked.

The long-haired student let his hand fall down to the desktop. He grinned and shrugged. 'Nah. I try to avoid doing anything unnecessary. I'm in physics, you know. We just use the theorems you mathematicians come up with. I'll leave working out the proofs to you.'

'But you do understand what it – what this – means?' Ishigami asked, gesturing at his notebook page.

'Yes, because it's already been proven. No harm in knowing what has a proof and what doesn't,' the student explained, steadily meeting Ishigami's gaze. 'The four-colour problem? Solved. You can colour any map with only four colours.'

'Not any map.'

'Oh, that's right. There were conditions. It had to be a map on a plane or a sphere, like a map of the world.'

It was one of the most famous problems in mathematics, first put into print in a paper in 1879 by one Arthur Cayley, who had asked the question: are four colours sufficient to colour the contiguous countries on any map, such that no two adjacent countries are ever coloured the same? All one had to do was prove that four colours were sufficient, or present a map where such separation was impossible – a process which had taken nearly one hundred years. The final proof had come from two mathematicians at the University of Illinois, Kenneth Appel and Wolfgang Haken. They had used a computer to confirm that all maps were only variations on roughly 150 basic maps, all of which could be coloured with four colours.

That was in 1976.

'I don't consider that a very convincing proof,' Ishigami stated.

'Of course you don't. That's why you're trying to solve it there with your paper and pencil.'

'The way they proved it would take too long for humans to do with their hands. That's why they used a computer. But that makes it impossible to determine, beyond a doubt, whether their proof is correct. It's not real mathematics if you have to use a computer to verify it.'

'Like I said, a true adherent of Erdös,' the long-haired student observed with a chuckle.

Paul Erdös was a Hungarian-born mathematician famous for travelling the world and engaging in joint research with other mathematicians wherever he went. He believed that the best theorems were those with clear, naturally elegant proofs. Though he'd acknowledged that Appel and Haken's work on the four-colour problem was probably correct, he had disparaged their proof for its lack of beauty.

Ishigami felt like this peculiar visitor had somehow peered directly into his soul.

'I went to one of my professors the other day about an examination problem concerning numbers analysis,' the other student said, changing the subject.

'The issue wasn't with the problem itself. It was that the answer wasn't very elegant. As I suspected, he'd made a mistake typing up the problem. What surprised me was that another student had already come to him with the same issue. To tell the truth, I was a little disappointed. I thought I was the only one who had truly solved the problem.'

'Oh that? That was nothing—' Ishigami began, then closed his mouth.

'—Nothing special?' the other finished for him. *'Not for a student like Ishigami* – that's what my professor said. Even when you're at the top, there's always something higher, eh? It was about then that I figured I wouldn't make it as a mathematician.'

'You said you're a physics major, right?'

'Yukawa's the name. Pleased to meet you.' He extended a hand towards Ishigami.

Ishigami took his hand, wondering at his peculiar new acquaintance. Then, he began to feel happy. He'd always thought he was the only weird one.

He wouldn't have called Yukawa a 'friend', but from then on, whenever they chanced to meet in the hall, they would always stop and exchange a few words. Yukawa was well read, and he knew a lot about fields outside of mathematics and physics. He could even hold his own in a conversation about literature or the arts – topics that Ishigami secretly despised. Of course, lacking any basis for comparison, Ishigami didn't know how deep the man's knowledge of such things went.

Besides, Yukawa soon noticed Ishigami's lack of interest in anything other than maths, and the scope of their conversations rapidly narrowed.

Nonetheless, Yukawa was the first person Ishigami had met at university with whom he felt he could talk intelligently and whose ability he respected.

Over time, however, their chance encounters became less and less frequent. Their paths took them in different directions, one in the maths department, the other in physics. A student who maintained a certain grade point average was allowed to switch departments, but neither of them had any desire for such a switch. *This is really the proper choice for both of us*, Ishigami thought. *Each on the path that suits him best.* They shared a common desire to describe the world around them with theorems, but they approached this task from opposite directions. Ishigami built his theorems with the rigid blocks of mathematical formulas while Yukawa began everything by making observations. When he found a mystery, he would go about breaking it down. Ishigami preferred simulations; Yukawa's heart was in actual experimentation.

As time went on Ishigami occasionally heard rumors about his acquaintance. He was filled with genuine admiration when he heard, in the autumn of their second year in graduate school, that a certain American industrial client had come to buy the rights to the 'magnetized gears' Yukawa had proposed in a thesis.

Ishigami didn't know what had become of

Yukawa after their master's programme was finished; he himself had already left the university by then. And so the years had slipped by.

'Some things never change, eh?' Yukawa said, looking up at the bookshelves in Ishigami's apartment.

'What's that?'

'Your love of maths, for one. I doubt anyone in my whole department has a personal collection of materials this thorough.'

Ishigami didn't dispute it. The bookshelves held more than just books. He also had files of publications from different research centers around the world. Most of them he had obtained over the Internet, but even so, he thought of himself as being more in touch with the world of mathematics than the average half-baked researcher.

'Well, have a seat,' he said after a moment. 'Want some coffee?'

'I don't mind coffee, but I did bring this,' Yukawa said, pulling a box from the paper bag in his hand. It held a famous brand of sake.

'You didn't have to go out of your way like that.'

'I couldn't come meet a long-lost friend empty-handed.'

'Well, then, how about I order out some sushi? You haven't eaten yet, have you?'

'Oh, don't worry about me.'

'No, I haven't eaten yet either.'

Ishigami picked up the phone and opened the

file where he kept all his menus from local places that delivered. He perused one briefly, then ordered a deluxe assortment and some sashimi on the side. The person taking the order sounded almost shocked to hear a request for something other than the cheap basic selection usually ordered from his telephone number. Ishigami wondered how long it had been since he had entertained a proper visitor.

'I have to say it's quite a surprise you showing up, Yukawa,' he said, taking his seat.

'Out of the blue I heard your name from a friend the other day, and thought I'd like to see you again.'

'A friend? Who could that have been?'

'Er, well, it's a bit of a strange story, actually.' Yukawa scratched his nose. 'A detective from the police department came by your apartment, right? Guy named Kusanagi?'

'A detective?' Ishigami felt a jolt run through him, but he took care not to let his surprise show on his face. He peered at his old classmate. *What does he know?*

'Right, well, that detective was a classmate of mine.'

Ishigami blinked. 'A classmate?'

'We were in the badminton club together. I know, he doesn't seem the Imperial University type, does he? I think he was over in the sociology department.'

'Ah . . . no kidding.' The cloud of unease that

had been spreading in Ishigami's chest vanished in a moment. 'Now that you mention it, I remember him looking at a letter that came to me from the university. That must've been why he asked about it. Wonder why he didn't tell me he was a fellow alum?'

'Well, honestly, he doesn't consider graduates from Imperial University sciences to be his class-mates. Sometimes, I don't even think he thinks of us as the same species.'

Ishigami nodded. He felt the same way about those in the humanities. It was strange to think of the detective as someone who had been at the same university at the same time.

'So Kusanagi tells me you're teaching maths at a high school?' Yukawa asked, staring directly at Ishigami's face.

'The high school near here, yes. You're at the university, Yukawa?'

'Yeah. Lab 13,' he replied simply.

Yukawa wasn't trying to ring his own bell, Ishigami realized; he didn't seem to have any desire to boast.

'Are you a professor?'

'No. I'm just futzing around as an assistant professor. It's pretty crowded at the top, you know,' Yukawa said, without any discernible ire.

'Really? I figured you would be a full professor for sure by now, after all that hype about those magnetic gears of yours.'

Yukawa smiled and rubbed his face. 'I think

108

you're the only one who remembers all that. They never did make a working prototype. The whole thing ended as an empty theory.' Yukawa picked up the sake bottle and began to open it.

Ishigami stood and brought two cups from the cupboard.

'But you,' Yukawa said, 'I had you pegged as a university professor, holed up in your office, taking on the Riemann hypothesis or some such. So what happened to Ishigami the Buddha? Or are you truly following in the footsteps of Erdös, playing the itinerant mathematician?'

'Nothing like that, I'm afraid,' Ishigami said with a light sigh.

'Well, let's drink,' Yukawa offered, ending his questions and pouring Ishigami a glass.

The fact of it was, Ishigami had planned on devoting his life to mathematics. After he got his master's, he had planned to stay at the university, just like Yukawa, earning his doctorate. Making his mark on the world.

That hadn't happened, because he had to look after his parents. Both were getting on in years and were in ill health. There was no way he could have made ends meet for all of them with the kind of part-time job he could have held while attending classes. Instead, he had looked around for steadier employment.

Just after his graduation, one of his professors had told him that a newly established university was looking for a teaching assistant. It was within commuting distance of his home, and it would allow him to continue his research, so he'd decided to check it out. It was a decision that quickly turned his life upside down.

He found it impossible to carry on with his own work at the new school. Most of the professors there were consumed with vying for power and protecting their positions, and not one cared the least bit about nurturing young scholars or doing groundbreaking research. The research reports Ishigami slaved over ended up permanently lodged in a professor's untended in-box. Worse still, the academic level of the students at the school was shockingly low. The time he spent teaching kids who couldn't even grasp high school level mathematics had detracted enormously from his own research. On top of all this, the pay was depressingly low.

He had tried finding a job at another university, but it wasn't easy. Universities that even had a mathematics department were few and far between. When they did have one, their budgets were meagre, and they lacked the resources to hire assistants. Maths research, unlike engineering, didn't have major corporations waiting in line to sponsor it.

Ishigami had soon realized he had to make a change, and fast. He had decided to take his teaching credentials and make those his means of support. This had meant giving up on being a career mathematician.

He didn't see any point in telling Yukawa all this, though. Most people who had been forced out of research had similar stories. Ishigami knew his was nothing special.

The sushi and sashimi arrived, so they ate, and drank a little more. When the bottle of sake Yukawa had opened was dry, Ishigami brought out some whiskey. He rarely drank much alcohol, but he did like to sip a little to ease his head after working on a particularly difficult mathematics problem.

Though the conversation wasn't exactly lively, he did enjoy discussing their old school days, as well as a bit about mathematics. Ishigami realized how little of the last two decades he had spent just chatting. This might've been the first time he had talked this much to another person since graduating. Who else could understand him but Yukawa? Who would even recognize him as an equal?

'That's right, I almost forgot the most important thing I wanted to show you,' Yukawa said suddenly, pulling a large brown envelope from his paper bag and placing it in front of Ishigami.

'What's this?'

'Open it and find out,' Yukawa said with a grin.

The envelope held a sheet of paper covered with mathematical formulas. Ishigami glanced over it, recognizing it almost instantly. 'You're trying a counterexample to the Riemann hypothesis?'

'That was quick.'

The Riemann hypothesis was widely considered

to be one of the most important unresolved problems confronting modern mathematics. The challenge was to prove a hypothesis proposed by the German mathematician Bernhard Riemann; no one had been able to do it so far.

The report Yukawa brought was an attempt to show that the hypothesis was false. Ishigami knew there were powerhouse scholars elsewhere in the world trying to do this very thing. Of course, none had succeeded yet.

'One of the professors in our maths department let me copy this. It hasn't been published anywhere yet. It's not a complete counterexample, but I think it's heading in the right direction,' Yukawa explained.

'So you think that the Riemann hypothesis is wrong?'

'I said it was heading in the right direction. If the hypothesis is right, then of course it means there's a mistake in this paper.'

Yukawa's eyes glittered like those of a young miscreant watching a particularly elaborate practical joke unfold. Ishigami realized what he was doing. This was a challenge. He wanted to see just how soft Ishigami the Buddha had grown.

'Mind if I take a look?'

'That's why I brought it.'

Ishigami pored over the paper intently. After a short while he went to his desk and got out a fresh piece of paper. Laying it down before him, he picked up a ballpoint pen.

'You're familiar with the P = NP problem, right?'
Yukawa asked from behind him.

Ishigami looked around. 'You're referring to the question of whether or not it is as easy to determine the accuracy of another person's results as it is to solve the problem yourself – or, failing that, how the difference in difficulty compares. It's one of the questions the Clay Mathematics Institute has offered a prize to solve.'

'I figured you might be.' Yukawa smiled and tipped back his glass.

Ishigami turned back to the desk.

He had always thought of mathematics as a treasure hunt. First, one had to decide where to dig; then one had to determine the proper excavation route that led to the answer. Once you had a plan, you could make formulas to fit it, and they would give you clues. If you wound up empty-handed, you had to go back to the beginning and choose another route. Only by doing this over and over, patiently, yet boldly, could you hope to find the treasure – a solution no one else had ever found.

Therefore, it would seem that analyzing the validity of someone else's solution was simply a matter of following the routes they had taken. In fact, however, it was never that simple. Sometimes, you could follow a mistaken route to a false treasure, and proving that it was false could be even harder than finding the real answer.

Which was why someone had proposed the exasperating P = NP problem.

Ishigami immersed himself in the problem and soon lost track of time. He was an explorer heading out on safari, a soldier diving headlong into battle, an engine fuelled by excitement and pride. His eyes never left the formulas for a moment, his every brain cell devoted to their manipulation.

'Ah!' Ishigami stood suddenly. Report paper in hand, he whirled around. Yukawa had put on his coat and was curled up in a ball on the floor, sleeping. Ishigami walked over, stopped, and shook his shoulder. 'I figured it out.'

Yukawa sat up, eyes bleary with sleep. He rubbed his face and looked up at Ishigami. 'What's that?'

'I figured it out. I'm sorry to report that this counterexample is wrong. It was an interesting approach, but there was a fundamental flaw in the distribution of prime numbers—'

'Hold on a second. Hold on.' Yukawa held up his hands. 'My brain is nowhere near awake enough to understand whatever you just said. I'm not sure I would understand even after a few cups of coffee, for that matter. To be honest, I don't know the Riemann hypothesis from a hole in the ground. I just brought that because I thought you'd be interested.'

'But you said you thought it was heading in the right direction?'

'I was just repeating what the professor over in the mathematics department said. Actually, he knew about the flaw in his counterproof. That's why he didn't publish it.'

'Oh. No wonder I found it,' Ishigami said, crestfallen.

'No, it is a wonder. I'm impressed. The professor told me that even a top-flight mathematician would never find that error in one sitting.' Yukawa looked at his watch. 'And you did it in only . . . six hours. Impressive!'

'Six hours?' Ishigami looked out the window. The sky was already whitening. He glanced at the alarm clock to see that it was almost five A.M.

'Ishigami the Buddha lives on!' Yukawa cheered. 'Some things never change. Which is kind of a relief.'

'Sorry, Yukawa. I totally forgot you were still here.'

'Oh, I don't mind. Still, you should probably get some sleep. You've got school, don't you?'

'That I do. But now I'm too excited to sleep. I haven't concentrated on something like this for a long time. Thank you.' Ishigami extended a hand.

'I'm glad I came,' Yukawa said, giving him a firm shake.

'Me, too.' Ishigami nodded. 'There's not much to do here, but feel free to make yourself at home until the trains start running again.'

Ishigami slept until seven o'clock. He slept deeply, either because his brain was tired or from a deep psychological satisfaction, and when he woke his mind was unusually clear.

He was bustling about, getting ready for work, when Yukawa commented, 'Your neighbour was up early.'

'My neighbour?'

'I just heard them leaving. A little after six thirty, I guess.'

So Yukawa had been awake.

Ishigami was wondering if he should say something when Yukawa continued, 'That Detective Kusanagi I was telling you about says that she's a suspect. That's why he dropped in on you, isn't it?'

Ishigami assumed an air of calm and put on his suit jacket. 'He tells you about his cases, does he?'

'Now and then. It's more like him dropping by to shoot the breeze, then complaining to me about work before I can get rid of him.'

'I still don't know what the whole thing is about. Detective . . . Kusanagi, was it? He didn't give me any details.'

'Well, apparently, a man was murdered. Your neighbour's ex-husband.'

'Huh. Never would have guessed it,' Ishigami said, his face expressionless.

'You talk to your neighbour much?' Yukawa asked.

Ishigami's brain went into overdrive. Judging from the tone of his voice, Yukawa didn't suspect anything. That wasn't why he was asking questions. Simply brushing him off was an option here. But Yukawa knew the detective – he had to

116

consider that. Yukawa might mention his visit here. Ishigami had to answer.

'I wouldn't say "much", but I do frequent the lunch box shop where Ms Hanaoka – that's her name – works. Forgot to mention that to Detective Kusanagi, now that I think about it.'

'So, she's a seller of lunch boxes,' Yukawa mused.

'I don't go there because my neighbour works there – she just happens to work at the store where I buy my lunch, if you follow. It's near the school.'

'I hear you. Still, I can't imagine it's all that pleasant having a murder suspect in the neighbourhood.'

'It wasn't me she murdered, so I don't see how it's any of my business.'

'How very true,' Yukawa said, without a shred of suspicion.

They left the apartment at seven thirty. Yukawa decided not to head for the nearest station, instead saying he'd walk with Ishigami to his school and take the train from there, a route that would save him from having to make a transfer.

Yukawa didn't speak of the case or Yasuko Hanaoka again. At first Ishigami had wondered if Kusanagi had sent him to get information, but now he decided he'd probably been overthinking the situation. Kusanagi would have no reason to go to such lengths to get information from him anyway.

'Interesting commute you have here,' Yukawa commented. They crossed under the Shin-Ohashi

Bridge and began to walk along the slow-flowing Sumida River, past the ramshackle village set up by the homeless.

The grey-haired man with the ponytail was hanging up his laundry. Beyond him, the Can Man was well into his daily routine.

'It's the same thing every day,' Ishigami said. 'This entire past month, nothing's changed a bit. You could set your watch by these people.'

'That's what happens when you free people from the restraints of time. They make their own rigid schedule.'

'I couldn't agree more.'

They went up the stairs just before Kiyosu Bridge, in the shadow of a nearby office building. Seeing their reflection in a glass door on the first floor, Ishigami shook his head. 'How have you managed to stay so young, Yukawa? You still have a full head of hair. How different we two are!'

'Not as full as it used to be. And what's underneath it is slowing down, too.'

'Good thing it was going too fast to begin with.'

While they chatted, Ishigami felt himself growing tense. If they kept on like this, Yukawa would come with him all the way to Benten-tei. He started to worry that this genius observer of the natural world might notice something between him and Yasuko Hanaoka if he happened to see the two of them together. And he didn't want to fluster Yasuko by suddenly arriving with a stranger.

When he saw the sign he pointed it out. 'There is the lunch box place I was telling you about.'

'Benten-tei, huh? Interesting name. The owners must have hoped that Benten, the goddess of wealth, would smile down on them.'

'Well, they have my business. I'll be buying one there again today.'

'Right. Well, I suppose I'd best be off, then.' Yukawa stopped.

This was unexpected – and welcome, Ishigami thought. 'I'm sorry I wasn't the best host.'

'Not at all. You sell yourself short.' Yukawa narrowed his eyes. 'You ever think about going back to the university to continue your research?'

Ishigami shook his head. 'Anything I can do at a university I can do on my own. And I doubt any place would be willing to take me at my age.'

'You might be surprised, but I won't twist your arm. Good luck, Ishigami.'

'You, too, Yukawa.'

'It was good seeing you again.'

The two shook hands, and Ishigami stood on the pavement to see his friend off. He wasn't being sentimental. He just didn't want Yukawa to see him go into Benten-tei. When Yukawa had disappeared into the distance, Ishigami turned and walked swiftly towards the shop.

CHAPTER 7

Yasuko breathed a sigh of relief when she saw Ishigami's face. He looked calm, and that made her calm somehow. She had noticed that he had a visitor the night before and that the lights in his apartment were on late into the night. She was afraid that the detective had come back to question him again.

'I'll take the special.' He placed the order in his usual monotone. As always, he did not so much as glance up at Yasuko.

'One special, coming up. Thank you,' she said. Then she added in a low voice, 'You had a visitor yesterday?'

Ishigami stammered, then glanced up at her, blinking. He looked around the room quickly. 'We shouldn't speak like this,' he whispered. 'They might be watching.'

'I'm sorry,' Yasuko said, withdrawing behind the counter.

The two said nothing while they waited for the lunch to be ready. They didn't even exchange glances.

Yasuko glanced out at the street but couldn't

see anyone watching. Of course, if the police really were out there, they wouldn't be so obvious about it.

The boxed lunch arrived from the back. She handed it to Ishigami.

'He was an old classmate,' Ishigami said abruptly as he was paying.

'What?'

'An old classmate from university came to visit. I'm sorry if it alarmed you.' Ishigami talked without moving his lips.

'Oh, no . . . I'm fine,' Yasuko said, smiling despite herself. Then she looked down at the floor, so that anyone watching from outside would not see her mouth. 'I see. I wondered – you don't seem to have many visitors.'

'He was my first, actually. It was a surprise to me.'

'Well, I'm glad for you, then.'

'Right, thanks,' Ishigami said awkwardly as he took the bag with his lunch in it from her. 'Tonight, then.'

Which meant he would be calling her again this evening. Yasuko nodded, smiling.

She watched the back of his stocky figure as he stepped out onto the street, wondering that even a man who was as much of a hermit as he was should have friends.

When the morning rush had subsided, she went to take her usual break in the back of the shop with Sayoko and her husband. Sayoko had a sweet tooth; she put out a couple of sweet bean cakes for her and Yasuko. Mr Yonazawa, whose tastes ran more

121

towards the salty and savoury, looked at the cakes without interest and sipped at his tea. The part-timer, Kaneko, was out making deliveries.

'Did they bug you again yesterday?' Sayoko asked after a sip of tea.

'Who?'

'Them. The cops.' Sayoko frowned. 'They had no end of questions for us during the day, you know. I figured they might drop by your place again at night. That's what we thought,' she said, looking to her husband. The taciturn Yonazawa merely nodded.

'No, no. Nothing since that time I told you about.'

Actually, Misato had been questioned outside her school, but Yasuko didn't see the need to tell them that.

'Well then, I'm glad. They can be very persistent.'

'All they were doing was asking a few questions,' Yonazawa said. 'It's not like they really suspect Yasuko of anything. They just have to follow procedure.'

'I suppose the police are public servants, after all. Still, even if she isn't a suspect, I'm sure glad that her ex didn't come here. If he had stopped in before he was killed, then the cops would be after Yasuko something fierce.'

'Now don't go scaring her with your foolishness,' Yonazawa scoffed at his wife.

'You never know! Wasn't the detective saying that Togashi had been asking around at Marian for Yasuko?' Marian was the club in Kinshicho where Yasuko and Sayoko had worked. 'He said it would have made sense for him to come here next. He was suspicious of something. I saw it on his face.'

'Well, maybe – but that Togashi never did show up here, so we don't have to worry about it, do we?'

'That's why I said I'm glad he didn't. If he had, then mark my words, the poor girl wouldn't get a moment's peace.'

Yonazawa frowned and shook his head, unconcerned. Yasuko wondered how he'd react if he found out that Togashi really had come to the shop. She felt a knot form in her stomach.

'Well, either way, it can't be pleasant. You just need to hang in there, Yasuko,' Sayoko said brightly. 'Of course the police will be investigating you; he was your ex-husband, after all. But once they are satisfied you had nothing to do with it, they'll leave you be. And then you'll be really free at last. I know Togashi was still hanging around your neck.'

Yasuko forced herself to smile.

'To be perfectly honest, I'm glad he got himself killed,' Sayoko said emphatically.

'Hey now.' Yonazawa frowned.

'Oh, what's the harm in telling it like it is? You just don't know how much trouble poor Yasuko went through on that man's account.'

'And you do?'

'Well, I have an idea – Yasuko's told me quite a bit. She started working at Marian just to get away

123

from him, isn't that true? And when I think about him snooping around there looking for her – why, it just gives me the shivers. I don't know who killed him, but I'd like to shake their hand.'

Yonazawa rolled his eyes and stood. Sayoko, looking disgruntled, watched him leave, then turned to Yasuko. 'Still, you have to wonder what did happen. Maybe some loan shark finally caught up with him?'

'Who knows?' Yasuko shrugged.

'Well, I hope you're spared the worst of it. That's all I'm concerned about,' Sayoko said quickly, picking up the last bit of bean cake and popping it in her mouth.

Yasuko returned to the front of the shop, the conversation weighing on her spirit. It was clear that the Yonazawas didn't suspect anything. To the contrary, they were concerned that the whole investigation was going to be a nuisance for her. It hurt to deceive them, but they would be in for far more trouble if she were arrested. That would be sure to hurt business at Benten-tei. She really had no other choice but to continue to conceal the truth from them.

She went about her work mechanically as the afternoon wore on, haunted by thoughts of her predicament. Each time her mind began to wander, she forced herself to focus on the task at hand, concentrating on the customers as best she could.

It was approaching six o'clock, and no customers

had been in for a while, when the shop door swung open.

'Welcome,' Yasuko said reflexively. Then she glanced at the new arrival. Her eyes widened. 'My . . .'

'Heya.' The man who stood before her smiled, wrinkles forming at the corners of his eyes.

'Mr Kudo!' Yasuko put her hands to her open mouth. 'What are you doing here?'

'What do you mean? I'm here to buy a lunch box,' Kudo said, looking up at the row of pictures showing the various boxed lunches they had for sale. 'Say, pretty nice selection you got here.'

'They told you where to find me at Marian.'

'Something like that.' He grinned. 'I dropped by there the other day. First time in a while.'

Yasuko called into the back of the shop, 'Sayoko! Come quick! You're never going to believe this!'

'What is it? What's wrong?' Sayoko asked, rushing out.

'It's Mr Kudo!' Yasuko answered, smiling. 'He's come to visit!'

'What? Mr Kudo . . . ?' Sayoko came out from the back, taking off her apron. When she saw the man standing there in his coat, smiling, her mouth opened wide. 'Why, Kudo! It is you!'

'You both look well. How are you and the old man getting along, *mama*? From the looks of your place, I'd say quite well.'

'Oh, we get by. It's so nice to see you again! To what do we owe the honour?'

125

'Nothing much, I just wanted to see your faces again,' Kudo replied, with a glance at Yasuko. He was scratching the tip of his nose – an old habit. Yasuko remembered that was something he did when he was feeling particularly shy about something.

Kudo had been a regular at the club in Akasaka when Yasuko first started working there. He had always asked for her at the club, and once or twice, they had even gone to dinner before her shift started. Sometimes, when club hours were over, they had gone out drinking. When she had moved on to Club Marian in Kinshicho to escape Togashi, Kudo was the only customer she had told. He'd quickly become a regular at her new workplace. He was also the first she had told when she quit Marian. She remembered the sad look on his face. 'Work hard, and be happy,' he had said.

She hadn't seen him since.

Yonazawa came out from the back of the shop, and soon they were all exchanging old stories. The two men knew each other well, both having been regulars at Club Marian.

After they had all talked for a while, Sayoko suggested that Yasuko leave early so that she and Kudo could go out for tea. Yonazawa nodded in assent.

Yasuko looked at Kudo.

'Only if you have time?' he asked. Of course, he had probably come close to closing time with this in mind.

'Just for a little while, then,' she replied, smiling.

They left the shop, walking towards Shin-Ohashi Road.

'Truth be told, I'd rather be taking you out to dinner, but I'll let you off the hook today. I'm sure your daughter's expecting you at home,' Kudo said as they walked. She had told him about her daughter shortly after getting to know him at Akasaka.

'Speaking of which, how's your son?'

'Great. He's a senior already. Makes my head hurt just thinking about college exams,' he said, grimacing for effect.

Kudo was the manager of a small printing company. He lived in Osaki, in southern Tokyo, with his wife and son.

They went into a coffee shop along the road. Yasuko avoided the family restaurant near the intersection where she had met with Togashi.

'I went to Marian to ask after you,' Kudo told her. 'I remember you telling me that you were going to work at a lunch box place with *mama* Sayoko after you quit, but I didn't know where that was.'

'You just remembered me, out of the blue?'

'Yeah, well, not exactly.' Kudo lit a cigarette. 'I heard about the murder on the news, and started to worry about you. Sorry to hear about your ex.'

'Oh . . . I'm surprised you knew it was him.'

Kudo chuckled, blowing out smoke. 'Of course I knew it was him. The name "Togashi" was right up there on the screen, and I'd never forget that face.'

'. . . I'm sorry.'

'Nothing for you to apologize about,' Kudo laughed, waving his hand dismissively.

She knew Kudo had a thing for her, of course. In truth, she was rather fond of him, too. Yet their relationship had always been strictly platonic. On more than one occasion he had invited her to join him at a hotel, but she had always refused as pleasantly as she could. She lacked the courage to have an affair with a man who was married with children, and she was, at the time, married, too, though she hid that from Kudo and her other customers.

Kudo had finally met Togashi once when seeing Yasuko home. She always had the taxi drop her off a short distance from her apartment, and that night was no exception. But she had left her cigarette case behind in the taxi. Kudo had discovered it and followed her out of the taxi to return it. He had seen her go inside the apartment, so he'd knocked on the door. But when the door opened, it wasn't Yasuko, but a stranger who had answered – Togashi.

Togashi had been drunk. When he saw Kudo standing there outside the door, breathless, he had immediately assumed it was one of her customers who just couldn't take no for an answer. Before Kudo could even explain himself, Togashi had flown into a rage and started throwing punches.

128

If Yasuko hadn't come out of the shower to stop them, there was no knowing how far it would have gone.

A few days later, Yasuko took Togashi with her to Kudo's workplace to apologize. Togashi had been on his best behaviour. He knew full well what would happen if Kudo filed a police report.

Yet Kudo had shown no rancour. All he had done was warn Togashi that he couldn't let his wife work at nightclubs forever. Although Togashi clearly didn't appreciate the criticism, he'd said nothing in return and merely bowed his head.

Even after that, Kudo had continued coming to the club as usual, always treating Yasuko exactly the same as before. But they had never met outside of club hours again.

As time wore on, every once in a while, Kudo had asked about Togashi when no one else was around – usually about whether he had found work. All Yasuko had been able to do was shake her head.

Kudo had been the first to notice when Togashi grew more violent. She had done the best she could to hide the bruises with makeup, but while it might have been good enough to deceive most customers, she never fooled him.

You should get an attorney, I'll pay for it, he once offered.

Now, years later, as they sat down with their coffee, Kudo looked over her shoulder and asked, 'So, what about this whole thing? I hope you didn't get caught up in it?'

'Well, the police have been by a few times, but that's about all.'

'I figured they might,' Kudo said with a sigh.

'It's really nothing to worry about,' Yasuko assured him, laughing.

'And the media haven't been after you as well?'

'No, not at all.'

'Well, that's good news, at least. I didn't think Togashi's murder was the kind of spectacular event that the media hounds tend to jump on, but you never know. If you were having trouble with them, I thought there might be something I could do to help.'

'Thank you. You're too kind, as always.'

Kudo blushed. Looking down at the table, he reached for his coffee cup. 'Well, I'm just glad to hear that you didn't have anything to do with it.'

'Of course I didn't. What, you thought I did?'

'Not like that. As soon as I heard the news, I was worried about you. Someone murdered your ex, after all. I don't know who killed him or for what reason, I was just worried that it might come back around to you somehow.'

'Sayoko said the same. You all worry far too much on my account.'

'Well, seeing how good you look, I'm starting to think that maybe I *was* worrying about the whole thing a bit too much. You've been divorced from him for a few years now, too. Had you seen him recently?'

'Seen him?'

'Yeah, Togashi.'

'Not at all,' she replied, feeling the muscles in her face tighten.

Thankfully, Kudo switched topics and began talking about his life. The economy was in a downturn, but his company had managed to tread water so far. When he talked about his home life, he only mentioned his son. This had always been the case. Yasuko knew nothing about Kudo's relationship with his wife, though she had always imagined them getting along well. One thing Yasuko had discovered during her time working as a hostess was that men who were good listeners and truly cared about other people's problems generally came from happy homes.

When they left the coffee shop, it was raining.

'This is my fault,' Kudo apologized to Yasuko. 'You could have beat the rain if you'd gone straight home.'

Yasuko shook her head. 'Don't be silly.'

'You live far from here?'

'Only about ten minutes by bicycle.'

'Bicycle? Oh dear.' Kudo bit his lip, looking up at the clouds.

'It's okay. I have a folding umbrella in my bag, and my bicycle's at the shop. I'll walk home and just go in a little early tomorrow.'

'Let me give you a lift.'

'No, it's all right.'

But Kudo was already stepping out into the street, hailing a cab.

'Let's have dinner next time,' Kudo said as the taxi pulled out into the street, the two of them in the back. 'Your daughter can come along, too, if that works better.'

'You don't have to worry about her – but what about you?'

'Oh, I'm fine anytime. Not that busy these days.'

'Oh. Right.'

What she had meant was, *What about your wife?* but she decided not to press the matter. She sensed that he got her drift but was avoiding the topic.

He asked for her mobile number, and she gave it to him. She couldn't think of a good reason not to.

Kudo had the taxi take them right to her apartment. She was sitting on the inside, by the door that didn't open, so they both had to get out.

'Jump back in or you'll get wet,' she said, standing out on the pavement.

'Right. Till next time.'

Yasuko merely nodded and smiled.

As Kudo got back into the taxi, he glanced past her, his eyes fixing on something. She turned around to see what it was, and discovered a man standing at the bottom of the stairs, umbrella in hand. It was too dark to see his face, but from the shape of his body she realized it was Ishigami.

Ishigami started walking down the street now, moving slowly. From the look on Kudo's face, Yasuko imagined that Ishigami had been standing there watching the two of them as they got out of the taxi.

'I'll call,' Kudo said through the window before signalling for the driver to leave.

Yasuko watched the taillights of the cab as it pulled away. Only then did she realize that her heart was fluttering. How many years had it been since she had spent time with a man who actually made her happy?

She watched as the taxi drove past Ishigami on his way down the pavement.

When she got back to her apartment, Misato was watching television.

'Anything happen today?' Yasuko asked.

Misato knew perfectly well she wasn't asking about school.

'Nope. Nothing. Mika didn't say anything, either. I don't think the police have talked to her yet.'

'Okay.'

Moments later, Yasuko's mobile phone rang. The display showed that the call was coming from a public phone.

'Yes, it's me.'

'Ishigami here,' came the low, familiar voice. 'Anything happen today?'

'Nothing in particular. Nothing with Misato, either.'

'I see. Please, be careful. The police still suspect you. They'll be doing the groundwork now, checking into everything and everyone around you.'

'I understand.'

'Did . . . anything else happen?'

'What?' Yasuko asked, flustered. 'No, nothing. I just said nothing happened.'

'Right . . . all right. Sorry. I'll talk to you again tomorrow.' Ishigami hung up.

Yasuko put down her mobile phone, wondering what that was all about. She had never heard Ishigami sound so uncertain before. Then it dawned on her that it must have been because he had seen Kudo. He had to have wondered who the man was who was talking to her so familiarly. No doubt that was why he had pressed her at the end – he wanted to know about Kudo.

Yasuko knew why Ishigami was going so far out of his way to help her and her daughter. Like Sayoko had said, he had a thing for her.

Suddenly she wondered what would happen if she got close to another man. Would Ishigami keep helping her like he had? Would he keep solving all their problems? Yasuko decided that it might be best not to have dinner with Kudo. And if they did meet, not to let Ishigami know about it. But as soon as the thought came, a strange feeling of anxiety seized her. How long would this last? How long would she have to avoid Ishigami's watchful eyes?

Would she be barred from seeing another man until the statute of limitations on Togashi's death ran out?

CHAPTER 8

From outside the gym door, Kusanagi could hear the squeaking of sneakers on polished hardwood, punctuated by what sounded like tiny percussive explosions. Familiar sounds.

He stopped in the doorway and looked inside. On the nearest tennis court he saw Yukawa poised on the near half of the court, racquet held at the ready, prepared for the next serve. The muscles in his thighs weren't as toned as they had been back when the two of them were in school, but his form was as good as ever.

His opponent was a student. He was apparently very skilled, and he had deftly countered Yukawa's usual devious attacks and answered his every move.

In one smooth motion, the younger man tossed the ball in the air and then smashed it into the corner. The game was over, and Yukawa sat down on the spot. He chuckled and said something to his victorious opponent. Then his eyes caught sight of Kusanagi. He called a thanks to the student, waved goodbye, pulled himself shakily to his feet, and, racquet in hand, headed over to the waiting detective.

'What is it now?'

Kusanagi took a half step back. 'Hey, that's my line. It was you who called me.'

There had been a call from Yukawa on the calls-received list on Kusanagi's mobile phone.

'Oh, that's right. When I tried to get ahold of you my call went direct to voice mail, but it wasn't important enough to leave a message. I figured you must be busy.'

'Actually, I had my phone turned off because I was watching a movie.'

'During business hours? You're really letting your hair down.'

'I wish. I was checking into the mother and daughter's alibi. Figured I might as well see what kind of movie the ladies went to see. After all, I can't really tell if the suspect is telling the truth if I don't know my facts.'

'Still, it's hard to beat getting paid to watch movies.'

'That's the irony of it. It's no fun at all when you're doing it for work. Anyway, I'm sorry I came all the way down here if it wasn't important. I tried to find you at the lab, but they told me you were here.'

'Well, since you're here anyway, how about getting something to eat? I do have to ask you something, after all.' Yukawa walked over to the door, where he slipped out of his gym sneakers and into his regular shoes.

'And what might that be?'

'It has to do with where you were this afternoon,' Yukawa said, walking.

'Where I was?'

Yukawa stopped and levelled his racquet at Kusanagi. 'The cinema.'

They stopped in at a bar near campus. It was a newer place, one that hadn't been there when Kusanagi was at school. They sat down at a table at the back.

'The suspect says she went to the movies on the tenth of this month – the day Togashi was murdered. Now, the daughter told one of her friends at school about it on the twelfth,' Kusanagi said, pouring Yukawa a glass of beer from a bottle. 'I just confirmed that with the friend. Which is why I went to see the movie – to see if what she said about the movie checked out.'

'Yes, yes, I'm sure you had every reason to be watching drivel on the public's dollar. So what did the daughter's friend have to say for herself?'

'Nothing helpful. According to her, there was nothing unusual about anything the daughter said. Her friend's name is Mika Ueno. Mika told me she had seen the movie, too, so they had had a lot to talk about.'

'Odd that she would wait a day after seeing it,' Yukawa noted.

'Isn't it? If she wanted to chat about it with her friends, why wouldn't she do that the next day?

137

So I started thinking, what if they really went to see that movie on the eleventh?'

'Is that possible?'

'Can't rule it out. The suspect works until six o'clock, and if the daughter came home right after badminton practice, they could make the seven o'clock show. Which is what they allegedly did on the tenth.'

'Badminton? The daughter's in the badminton club?'

'Yeah. I figured that out the first time I went to visit them. Saw her racquet in the apartment. Incidentally, the whole badminton thing bothers me, too. It's a pretty intense sport, and even if she is in junior high, she should be bushed after practice.'

'Not if she's a slacker like you who lets everyone else do the heavy lifting,' Yukawa commented, smearing some hot mustard on a rubbery cube of steamed konnyaku.

'Don't try to derail the conversation with your little jokes. What I'm trying to say is—'

'It's remarkable that a schoolgirl, worn out from badminton practice, would go off to the movies, then sing late into the night at a karaoke joint, right?'

Kusanagi blinked at his friend. That was exactly his point.

'Still, it's not entirely inconceivable. She's a healthy enough girl, right? And young.'

'That's true. But she's skinny – doesn't look like she has much stamina.'

'I don't know that that's a valid assumption, and besides, maybe practice wasn't so hard that day. And you confirmed they went to the karaoke place on the night of the tenth, didn't you?'

'Yeah.'

'Well, what time did they go into the karaoke place?'

'9:40 P.M.'

'And you confirmed that the mum works at the lunch box store until six, right? If the crime was committed in Shinozaki, then allowing for a round trip, they had two hours to do the deed and still get to karaoke. I suppose it's possible.' Yukawa folded his arms, chopsticks still in hand.

Kusanagi stared at him, wondering when he had told Yukawa that the suspect worked at a lunch box shop. 'Tell me,' he said after a moment, 'why are you so interested in this case all of a sudden? You never ask me how my other investigations are going.'

'I wouldn't call it "interest", per se. It was just on my mind. I like this business of chipping away at ironclad alibis.'

'It's less ironclad then simply hard to pin down – which is why we're working on it.'

'But you have no evidence against her, nothing that would lead you to suspect her yet, right?'

'True enough. But the fact is, we have no one else worth suspecting right now. Togashi didn't leave much of a trail. He didn't have a lot of friends, but no real enemies either. That, and doesn't it strike

139

you as a little bit too convenient that they happened to go to the movies *and* karaoke on the night of the murder?'

'I see what you mean, but you need to make some logical decisions here. Maybe you should look at something other than the alibi?'

'Don't feel you have to tell me how to do my job. We're doing all the groundwork, believe me.' Kusanagi pulled a photocopy from the pocket of his coat where it hung on his chair and spread the paper out on the table. It was a drawing of a man's face.

'What's that?'

'An artist's depiction of the victim when he was still alive. We have a few men around Shinozaki Station asking if anyone saw him.'

'That reminds me – you were saying some of the man's clothing escaped burning? A navy jacket, grey sweater, and black pants, was it? Sounds like something just about anybody might wear.'

'Doesn't it? Apparently they have a mountain of reports of people saying they saw someone a lot like him. We don't know where to start.'

'So, nothing useful at all?'

'Not really. The closest thing we have to a useful tip is one woman who says she saw a suspicious-looking guy wearing clothes like that near the station. An office lady on her way home from work; she saw him loitering there. She called it in after seeing one of the posters we put up at Shinozaki.'

'It's good to see the people here are being helpful. So why don't you question her? Maybe you can get something more out of her.'

'We did, of course. The problem is, the man she saw doesn't sound like our victim.'

'How so?'

'Well, first of all, the station she saw him at wasn't Shinozaki, but Mizue – one station before it on the same line. That, and when we showed her the picture, she said his face looked rounder than the one in our illustration.'

'Rounder, huh?'

'One thing you come to realize as a police detective is that a lot of our work consists of barking up the wrong tree. It's not like your world, where once the logic fits, you have your proof and you can call it a day.' Kusanagi busied himself with fishing for leftover chunks of potato with his chopsticks. He was expecting a snappy comeback, but Yukawa didn't say anything. When he looked up he saw his friend staring off into space, his hands lightly clasped together.

Kusanagi had seen this look before: it was a sure sign that the physicist was deep in thought – though whether the sudden revery had anything to do with the matter at hand remained to be seen.

Gradually Yukawa's eyes regained their focus. He looked at Kusanagi. 'You said the man's face was crushed?'

'Yep. His fingerprints were burned off, too. They

141

must have been trying to keep us from identifying the body.'

'What did they use to crush the face?'

Kusanagi glanced around to make sure no one was eavesdropping, then he leaned across the table. 'We haven't found anything, but we suspect the killer used a hammer. Forensics thinks the face was struck several times to break the bones. The teeth and jaw were completely destroyed, too, making it impossible for us to check them against his dental records.'

'A hammer, huh?' Yukawa muttered, using the tips of his chopsticks to split a soft stewed daikon radish.

'What about it?' Kusanagi asked.

Yukawa put down his chopsticks and rested his elbows on the table. 'If this woman from the lunch box shop *was* the killer, what exactly do you think she did that day? First, you're assuming that she didn't really go to that movie, right?'

'I'm not certain she did or didn't go, if that's what you're asking.'

'Never mind what really happened. I just want to hear some deductive reasoning.' Yukawa made an encouraging motion with one hand while lifting his beer to his lips with the other.

Kusanagi frowned. 'Well, it's more conjecture than anything solid, but here's what I think. The lunch box lady – let's just call her Ms A for short – well, Ms A gets off work and leaves the shop after six. It takes her ten minutes to walk from there to Hamamatsu Station. It's another twenty minutes from there on the subway to Shinozaki Station. She takes a bus or taxi from the station to someplace near the Old Edogawa River, which would put her near the scene of the crime at around seven o'clock.'

'And what's the victim doing during this time?'

'The victim's heading towards the scene, too. He's going there to meet with Ms A. But the victim comes from Shinozaki Station by bicycle.'

'Bicycle?'

'Yeah. There was a bicycle abandoned near where the body was found, and the prints on the bicycle matched those of the victim.'

'The prints? I thought you said his fingertips had been burned off?'

Kusanagi nodded. 'After we figured out who the John Doe was, we got some useable prints. What I should have said was the prints on the bicycle matched those we found in the room where the victim was staying. Aha! I know what you're getting at. You're going to tell me that even if we could prove the man renting the room was the same one who used that bicycle, that doesn't mean they were the victim, right? What if the man staying in the room was the real killer, and he used the bicycle? Plausible enough, I suppose. But we also found some hair in his room. It matched the hair on the victim's body. We even did DNA analyses of both and they were a match.'

Yukawa chuckled. 'No, I wasn't going to suggest

that the police had made a mistake identifying the body. I'm more concerned about the idea of him using this bicycle. Did the victim leave his bicycle at Shinozaki Station?'

'No, actually—'

Kusanagi went on to explain what he'd learned about the stolen bicycle. Yukawa's eyes widened slightly behind his wireframe glasses.

'So the victim went out of his way to steal a bicycle at the station just to go to the scene of the crime? Why not take a bus or a taxi?'

'I don't know why he stole the bike, but that's what he must've done. The guy was unemployed, after all, without a whole lot of money to his name. He probably wanted to avoid paying the bus fare.'

Yukawa, looking unconvinced, crossed his arms and gave a faint snort. 'Well, okay – however he did it, the victim went to meet with our Ms A at the scene of the crime. Go on.'

'I figure they had planned some sort of rendezvous but Ms A got there a little early and was hiding somewhere. When she saw the victim approach, she snuck up behind him, wrapped a rope around his neck, and strangled him to death.'

'Stop right there!' Yukawa raised both hands. 'How tall was the victim?'

'One hundred and seventy centimetres plus change,' Kusanagi said, resisting the urge to curse. He knew what Yukawa was going to say next.

'And Ms A?'

'About one sixty.'

'So he was over ten centimetres taller,' Yukawa said with a slight grin, resting his chin on his hand. 'You see what I'm getting at here.'

'Sure, it's hard to strangle someone taller than you. And from the angle of the marks on the victim's neck, it's pretty clear whoever strangled him was pulling upward. But the victim could have been sitting. Maybe he was still on the bicycle.'

'Well, I'm glad you had a sad excuse for your scenario ready.'

'Nothing sad about it,' Kusanagi said emphatically, bringing his fist down on the tabletop.

'So what happened next? She took off his clothes, smashed in his face with the hammer she also brought, and burned off his fingertips with a lighter? Then she set fire to his clothes, and fled the scene. That's about it?'

'She still could've made it to Kinshicho by nine o'clock.'

'Theoretically, yes. But I can't help thinking you're grasping at straws. Don't tell me that the entire department is backing your little scenario?'

Kusanagi's mouth curled into a frown. He downed the rest of his beer and waved to the waitress for another round, then turned back to Yukawa. 'Yeah, well, a lot of the men wonder if a woman really could have pulled it off.'

'As well they should. Even if she did catch him by surprise, it's not easy to strangle a grown man who is fighting back. And believe me, he would

145

have done everything in his power to stop her. Besides, it would be difficult for a woman of average size and strength to dispose of a grown man's body after the deed was done. I'm sorry, but I have to join the crowd that thinks your theory is full of holes.'

'Yeah, I figured you'd say that. I don't much believe it myself. I'm just saying it's one of several possibilities.'

'Which suggests you have some other ideas. Well, don't keep them all to yourself. Let's hear another theory.'

'I'm not claiming that I've got much of anything right now. But the scenario I just gave you assumes that the man was killed near where he was found. It's also possible he was killed somewhere else and then his corpse was dumped there. Truth be told, most of the department thinks that's what happened. Regardless of whether Ms A did it or not.'

'It does seem to be the more reasonable assumption. But it wasn't the one you offered up first. Why?'

'Simple. If Ms A was the killer, she couldn't have done it someplace else. She doesn't have a car or access to one. She can't even drive. There was no way she could have transported the body to the riverbank.'

'I see. That strikes me as an important point.'

'And then there's the matter of the bicycle. We could assume whoever left it there did so on purpose to make us think that the murder took place on the riverbank, but then there would have been no reason to go to the effort to put the victim's fingerprints on it. Especially since they went to the trouble of burning fingertips off the body.'

'The bicycle *is* a mystery. For a number of reasons.' Yukawa tapped his fingers on the tabletop like he was playing the piano. Then he stopped and said, 'Either way, isn't it better to assume that a man probably did it?'

'That's what most people at the department think. But I still think Ms A was involved.'

'So Ms A had a male accomplice?'

'We're looking into people connected to her now. She used to be a hostess at a nightclub, after all. There have to be *some* men in her life.'

'An interesting assumption. I can hear the uproar from hostesses across the country already,' Yukawa said with a grin. He took a swallow of beer, then, a serious look returning to his face, asked to see the illustration again.

Kusanagi handed him the artist's depiction of the victim. It was a rendering of Togashi as he might have appeared dressed in the clothes they'd found near the crime scene.

Yukawa stared at it intently. 'Why did the killer feel the need to strip the body, I wonder?' he muttered.

'To help hide the victim's identity. Same reason he crushed the face and got rid of the fingerprints.'

147

'Then why didn't he take the clothes with him when he left? It's only because he tried to burn them and failed that you were able to come up with that illustration there.'

'Well, he was probably in a hurry. Or he made a mistake.'

'I agree that you can tell someone's identity from their wallet or driver's licence, but can you really identify someone from their clothes or shoes? It seems like the risk involved in taking the time to take off and burn his clothes would outweigh any benefits. Wouldn't the killer want to get away as quick as he could?'

'What are you driving at? You think there's another reason they stripped him?'

'I can't say for sure. But if there was, then until you figure out that reason, you won't be able to pin down your killer.' Yukawa traced a large question mark on the illustration with his fingertip.

The performance of the junior-year group 2 maths class on the year-end exams was appalling. And group 2 wasn't the only sad story; the entire junior class had done poorly. To Ishigami it seemed like the students were getting dumber by the year.

After he'd passed out the answers, the maths teacher put up a schedule for make-up exams. The school had set a lowest acceptable score for each subject, and those students who didn't reach it wouldn't go on to the next grade. Of course, they prevented all but the most hopeless cases from failing and being held back a year by making them take as many make-up exams as they needed to pass.

Shouts of protest rose from the class when they saw the grades he'd given them. Ishigami ignored the outcry as usual, but one comment rose above the noise and reached his ears.

'Hey, Teach, aren't there universities that don't require a maths test to get in?' one of the students was saying. 'Why should us guys who are going to those schools have to pass maths?'

Ishigami looked in the direction of the student, a boy named Morioka. He was leaning back in his chair, scratching his head and looking around at the other students for support. He was a short kid, but he filled the role of class crime boss – even Ishigami, who didn't have this bunch for homeroom, knew his reputation. The boy already had a long history of warnings for riding to school on a motorbike, which was strictly forbidden.

'Are you going to art school, Morioka?' Ishigami asked.

'Well, I mean . . . if I do go to university, it'll be one without a maths exam for sure. Not that I plan on going. Besides, I'm not taking the optional maths class next year, so what's my grade this year matter? Hey, don't get me wrong, I'm thinking about you, too, Teach. Can't be much fun teaching with idiots like me in the class. So, I was thinking, maybe we could kind of come to an understanding about this. An agreement between adults, like.'

That last line got a laugh from the class. Ishigami chuckled wryly. 'If you're so worried on my account, then pass your make-up exam. It's only differential and integral calculus. That can't be too hard.'

Morioka scoffed loudly. He crossed his legs off to the side of his chair. 'What good's differential and integral calculus gonna do me? It's a waste of time.'

Ishigami had turned to the blackboard to begin an explanation of some of the trickier problems on the year-end exam, but Morioka's comment made him stop and turn around. This wasn't the kind of thing he could let slide. 'I hear you like motorbikes, Morioka. Ever watched a race?'

Morioka nodded, clearly taken aback by the sudden question.

'Well, do racers drive their bikes at a set speed? No, they're constantly adjusting their speed based on the terrain, the way the wind's blowing, their race strategy, and so on. They need to know in an instant where to hold back and where to accelerate in order to win. Do you follow?'

'Yeah, sure, I follow. But what's that got to do with maths?'

'Well, exactly how much they accelerate at a given time is the derivative of their speed at that exact moment. Furthermore, the distance they travel is the integral of their changing speed. In a race, the bikes all have to run roughly the same distance, so in determining who wins and who

150

loses, the speed differential becomes very important. So you see, differential and integral calculus is very important.'

'Yeah,' Morioka said after a confused pause, 'but a racer doesn't have to think about all that. What do they care about differentials and integrals? They win by experience and instinct.'

'I'm sure they do. But that isn't true for the support team for those racers. They run detailed simulations over and over to find the best places to accelerate – that's how they work out a strategy. And in order to do that, they use differential and integral calculus. Even if they don't know it, the computer software they're using does.'

'So why not leave the mathematics to whoever's making the software?'

'We could do that, but what if it was you who had to make the software, Morioka?'

Morioka leaned further back in his chair. 'Me? Write software? I don't think so.'

'Even if you don't become a software engineer, someone else in this class might. That's why we study mathematics. That's why we have this class. You should know that what I'm teaching here is only the tip of the iceberg – a doorway into the world of mathematics. If you don't even know where the door is, how can you ever expect to be able to walk through it? Of course, you don't have to walk through it unless you want to. All I'm testing here is whether or not you know where the doorway is. I'm giving you choices.'

As he talked, Ishigami scanned the room. Every year there was someone who asked why they had to study maths. Every year, he gave the same explanation. This time, since it was a student who liked motorbikes, he'd used the example of motorbike racing. Last year, it was an aspiring musician, so he talked about the maths used in designing musical technology. But no matter the specifics of the discussion, which changed from year to year, it was all old hat for Ishigami.

When he returned to the teachers' room after class, Ishigami found a note stuck to his desk. It was hastily scrawled, and it read, 'Call Yukawa.' With a mobile number written below, he recognized the handwriting as belonging to another one of the school's maths teachers.

What does Yukawa want? he wondered, swallowing to clear the sudden catch in his throat.

Mobile phone in hand, he went out into the hallway. He dialled the number on the memo. Yukawa picked up after the first ring.

'Sorry to bother you during school hours.'

'Is it something urgent?'

'I guess you could call it urgent, yeah. Do you think we could meet today?'

'Today? Well, I have a few more things to take care of here. I suppose if it was after five o'clock . . .' He had just finished his sixth-period class, and all the students were in homeroom. Ishigami didn't have a homeroom class of his own, so he could leave the keys to the judo dojo with another teacher and get out early if he had to.

'Great. I'll meet you at the front gate at five, then. Sound good?'

'That's fine – where are you now?'

'In the neighbourhood. See you soon!'

'Right, see you.'

After Yukawa hung up, Ishigami clutched his mobile phone with tense fingers, staring down at it. What could possibly be so urgent that it would drive the physicist to come see him here at school? Ishigami puzzled over it as he walked back to his desk.

By the time he had finished grading his few remaining exams and had gotten ready to leave it was already five. Ishigami walked out of the teachers' room and cut across the schoolyard towards the front gate.

Yukawa was standing near the gate next to the crosswalk. His black coat fluttered in the wind. When he saw Ishigami, he waved and smiled. 'Sorry to drag you out like this,' he called out cheerfully.

'I was just wondering what was so urgent that you came all the way out here to see me about it,' Ishigami said, his expression softening.

'Let's talk while we walk.' Yukawa set off down Kiyosubashi Road.

'No, this way is faster,' Ishigami said, indicating a side road. 'If we go straight through here it will get us right to my apartment building.'

'Yeah, but I want to go to that lunch box shop,' Yukawa explained.

'The lunch box shop? Why go there?' Ishigami asked, feeling the muscles in his face tighten.

'Why? To get a lunch box. Why else? I don't think I'll have time to get a proper dinner anywhere tonight, so I thought I might get something easy ahead of time. The lunches are good there, aren't they? I'd hope so, seeing as how you buy them every day.'

'Oh . . . right. Off we go, then.' Ishigami turned towards Benten-tei.

They headed off in the direction of Kiyosu Bridge. As they walked along, a large truck rattled past them on the road.

'So,' Yukawa was saying, 'I met with Kusanagi the other day – you remember, the detective that dropped in on you?'

Ishigami tensed, his premonition growing steadily worse.

'What'd he have to say?'

'Nothing big. Whenever he runs into a dead end, you see, he always comes whining to me. And never with the easy problems, either. Once he even wanted me to solve a poltergeist haunting. See what I mean?'

Yukawa began to tell him the story of the poltergeist haunting. It sounded interesting enough to Ishigami. But he knew that Yukawa hadn't come all the way here to relate a would-be ghost story.

The maths teacher was on the verge of asking

his old friend what he had really come for when the sign for Benten-tei came into view. Another wave of unease washed over him. How would Yasuko react when she saw them? It was unusual under any circumstances for Ishigami to show up at this time of day, and if he came with a friend, she would be sure to suspect the worst. He just hoped she had the sense to act naturally.

Yukawa stepped up to the sliding glass door to Benten-tei, opened it, and went inside. Ishigami followed, somewhat hesitantly. He saw Yasuko behind the counter, in the middle of helping another customer.

'Welcome!' she said brightly to Yukawa. Then she turned to look at Ishigami. A look of bewilderment came into her eyes, and her smile froze on her face.

'Did my friend do something?' Yukawa asked.

'No – nothing,' Yasuko shook her head, still smiling uncomfortably. 'He's my neighbour. He always buys his lunch here . . .'

'So I'm told. I'm here on his recommendation.'

'Thank you, then,' Yasuko said, nodding politely.

'We were classmates back in university,' Yukawa went on, turning to Ishigami. 'I was just over at his place the other day.'

'Oh, right.' Yasuko smiled and nodded again.

'Oh, he told you?'

'Yes, in passing.'

Yukawa nodded, smiling. 'So, what do you recommend? No, what does he usually buy?'

'Mr Ishigami almost always gets the special, but I'm afraid we're sold out . . .'

'That's too bad. Let's see, then. They all look so good . . .'

While Yukawa selected a boxed lunch, Ishigami stood looking out through the sliding glass door. He wondered if the detectives were watching from somewhere nearby. If possible, he didn't want them to see him being friendly with Yasuko.

Then another thought occurred to him, and he gave Yukawa a sidelong glance. Could Yukawa be trusted? Did he need to be on his guard around this old friend? *If he's friends with Kusanagi, anything he sees here might eventually wind up back with the police.*

Yukawa had finally decided on a lunch box. Yasuko had just gone back with his order when the glass door slid open again and a man in a dark brown jacket stepped into the shop. Ishigami glanced behind him as casually as he could. He felt his jaw clench involuntarily.

It was the man he had seen dropping Yasuko off the other day in front of their apartment building. From beneath his umbrella, Ishigami had watched them talking together. He had gotten the impression that they were old friends – or something more.

The man didn't seem to notice Ishigami. He was waiting for Yasuko to reappear. When she came back to the front and saw him, her eyes opened in surprise. The man merely nodded, smiling, with a look that said, *We'll talk after you've dealt with these customers.*

Who is he? Ishigami wondered. *When did he show up, and how did he get so close to Yasuko Hanaoka?* Ishigami vividly remembered the look on Yasuko's face when she had stepped out of the taxi the night before. He had never seen her looking so full of life. Her face hadn't been the face of a mother or an employee at a lunch box shop. It had been her true face, he thought. A woman's face.

A face she wore for this man, and would never wear for Ishigami—

Ishigami's gaze darted between the mystery man and Yasuko. He thought he could feel the atmosphere shift between them. A feeling of anxiety clutched at the maths teacher's chest.

Yukawa's lunch box was ready. He paid, took the bag, and turned to Ishigami. 'Thanks for waiting.'

They left Benten-tei and went down to the Sumida River at the stairs by Kiyosu Bridge. They began to walk along the river.

'So who was that guy?' Yukawa asked.

'Huh?'

'The guy that came into the shop. It looked like you recognized him.'

Internally, Ishigami cursed his old friend's powers of observation. 'Really? Can't say that I did,' he replied, striving to maintain his composure.

157

'Oh, well, never mind then.' Yukawa said.

'So what is the urgent business all about, anyway? Don't tell me you came all this way just to buy a lunch box?'

'Oh, right. I hadn't gotten to why I came, had I?' Yukawa frowned. 'Like I said before, that Detective Kusanagi has a habit of bringing me all of his annoying loose ends. Anyway, this time he came because he found out I knew you, and you're her neighbour. It turns out he has a . . . well, a rather unpleasant request.'

'What's that?'

'To put it bluntly, the police are still investigating the murder of your neighbour's ex-husband, and they have suspicions about your neighbour. Unfortunately, they haven't got a shred of evidence linking her to the crime. So, they'd like to keep tabs on her, watch what she does – you know, *observe*. But there are limits to how far they can take that. Which is where we come to you.'

'Wait, they don't want me to watch her for them, do they?'

Yukawa scratched the back of his head sheep-ishly. 'Er, well, yes, actually they do. It's not like they want you to observe her all the time, twenty-four seven. They just want you to keep an eye on the place next door, and let them know if you notice anything. I know, it's a serious imposition, but that's how they are.'

'So that's why you came out here to talk to me?'

'Well, I expect the police will make a more

formal request soon enough. They just wanted me to feel you out about it first. Personally, I wouldn't care if you said no – in fact, I almost think you should, but I thought I owed my detective friend at least a preliminary chat with you.'

Yukawa looked sincerely put upon. Secretly, though, Ishigami wondered if the story was really true. Would the police really go to a civilian with a request like that?

'Is that why you wanted to go to Benten-tei, too?'

'Honestly, yes. I wanted to see this suspect for myself. And I gotta say, now that I have, I don't think she's capable of killing someone.'

Ishigami was about to tell him that he agreed, but he held back. Instead, he said, 'Well, they say you shouldn't judge a book by its cover.'

'True enough. So, what do you say? How *would* you answer if the police asked you to spy for them?'

Ishigami shook his head. 'Honestly, I'd rather not get involved. I'm not in the habit of prying into other people's lives, and besides, I barely have the time. It might not look it, but I'm rather a busy man.'

'So I thought. Look, I'll just tell Kusanagi what you said. That should put an end to the whole idea. Sorry if I made you uncomfortable at all.'

'No, not a bit.'

They were approaching Shin-Ohashi Bridge. They could already see the homeless people's shanties along the riverside.

'So the murder happened on March tenth, I think he said,' Yukawa said. 'Kusanagi mentioned you came home kind of early that day?'

'Yeah. I didn't have anything scheduled that night. I think I got back around seven – I believe that's what I told him.'

'After which you holed up in your room, doing battle with those mathematical problems of yours?'

'Something like that.'

As he talked, Ishigami wondered if Yukawa was actually trying to see if he had an alibi. If that was the case, then he already suspected Ishigami of being involved.

'Which reminds me, I have no idea if you have any other hobbies. I mean something other than maths.'

Ishigami snorted. 'Hobbies? Not really. Maths is about all I do.'

'What you do to blow off steam, then? Do you like going for drives?' Yukawa pantomimed gripping a steering wheel.

'No, no. Even if I wanted to, I couldn't. I don't own a car.'

'But you have a driver's licence?'

'Is that a surprise?'

'Not particularly. You're not so busy that you couldn't find the time to go to driving school, are you?'

'I got it right after I found out I wasn't getting a university job. I figured it might be of help in finding work. Of course, it ended up not helping at all,' Ishigami said with a sidelong glance at Yukawa. 'What, are you trying to figure out whether I could drive a car?'

Yukawa blinked. 'No. Why would I?'

'Given your questions, I just thought you might be.'

'Well I didn't mean anything by it. I was just wondering if you like to go for drives. Or, more to the point, if you had anything you like to discuss other than mathematics once in a while.'

'Other than mathematics and murder mysteries, you mean.'

Yukawa laughed. 'Well said.'

They passed beneath Shin-Ohashi Bridge. The man with grey hair pulled into a ponytail was boiling something in a pot over a makeshift burner. He had a small oil can sitting next to him. A few of the other homeless were out and about.

As they made their way up the stairs by the bridge, Yukawa turned to Ishigami and said, 'Well, I'd better be getting back home. Sorry for troubling you with the whole investigation thing.'

'Just apologize to Detective Kusanagi for me. I'm sorry I couldn't help him.'

'I don't think there's any need to apologize. And, I hope you don't mind if I drop in again?'

'No, I don't mind.'

'Great. We can drink sake and talk maths.'

'You mean talk maths and murder.'

Yukawa shrugged and wrinkled his brow. 'Maybe

161

so. Though I did come up with a new problem for you. Maybe something you can think about in your spare time?'

'That being?'

'Which is harder: devising an unsolvable problem, or solving that problem? And it's not an empty question. Unlike the Clay Mathematics Institute prize people, I guarantee this puzzle has an answer. Interesting, no?'

'Very interesting,' Ishigami said, trying to read Yukawa's expression. 'I'll think about it.'

Yukawa nodded, then turned and walked back towards the main road.

CHAPTER 9

They had eaten the last of the shrimp, and the wine bottle was empty. Yasuko drank the last sip of wine from her glass and breathed a sigh of contentment. She couldn't remember the last time she had been out for real Italian food.

'Something more to drink?' Kudo asked her, a line of red showing beneath his eyes.

'I'm fine, thanks. Why don't you order something?'

'No, I'll pass. Save it for dessert.' He smiled and dabbed at his mouth with a napkin.

Yasuko had gone out to dinner with Kudo several times back when she was a hostess. Whether the meal was French or Italian, he had never stopped at the first bottle of wine.

'Drinking less these days?'

Kudo nodded thoughtfully. 'I suppose I am. Less than before, at any rate. Maybe I'm getting old.'

'There's nothing wrong with moderation. You have to take care of yourself.'

'Thanks.' Kudo laughed.

He had called her mobile phone earlier that day

to ask her out to dinner. At first, she hesitated, but then she accepted. The murder investigation had given her pause. It felt wrong, somehow, to go out to dinner at a time like this. Wrong for her, and especially for her daughter, who was surely even more frightened by the whole thing than she was. There was also the matter of Ishigami, and his help in covering up Togashi's death. She wondered how long his assistance would remain unconditional.

Then again, she thought, maybe it was precisely at times like these that she should do her best to act normal. If she didn't have a particular reason not to go, wouldn't it be 'normal' to accept an old friend's offer to go to dinner? It would be more unnatural for her to refuse, and if word of it reached Sayoko, then she might grow suspicious.

Whatever the line of reasoning she came up with to rationalize it to herself, Yasuko knew it was all a pretense. The real reason she had accepted Kudo's offer was that she'd wanted to see him again.

She wasn't sure if she had romantic feelings for him. In fact, before he had showed up the other day, she had scarcely thought of him in the last year. She was fond of him, that was true, but at present, it went no further.

Yet she couldn't deny that after he had invited her out, she had felt elated – an elation very similar to what she remembered feeling when making a date to meet a lover. She had even felt her body warming. Heart aflutter, she had asked Sayoko if she could get out of work early.

It was possible that all she really wanted was an escape from the worrying that had become a constant in her life. Or perhaps she wanted once again to be treated like a woman, to feel those things she had not felt in so long.

Regardless of the reasons, Yasuko didn't regret accepting Kudo's invitation. Though she couldn't help feeling like she was sneaking away from something else she should have been doing, it was undeniable that she was having fun.

'What did your daughter do for dinner tonight?' Kudo asked, taking a sip of coffee.

'I left her a message telling her she could order out. I'm guessing pizza – it's her favourite by far.'

'Hmph. Poor girl. Eating pizza while we're here with this feast.'

'I don't know. I think she prefers watching TV and eating pizza to a place like this. She's not fond of formal dining – or anything else where you have to act proper.'

Kudo nodded, frowning. He scratched at the side of his nose. 'That may be, that may be. I doubt she'd like to share a meal with some strange old man, either. But maybe next time I could take the both of you out to something simpler. A sushi-go-round, perhaps?'

'Thanks. But you don't have to worry on our account.'

'It's not worrying. I'd like to meet her – your daughter.' Kudo raised his eyes shyly from his coffee.

When he had first invited her out, he'd insisted that she bring her daughter along. And Yasuko had been sure of his sincerity, which made her happy.

Yet she had known at once that she couldn't bring Misato. It was true that the girl didn't like places like the restaurant Kudo had chosen. That, and Yasuko didn't want her daughter to have to deal with people at a time like this. If the conversation had chanced to drift to the murder, she didn't know whether Misato would be able to keep her cool. She also didn't want her daughter to see her mother as she was now – a single woman out with a man.

'What about you, Kudo? Is it all right for you to skip out on dinner with your family?'

'What about me, indeed.' Kudo set down his coffee cup and rested his elbows on the table. 'Actually, one of the reasons I invited you out to dinner today was to talk about that.'

Yasuko lifted an eyebrow, looking into his eyes.

'That is to say – actually, I'm single now.'

Yasuko gasped out loud.

'My wife got cancer. Pancreatic. She had surgery, but it was too little, too late. She passed away last summer. She was young, but once it started it went quickly. It was over in the blink of an eye.'

He spoke evenly, which had the effect of making

166

his story sound almost unreal to Yasuko's ears. For several seconds, she merely sat there, staring at him.

'Really?' she finally managed.

'I wouldn't joke about something like that,' he replied with a wry smile.

'No, of course you wouldn't. I just don't know what to say—' She looked down at the table, then bit her lip before looking back up. 'I . . . I'm sorry for your loss. It must have been difficult.'

'It was. But, like I said, it was over quickly. She went to the hospital complaining of a backache. Then I got a call from the doctor and she was admitted. She went into surgery. I came in to be with her – one thing after the other, like we were on a conveyor belt. I was hardly aware of the days passing, and then suddenly she was gone. It wasn't hospital policy to tell patients about their cancer without family consent, so I'm not sure whether she ever knew what she had.' Kudo picked up a glass of water and drank.

'When did you first learn she had it?'

Kudo thought for a moment. 'Around the end of the year before last . . . so, two years ago.'

'I was still at Marian then . . . you were still coming to the club.'

Kudo laughed quietly, his shoulders shaking. 'Pretty insensitive, huh? Here my wife is on the brink of death, and I'm going out drinking.'

Yasuko froze. She didn't know what to say. All she could remember was Kudo's smiling face at the club.

'Well, if you want an excuse, let's just say I was tired. I needed a break, I wanted to see you.' He scratched his head, frowning.

Yasuko thought back to when she had quit the club. On her last day, Kudo had brought her a bouquet.

Work hard and be happy—

What had he meant when he said those words? How had he felt? He must've been in far more pain than she, yet he had never let it show. He'd sent her on her way with good wishes and flowers.

'Well, sorry for killing the mood,' Kudo said, pulling out a cigarette. 'What I was trying to say is, you needn't worry about my family.'

'What about your son, then? He's got exams coming up, doesn't he?'

'My parents are taking care of him for the time being. They live closer to his high school, and I'm pretty useless around the house. Can't even make the kid a proper dinner. I think my mother's happy to have someone to look after.'

'So you're living alone now?'

'If you call going back to the bedroom after work, falling on my face, and sleeping "living", then yeah, pretty much.'

'But you didn't say anything about that the last time we met.'

'Didn't think there was a need. I came to see you because I was worried about you, after all. But I figured if I asked you to dinner, you would worry about my family – and you certainly have a right to. So, that's the story and here we are.'

'I had no idea . . .' Yasuko lowered her eyes.

Kudo's intentions were clear now. He was letting her know that he wanted to see her more often. He wanted to date, officially this time. And dating with the possibility of a future together. No doubt that was why he wanted to meet Misato, too.

After that they left the restaurant, and Kudo gave her a ride home in a taxi just as he had the other night.

'Thanks for dinner,' Yasuko said before she got out.

'I hope it won't be the last?'

There was a pause, then Yasuko smiled and said, 'Yes.'

'Then, good night. My best to your daughter.'

'Good night,' she replied, but even as she spoke she was thinking about how difficult it would be to talk to Misato about her evening with Kudo. In the message on the answering machine, she had said she was going out to dinner with Sayoko and her husband.

She watched the taxi leave, then walked up the stairs to her apartment. Misato was sitting with her legs tucked under the kotatsu, watching television. An empty pizza box was on the table.

'Welcome back, Mum,' the girl said, looking up.

'Hi, honey. Sorry about tonight.'

Yasuko had trouble meeting her daughter's eyes. She was afraid her guilt at having gone out to dinner with a man would show on her face.

'You get a call?' Misato asked.

'A call?'

'Yeah, from Mr Ishigami next door?' Misato added, quietly. She meant the usual evening call.

'No, I had my phone off.'

'Oh,' Misato said glumly.

'Why, did something happen?'

'Nothing, just—' Misato's eyes glanced towards the clock on the wall. 'Ishigami's been going in and out of his apartment all night. I watched him from the window, and it looked like he was going down to the street. I figured he was going out to call you.'

'Oh . . .'

He probably had been, Yasuko thought. She had been worried about that very possibility, even while she was eating dinner with Kudo. And she was worried even more about the fact that Ishigami had run into Kudo at Benten-tei. Of course, to Kudo, Ishigami was nothing more than another customer.

She wondered why Ishigami had come to the store at such a time – on this day, of all days. And with his 'friend'. He never came with friends, and he never came after lunchtime.

Of course Ishigami would remember Kudo. He probably suspected something when he saw the same man who had dropped Yasuko off in a taxi the other day show up at Benten-tei. None of this made her look forward to Ishigami's next call.

She was hanging her coat on the hanger when the

doorbell rang. Yasuko froze and exchanged glances with Misato. For a moment, she thought it must be Ishigami. But then that didn't make much sense; he would never risk coming to her apartment.

'Yes?' she called out towards the door.

'Sorry to bother you so late at night, ma'am. I was wondering if I could ask a few questions?' It was a man's voice, but not one she remembered hearing before. Yasuko opened the door, leaving the chain on. Someone was standing outside the apartment. She recognized him even as he reached into his coat and pulled out a police badge.

'Detective Kishitani, Homicide, ma'am. I came by the other day with Detective Kusanagi?'

'Right, of course,' Yasuko said, remembering. She looked down the hallway but Kusanagi was nowhere in sight.

Yasuko closed the door and gave Misato a look. Misato got out from under the kotatsu and went silently into the back room. As soon as the sliding door was shut behind her, Yasuko undid the chain and opened the front door again. 'Can I help you with something?'

Kishitani nodded. 'Yes – it's about that movie you went to see, again . . .'

Yasuko frowned despite herself. Ishigami had warned her the police would get on her case about the cinema, and he was turning out to be more right than she had expected.

'What about the movie? I've already told you everything I know.'

'Yes, you've been very cooperative, ma'am. Thank you. I was just wondering if I could borrow those stubs?'

'Stubs? You mean the ticket stubs?'

'That's right. I believe Detective Kusanagi asked you to keep them in a safe place the last time we were here?'

'Just a moment.'

Yasuko went to the kitchen cupboard and pulled out the drawer. She took out an envelope and from it removed two ticket stubs. She handed both of them – one for her and one for Misato, over to the detective. He thanked her and took them. She noticed he was wearing white gloves.

'I'm a suspect, aren't I?' Yasuko asked suddenly.

Kishitani shook his head and waved his hands in front of his face. 'Not at all, not at all. In fact, we're having trouble finding a suspect. That's why we have to do this: we go around eliminating all the people connected with the victim, even the ones that aren't very suspicious.'

'How can those stubs help you do that?'

'Well, I can't really say, but they might be of some use. The best thing would be if we could prove that you did go to the movies on the day you say you did . . . tell me, you haven't thought of anything else, have you – anything unusual from that day?'

'No, nothing more than what I've already said.'

'Right, thank you,' Kishitani said, his eyes wandering around the room.

172

'Sure has been cold lately, hasn't it? You use that electric kotatsu there every winter?'

'The kotatsu? I suppose . . .' Yasuko said, turning around to glance at the heated table, in part to hide her shock from the detective. He couldn't have mentioned the kotatsu purely by accident.

'How long have you had that kotatsu for?'

'Oh, I don't know . . . four, maybe five years. Is there something wrong?'

'No, not at all,' Kishitani said, shaking his head. 'By the way, did you go someplace after work today? I noticed you came home late.'

Yasuko blinked, the question taking her by surprise. She realized that the police must have been waiting for her by her apartment. Which meant they had probably seen her getting out of the taxi.

I'd better not lie.

'I went out to dinner with a friend,' she answered, trying to keep her answer as vague as possible, but of course that wasn't enough to satisfy the detective.

'The man who was with you in the taxi? Right. I was wondering, how do you know him? If you don't mind me asking,' the detective said, almost bashfully.

'Do I have to tell you where I went to dinner, too?'

'If it's not a problem, ma'am. I'm sorry, I don't mean to pry into your personal affairs, but if I don't ask about it then my boss will complain

173

when I get back to the office, see?' Kishitani gave a sheepish grin. 'Be assured, we wouldn't think of troubling your friend – the man you were with. If you could just tell me where you went?'

Yasuko sighed deeply. 'His name is Kudo. He was a regular at the club where I used to work. He knew I had been married to Togashi and he was worried about me with the case on the news and all. He came to my work to check in on me.'

'What does he do, this Mr Kudo?'

'I heard he runs a printing company, but I don't know much more than that.'

'Do you have a number where we could reach him?'

Yasuko furrowed her brow and frowned.

'Please understand,' Kishitani said, nodding apologetically, 'we won't contact him unless there is some dire need – and even if we do, we will be very discreet, I assure you.'

Yasuko took out her mobile phone, not bothering to hide her displeasure, and quickly read off the number Kudo had given her. The detective hurriedly scribbled the number down.

Kishitani then asked her to tell him everything she knew about Kudo. All the while that they talked, even as he kept on prying, he maintained his sheepish demeanour. Eventually, Yasuko found herself telling him everything back to the first day when Kudo had appeared at Benten-tei.

After Kishitani left, Yasuko locked the door and

sat down in the entranceway. She felt overwrought, her emotions dragged out to exhaustion.

Then she heard the sound of the sliding door as Misato emerged from the back room. 'They still suspect something about the movie, don't they?' the girl said. 'Everything's happening just like Ishigami said it would. It's pretty incredible, you know.'

'I know.' Yasuko stood and brushed her fallen bangs out of her face.

'Mum. I thought you went out to eat with the people at Benten-tei?'

Yasuko looked up. Misato was frowning.

'You were listening?'

'Of course I was.'

'Oh . . .' Yasuko slid her legs under the kotatsu, her head hanging. She remembered the detective asking about the kotatsu.

'How could you go out to eat with someone at a time like this?'

'I couldn't say no. He – the person I went to dinner with – was very good to me in the past. And he came to find me because he was worried about me – about us. I'm sorry I didn't tell you about it before.'

'No, Mum, I'm fine. It's just—'

They heard the door to the next apartment open and shut. Then came the sound of footsteps, heading down the stairs. Yasuko and Misato exchanged glances.

'Mum, your mobile.'

'It's on.'

A few minutes later, Yasuko's phone began to ring.

Ishigami used the same public phone he always did when he made his third call that evening. The first two times he hadn't been able to get through to Yasuko's mobile phone. He was worried that something might have happened – he'd always gotten through to her before – but when she answered he realized immediately from her tone that his fears were misplaced.

Ishigami had heard the doorbell at the Hanaokas earlier – and as he'd suspected, it had been the police. Yasuko told him that the detective had asked her for the ticket stubs. Ishigami knew what they were after. They would try to match the stubs to their other halves, presumably in storage at the cinema. If they found stubs that matched the ones they got from Yasuko, they would check the finger-prints. If Yasuko's fingerprints were on them, that would prove that she and her daughter had at least been at the cinema that night – whether they had actually seen the movie or not. If there were no fingerprints, the police suspicion of the Hanaokas would go up a notch.

And the detective had asked about the kotatsu. This, too, Ishigami had predicted.

'I think they've determined the murder weapon,' Ishigami said into the receiver.

'The murder weapon?'

'The kotatsu cord. That's what you used, isn't it?'

The phone went silent on the other end. Maybe Yasuko was remembering the moment it had happened, when she had strangled Togashi.

'In any strangulation, marks from the murder weapon remain on the skin of the neck,' Ishigami explained. It felt harsh to lay it out so plainly, but this was no time for euphemisms. 'Forensics is quite advanced these days. They can usually tell the murder weapon used by looking at the marks it leaves.'

'So that's why the detective asked about the kotatsu?'

'I'd assume so. But there's no need to worry. I've already made arrangements.'

He had expected the police to identify the murder weapon. Which was why he had exchanged the Hanaokas' kotatsu with his own. Their old kotatsu – the real murder weapon – was packed away in his closet. As luck would have it, the cord on his old kotatsu was different from the one on theirs. If the detectives came back and examined that cord, they would immediately realize it was a dead end.

'What else did the detective ask you?'

'What else . . . ?' Yasuko's voice faded into silence.

'Ms Hanaoka? Hello?'

'Y . . . Yes?'

'Is something wrong?'

'No, nothing at all. I was just trying to remember

what else he said. There wasn't anything, I don't think. He mentioned that if they could prove that I went to the movies then I would no longer be a suspect, or something to that effect.'

'Yes, the cinema alibi is very important to them. That was part of my plan, of course. There's really nothing to be worried about.'

'Thank you. It's a great relief to hear you say that.'

Yasuko's words lit a fire somewhere deep in Ishigami's chest. For a brief moment, the tension he had been feeling pretty much around the clock eased a little.

It occurred to him then that he might ask about the man. The man who had dropped her off – the customer who had come into Benten-tei when he was there with Yukawa. Ishigami knew that he had given her a ride home tonight, too. He had seen them from his window.

'That's about all I have to report. What about you, Mr Ishigami? Is everything all right with you? Is something wrong?' Yasuko asked abruptly. Ishigami realized he hadn't said anything for some time.

'No, nothing at all. Please, try to live life as normally as possible. I'm sure the police will be back with more questions, but what's most important is that you don't panic.'

'Yes, I understand.'

'Great. Please give my best to your daughter. Good night.'

He waited for her reply, then hung up the handset. The phone spit out his telephone card from the slot below the receiver.

When Mamiya heard Kusanagi's report, the chief's despair was written on his face. He rubbed his shoulders and rocked in his chair. 'So this Kudo guy only met with Yasuko Hanaoka *after* the incident? You're sure about that?'

'That's what the couple at the lunch box store are saying. I don't think they have any reason to lie, either. They said Yasuko was just as surprised as they were when Kudo first showed up at the shop. Of course, it could be an act.'

'She *was* a hostess at a nightclub. Acting would be second nature to her.' Mamiya looked up at Kusanagi. 'Anyway, let's look into this Kudo a bit more. I don't like how he showed up right after all this happened.'

'Yeah,' said Kishitani, butting in, 'but according to Ms Hanaoka, Kudo came to see her because he heard about the murder. So, it's not like it was a coincidence. And I hardly think they'd go meeting in public or having dinner together if they were co-conspirators or something.'

'You never know. Could be a really gutsy diversion,' Kusanagi offered.

Kishitani frowned at his superior officer. 'Well, yeah, but—'

'You want us to try talking directly to Kudo?' Kusanagi asked, turning to Mamiya.

'I think so. If he was involved, he might let something slip. Check it out.'

Kusanagi nodded, and he and Kishitani headed out.

'You gotta stop saying things like that based on these assumptions of yours,' Kusanagi warned Kishitani as they left. 'The killers might be trying to use that against you.'

'What do you mean?'

'Your comment about Kudo and Ms Hanaoka. And the assumptions it's based on. For all we actually know, Ms Hanaoka and this Kudo might have been really close for years, but have been keeping it hidden. When it comes to committing this sort of crime, a hidden connection like that would be a big advantage. What better accomplice than someone no one else knows you have anything to do with?'

'Well, then why wouldn't they continue to keep it hidden?'

'Lots of reasons. Relationships always come out eventually. Maybe they thought this was the perfect chance for them to stage a little reunion.'

Kishitani nodded, but his face said he wasn't buying it.

They left the Edogawa police station and got into Kusanagi's car. 'Forensics thinks the murder weapon was some kind of electrical cord,' Kishitani said as he put on his seatbelt. 'A "textile braided insulated cord", specifically.'

'Right. The ones they use on heating appliances. Like an electric kotatsu.'

'They picked up the thread pattern on the cord from the wound.'

'Yeah, so?'

'Well, I glanced at the kotatsu in the Hanaokas' place. The cord wasn't textile insulated. It was what they call a "round braided" cord. Like a smooth tube of rubber.'

'Okay. So?'

'That's all.'

'There are a lot of electrical appliances other than a kotatsu, Kishitani. And the murder weapon doesn't have to be something the killer had around all the time. They might've picked up an electrical cord they found lying on the street.'

'Right . . .' Kishitani mumbled glumly.

Kusanagi and Kishitani had spent the previous day together, on stakeout, watching and tailing Yasuko Hanaoka. Their primary goal had been to watch everyone who crossed her path, looking for anyone who could possibly be an accomplice.

After she left work, from the time she had left the shop with a man in a taxi, they watched her every move. They had waited patiently for her to come out after the two went into a restaurant in Shiodome, near the harbour.

Eventually the couple had finished dinner and gotten back into the taxi. From there, they had gone straight back to Yasuko's apartment. The taxi had stopped, but the man hadn't gotten out. Kusanagi had sent Kishitani up to ask questions while he followed the taxi. Luckily, no one seemed to have noticed the tail.

The man lived in a large apartment in Osaki. Kusanagi had learned his name from the sign next to his door: 'Kuniaki Kudo.'

Kusanagi had already accepted that even if Yasuko was involved with Togashi's murder, she couldn't have done it alone. She would have needed a male accomplice – or perhaps it would be better to call him the actual killer, whoever he was.

So, could this Mr Kudo be the man? Even as Kusanagi described that possible scenario to Kishitani, he didn't half believe it himself. To the contrary, he felt like they were once again barking up the wrong tree.

And something else had been tugging at Kusanagi's brain: the two unexpected visitors he had seen while he was on stakeout outside Bententei. Manabu Yukawa and the maths teacher who lived next door to Yasuko Hanaoka.

CHAPTER 10

A little after six P.M. a green Mercedes pulled into the underground parking lot. Kusanagi had confirmed it was Kuniaki Kudo's car earlier that day. The detective stood up from his seat at the coffee shop across the street from the lot and fished a few yen out of his wallet to cover the two coffees he'd bought. The second cup was still on the table, almost full.

Kusanagi jogged across the street and into the apartment block's parking complex. The building had entrances on the first floor and the basement floor, both fitted with an autolock system. People who parked their cars here always used the more convenient basement entrance. Kusanagi wanted to catch Kudo before he disappeared inside the block of apartments. The detective wanted to avoid having to call up to Kudo's apartment via the intercom system. That would give Kudo time to prepare himself.

Luckily, Kusanagi got to the entrance first. He was standing off to the side, with one hand against the wall, catching his breath, when Kudo came up. Kudo, wearing a suit and carrying a briefcase, walked past him without a pause.

Kudo had his key out and was just putting it into the door when Kusanagi called out from behind. 'Excuse me, Mr Kudo?'

Kudo straightened up and pulled out the key. He turned around and took in the detective with a glance, sizing him up. A frown spread across Kudo's face. 'Yes?'

Kusanagi flashed his badge at him. 'Sorry to bother you like this. I'm with the police. I was wondering if you could help me.'

'The police . . . you're a detective?' Kudo lowered his voice, his eyes narrowing.

Kusanagi nodded. 'Yes. I was hoping I could talk to you about Ms Yasuko Hanaoka?'

Kusanagi was watching closely to see how Kudo would react when he heard Yasuko's name. Kudo should know about the case, and if he looked unduly surprised or startled, then Kusanagi would know something was fishy. Kudo frowned and nodded grimly. 'Very well. Do you want to come up to my place? Or is a café better?'

'Your apartment would be just fine, thanks.'

'Sure thing. It's a little messy . . .'

Not so much messy as desolate, Kusanagi thought when they got up to the apartment. There was hardly any furniture. Just two plush chairs, one of them large enough to seat two. Kudo waved Kusanagi towards it.

184

'Can I get you something to drink? Tea?' Kudo asked without taking off his suit jacket.

'No thank you. I won't be long.'

'All right,' Kudo said, but he went into the kitchen anyway and brought out two glasses and a plastic bottle of cold oolong tea.

'Do you have any family?' Kusanagi asked suddenly.

'My wife passed away last year. I have a son, but, for various reasons, my parents are taking care of him at their house,' Kudo explained, speaking evenly.

'I see. So you live alone?'

'Pretty much, yes,' Kudo said, his expression softening. He poured the tea into the two glasses and placed one in front of Kusanagi. 'Is . . . this about Mr Togashi?'

Kusanagi had been reaching for the glass, but now he pulled his hand back. If Kudo wanted to get to the heart of the matter, there was no point wasting time on pleasantries.

'That's right. As you know, Yasuko Hanaoka's ex-husband was murdered.'

'She had nothing to do with it.'

'That so?'

'Of course. They broke up a while ago, and they never saw each other. Why would she kill him?'

'As it happens, I'm inclined to agree with you, for the most part.'

'For the most part?'

'There are many couples in the world, and a lot

185

of divorces, and none of them fall apart exactly the same way. If every unhappy couple could just break it off cleanly, become total strangers in the space of a day and never see each other again, well, then we wouldn't have stalkers. Unfortunately, that's not the case. Often one party breaks off a relationship, but the other party doesn't. Even after the divorce papers have been filed.'

'Well, she told me she hadn't seen Mr Togashi at all,' Kudo stated, a look of defiance growing in his eyes.

'Have you talked to her about the murder?'

'I have. I mean, after all, that's why I went to see her.'

Which fits with Yasuko Hanaoka's testimony.

'So you had Ms Hanaoka on your mind, even before the incident?'

Kudo frowned. 'I'm not sure what you mean by "on my mind". Given that you came to me here at my apartment, I'm guessing you already know about my relationship with her. I was a regular at the club where she used to work. I even met her husband once, though that was by accident. That's when I found out his name was Togashi. When he was killed, I saw his name and photo on the news, so I got worried and went to see how Yasuko was doing.'

'I've heard you were a regular at her club, yes. Just, it's a little hard for me to imagine you going so far out of your way to see her just because of that. You run a business, don't you? I'd think you'd be rather busy.' Kusanagi knew how his questions sounded – cynical and leading. He didn't like talking like this, even though his job frequently demanded it.

Admittedly though, the technique worked. Kudo blanched. 'I thought you were here to ask about Yasuko Hanaoka. So far, all your questions have been about me. Am I a suspect?'

Kusanagi smiled and waved a hand. 'Not at all. I'm sorry to pry. I merely wanted to find out more about you, since it seemed like you were particularly close to Ms Hanaoka.'

The detective had spoken as gently as he could, but Kudo's glare only hardened. He took a deep breath, then nodded.

'All right. As I'd prefer to not have you poking around further, I'll be as frank as I can. I'm fond of Yasuko, romantically. When I heard about the murder, I thought it might be my chance to get closer to her. How's that? Does that satisfy your curiosity?'

Kusanagi chuckled wryly. It was an honest chuckle – not an act or an interrogation technique. 'There's no need to be defensive.'

'But that's what you wanted to know, isn't it?'

'We just need to understand who is connected to Yasuko Hanaoka, and how.'

'That's what I don't get. Why do the police suspect her?' Kudo shook his head.

'Togashi was trying to find her just before he was killed. Which means there's a chance they did 'meet,' Kusanagi told him, hoping the revelation would do more good than harm.

'What, so that means she killed him? Isn't that a little simplistic, even for the police?' Kudo snorted and shrugged.

'Sorry we're not very sophisticated. Of course, we have suspects other than Ms Hanaoka. It's just that we can't afford to remove her from the list at this point. Even if she isn't the key to solving this murder, someone around her might be.'

'Someone around her?' Kudo raised an eyebrow, then shook his head as though he had just realized something. 'Is that so,' he said.

'Is what so?'

'You think she went to someone and asked them to kill her former husband for her, don't you? That's why you came here. So now I'm a suspected assassin!'

'We're certainly not saying anyone is an assassin, yet . . .' Kusanagi protested, purposely letting his voice trail off. If Kudo had any bright ideas he wanted to share, Kusanagi didn't want to discourage him.

'If it's an accomplice you're looking for, you'll need to talk to a lot more people. I wasn't the only customer infatuated with her, that's for sure. She's quite a beauty. And I don't just mean when she was a hostess, either. To hear the Yonazawas tell it, they get customers at the lunch shop who come just to see her. Why don't you go talk to all of them, too?'

'If you have any names or contact information, I'll be happy to question them.'

'Sorry, but I don't. Nor would I wish that on anybody. It's against my policy to squeal on innocents,' Kudo said, chopping his hand through the air with finality. 'And even if you did manage to meet with all of them, I don't think you'd turn up much. She's not the kind of person to go looking for someone like that. She's no black widow, and she's no fool. In any case, I wouldn't be stupid enough to kill someone just because a beautiful woman asked me to. So, Detective . . . Kusanagi, was it? I'm sorry you've come so far out of your way only to leave empty-handed.' He then stood abruptly, putting a period at the end of his words.

Kusanagi got up from the sofa, his pen still poised over his notepad. 'Were you at work on March tenth?'

Kudo's eyes went wide with disbelief for a moment, then his face hardened. 'What, you want me to provide an alibi, now?'

'Yes, in fact,' Kusanagi replied, seeing no need to beat around the bush. Kudo was already angry, after all.

'Hold on a moment, then,' Kudo said. He went over to his briefcase and pulled out a thick notebook. He flipped through the pages and sighed. 'Well, I don't have anything on my calendar for that day, so I assume I went to work as usual. That means I probably left work around six

189

o'clock. If you need to confirm that, ask one of my employees.'

'And after you left work?'

'Like I said, I didn't write anything down, so I assume it was the same as every day. I came home, ate something, and went to bed. Too bad I live alone – no witnesses for you to question.'

'Could you try remembering just a little more about that day for me? You understand, I'm just trying to reduce the list of suspects we need to check.'

Kudo looked almost despondent now, and he opened up his calendar again. 'All right. The tenth, huh? Oh right . . .' he muttered half to himself.

'Did something happen?'

'Yes, I went to a client's after work. It was in the evening . . . that's right, he treated me to yakitori.'

'Do you know around what time that was?'

'Not exactly. I guess we were out drinking until nine or so. I went home straight after that. This is the client,' Kudo said, pulling a business card out of his notebook. The card bore the name of a designer's office.

'Thank you,' Kusanagi said, declining to take the card. 'I won't need that.' He then put away his pen and turned towards the door.

He was slipping into his shoes when Kudo called after him.

'Detective? How long are you going to be watching her?'

Kusanagi met his glare silently.

'That's how you knew I went to see her, right? Because you have her under surveillance? And then you tailed me back here.'

Kusanagi scratched his head. 'You got me.'

'Then can you please tell me how long you intend to keep following her?'

Kusanagi sighed. He gave up trying to smile and instead stared at Kudo. 'We'll follow her as long as there is a need to, sir.'

Kudo looked like he had something more to say, but Kusanagi turned his back on him, opened the door, and left the apartment.

Back out on the street outside the building, the detective waved down a taxi.

'Imperial University.'

The taxi driver nodded and pulled out. In the back, Kusanagi took out his notepad. Glancing over his own hastily scrawled notes, he reflected on his conversation with Kudo. He would have to check his alibi, but he had already come to a conclusion.

The man's innocent. He's telling the truth.

That, and Kudo really was in love with Yasuko Hanaoka. Just as he'd pointed out, there could be any number of other people who might have wanted to help her.

The front gate at Imperial University was closed. There were a few lights here and there, so it wasn't completely dark, but still the university at night had an eerie feel to it. Kusanagi went in through the student entrance and checked in at the security office. 'I'm supposed to meet with Assistant Professor Yukawa in Physics Laboratory 13,' he told the guard, though he didn't actually have an appointment.

The halls in the science building were deserted. Yet there were some people around – as he could see from the light streaming from beneath several of the laboratory doors. *Probably researchers and students working overtime on a project.* It reminded Kusanagi that Yukawa had once told him he sometimes spent the night in the lab.

Kusanagi had decided to check in on Yukawa tonight even before he met with Kudo. The university wasn't far from Kudo's apartment, and there was something he wanted to ask Yukawa.

Why had he gone to Benten-tei? And what was his connection to his old university classmate, the maths teacher? If he had figured out something about the case, Kusanagi wanted to know what it was. Or was he still just catching up with his old friend, and their visit to the lunch shop where their primary suspect worked coincidental?

Kusanagi didn't think Yukawa would just drop in on a suspect in an unsolved case unless he had something specific in mind. After all, Yukawa's policy had always been to avoid direct involvement in Kusanagi's cases – not because they annoyed him, as he claimed, but out of deference to Kusanagi's position.

There was a status chart on the door to Lab 13, where students working there, graduate students, and professors with access to the lab would indicate whether they were in or out. Yukawa was 'OUT'. Kusanagi clicked his tongue. If Yukawa wasn't in the lab this late in the evening, he had probably headed straight home after finishing whatever he was working on.

Kusanagi tried knocking on the door anyway. If the chart was correct, there should be two grad students in the lab.

'Come in,' said a thick voice. Kusanagi opened the door. A young man wearing glasses and a sweatshirt came out from the back of the lab – a grad student. The detective had seen him here before.

'Yukawa's gone home already?'

The grad student frowned and nodded. 'Yeah, just a little while ago. Did you want his mobile phone number?'

'No thanks, I already have it. It's nothing urgent anyway. I was just in the area and decided to drop in.'

'Right, okay,' the student said, his face brightening. The students in the lab were familiar with Kusanagi's visits.

'I know he works late a lot, so I figured I might be able to catch him here at the lab.'

'Usually, yeah, but he's been leaving early for the last two or three days. I think today he had somewhere he had to go.'

'You know where?' *Maybe the maths teacher's place again?* Kusanagi wondered.

'I'm not sure exactly, but he said something about Shinozaki.'

Kusanagi blinked. That was the last thing he had expected to hear. 'Shinozaki?'

'Yeah. He asked me the quickest way to get to the station there.'

'But he didn't tell you why he was going?'

'No. I asked, but he didn't say much.'

Kusanagi snorted. Then he thanked the student and left. He was beginning to suspect that something was afoot, he just didn't know what. Shinozaki Station was the closest to the murder scene. Why would Yukawa be going there?

Leaving the university behind, Kusanagi pulled out his mobile phone. He started to look up Yukawa's number, but on the verge of calling, he hesitated, then shut the phone with a snap and slipped it back into his pocket. Now wasn't the time to press his friend with questions. If Yukawa was on the case without so much as a nod from Kusanagi, he must be onto something.

Besides, he could hear the protest already.

What do you care if I do a little poking around myself?

Ishigami sighed. He was in the middle of grading make-up exams. They were terrible. He had designed the problems so they would be easy enough for everyone to handle – far easier than the ones on the real exam, so everyone taking the make-up test could pass – but he was hard-pressed to find a single decent answer in the pile. The students must not be studying, he decided.

They knew that no matter how badly they did on their tests, the school would pass them anyway. After all, the board rarely held anyone back. Even when a student or two just couldn't make the grade, the administration would find some reason to graduate the entire class.

Why don't they just remove maths from the list of required subjects, then? Ishigami wondered. Only a handful of people really understood mathematics anyway. There was no point in even teaching maths at this low level. Wasn't it enough to let them know there was this incomprehensible thing out there called mathematics, and leave it at that?

When he had finished grading, he looked at the clock. It was already eight P.M.

After checking that the dojo was locked up, Ishigami left the school for the night. He was standing at the crosswalk under the traffic light when a man approached.

'On your way home?' the man asked, smiling. 'When you weren't at your apartment I thought I might find you here.'

Ishigami recognized the man's face. It was the homicide detective.

'I'm sorry, you are . . . ?'

'Ah, you've probably forgotten.'

The man reached for his coat pocket, but Ishigami held up his hand and nodded. 'No, I remember you now. You're Detective Kusanagi.'

The light turned green and Ishigami began to walk. Kusanagi followed.

What's he doing here? Ishigami thought as he crossed the street. Was it about Yukawa's visit two days ago? Yukawa had told him that they wanted him to help with their investigation, but he had refused, hadn't he?

'Do you know a Manabu Yukawa?' Kusanagi asked.

'I do. He came to see me. He said you'd told him about me.'

'Actually, that's true. I told him that you'd gone to Imperial University – the same department he was in. I'm sorry if it was an imposition.'

'Not at all. I was glad to see him again.'

'What did you two talk about, if you don't mind me asking?'

'Old times, mostly. That was about all we talked about the first time he visited.'

'The first time?' Kusanagi lifted an eyebrow. 'Has he been back?'

'He's come to see me twice. The second time, he told me that you'd sent him.'

'*I* sent him?' Kusanagi blinked. 'Um, what exactly did he say I sent him to do?'

'He said you wanted me to help with your investigation, and that you thought it might be better if the request came from him.'

'Oh, right, help with the investigation.' Kusanagi scratched his head as he walked.

Ishigami noticed his uncertainty at once. The detective seemed confused. *Perhaps he didn't ask Yukawa to come talk to me after all?*

196

Kusanagi grinned sheepishly. 'I talk to him about a lot of things, so I get a little confused about exactly which cases he knows about and which he doesn't. What kind of help did he mention?'

Ishigami considered the detective's question. He hesitated to say Yasuko's name, but of course, he couldn't exactly play dumb. Kusanagi would surely cross-check whatever he said with Yukawa.

Ishigami told him about Yukawa's request that he spy on Yasuko Hanaoka.

Kusanagi's eyes went wide. 'He asked you to do that, did he?' he asked, sounding flustered. 'Right, right – ah, I guess I did talk to him about that, yes. About whether you might be able to help us. He must have thought he could help out by asking you, since you two have a connection. Right, that makes sense.'

To Ishigami, the detective's explanation sounded like a last-minute improvisation. Which meant that Yukawa had come on his own to prod Ishigami about the case. So what had he been after?

Ishigami stopped and turned to face Kusanagi. 'And you came out here today to ask me that? Or was there something else?'

'No, sorry, I was just getting to it.' Kusanagi pulled a photograph from his jacket pocket. 'Have you seen this man? I'm sorry the picture isn't very good, I had to take it with a telephoto.'

Ishigami looked at the photograph and swallowed. The man in the photograph was the person who had been foremost in his thoughts these past few days. He didn't know his name. He didn't know who he was. All he knew was that this man was close to Yasuko.

'Mr Ishigami?'

Ishigami wondered how to respond. He could just say he didn't know him and leave it at that. But then how would he ever find out who the man really was?

'You know, he looks somewhat familiar,' Ishigami said slowly. 'Who is he?'

'Can you think where you might have seen him?'

'Well, I'm not sure. I see a lot of people every day. If you told me his name or where he works, I might be able to come up with something.'

'His name is Kudo. He runs a printing company.'

'Kudo?'

'Yes. Like this—' Kusanagi described the Chinese characters used to write Kudo's name.

Kudo . . . Ishigami stared at the photograph. So why were the police checking him out? *He must be involved with Yasuko somehow.* In other words, the police suspected a connection – a special, maybe even intimate connection – between this Mr Kudo and Yasuko Hanaoka.

'Well? Do you remember anything?'

'Hmm. Not really. He does look familiar though.' Ishigami shook his head. 'I'm sorry I don't remember more than that. Maybe I'm mistaking him for someone else.'

'Right, no problem,' Kusanagi said, frowning

slightly and putting the photo back into his pocket. He pulled out a business card. 'If you think of anything, do you mind dropping me a line?'

'Certainly. Um, does he have something to do with the case?'

'I really can't say at this time. We're still looking into it.'

'Is he involved with Ms Hanaoka somehow?'

'They had some contact, yes,' Kusanagi said, being intentionally vague. He didn't want to divulge any more information than he already had. 'By the way, you were at Benten-tei with Yukawa the other day, yes?'

Ishigami looked up at the detective. The question was so unexpected, for a moment he didn't know how to respond.

'I happened to see the two of you there,' the detective went on. 'I was on the job. Sorry I didn't say hello.'

So they are staking out Benten-tei.

'That's right. Yukawa said he wanted to buy a lunch box, so I took him there.'

'Why go all that way? Don't they sell lunches at the convenience store by the school?'

'Well, you'd have to ask Yukawa. Benten-tei was his idea.'

'Did you discuss anything about Ms Hanaoka or the case?'

'Well, only what I told you before – that you wanted my help with the investigation.'

Kusanagi shook his head. 'I mean other than

that. As he probably told you, I ask Yukawa for advice on cases. Turns out he's more than just a physics genius, he's also a gifted sleuth. I was just hoping he might have said something about his thoughts on the case.'

Ishigami was confused. If they were meeting as often as it sounded like they were, then Yukawa and the detective should have been exchanging information. Why would the detective have to ask him what Yukawa thought?

'No, he didn't say anything in particular,' Ishigami said.

'I see. Very well. Sorry to bother you on your way home.'

Kusanagi nodded farewell and headed back along the way that they had come. Ishigami watched him go. A feeling rose inside him, making him queasy, as though an elaborate formula he'd thought was perfect was now giving false results because of an unpredictable variable.

CHAPTER 11

Kusanagi pulled out his mobile phone as he emerged from Shinozaki Station. He looked up Manabu Yukawa's number and pressed the call button. Then, phone to his ear, he looked around. It was three in the afternoon – the lull time between the lunch rush and the commuter hour – but there were still plenty of people out on the street. A line of bicycles stood in front of the supermarket across the way.

Kusanagi's mobile found a signal quickly, and he waited for the dial tone – but then, before the phone began to ring, he closed it with a snap. He had just spotted the man he was looking for.

Yukawa was sitting on a guardrail in front of a bookshop, eating an ice cream cone. He was wearing white trousers and a simple black long-sleeved shirt. He was wearing sunglasses, too – a sleek, fashionable pair.

Kusanagi crossed the street and approached him from behind. Yukawa wasn't moving. His eyes were fixed on the supermarket and its environs.

'Detective Galileo!' the detective exclaimed, hoping to get a rise out of his friend, but Yukawa's reaction was unusually subdued. Still licking his ice cream, he looked around, his head turning in slow motion.

'I see your nose is as keen as ever. Who says the police need bloodhounds to do their sniffing for them?' he said, his expression unchanging.

'What are you doing here?' Kusanagi asked. 'Oh, and before you say it, "I was eating ice cream" isn't an acceptable answer.'

Yukawa chuckled. 'I might ask you the same question, but there's no need. The answer's quite evident. You came looking for me. Or rather, you came here hoping to find out what I was up to.'

'Well, now that the jig is up, you can just come out and tell me what you're up to.'

'I was waiting for you.'

'Me? Yeah, right.'

'I'm quite serious. You see, I called the lab a little while ago, and one of the grad students said you'd been there asking after me. And I hear that you dropped by last evening, too, didn't you? So, I reasoned that if I waited here long enough, you'd show up. After all, my grad student told you I was here at Shinozaki, didn't he?'

This was all true enough, but it didn't answer the real question, and Kusanagi wasn't in the mood to let Yukawa off so easily.

'What I want to know is: why are you here in the first place?' he said, his voice rising a little. He was used to his physicist friend's circumlocutions, but still they could be maddening sometimes.

'No need to get impatient. How about some coffee? All I can offer is what's in those vending machines over there, but it's bound to be better than the instant stuff back at the lab.' Yukawa stood, tossing the rest of his ice cream cone into a nearby dustbin.

With Kusanagi following he ambled over to the supermarket, where he bought two coffees out of one of the vending machines. He passed one to the detective, and then, carelessly straddling a nearby parked bicycle, he began to sip his own drink.

Kusanagi remained standing. He looked around as he opened the top on his can. 'You shouldn't sit on other people's bicycles like that. What if the owner comes back?'

'She won't. Not for some time.'

'How do you know that?'

'Because the owner of this bicycle left it here, then went into the subway station. Even if she was only headed to the next station over, it would take her at least thirty minutes to get there, do whatever it was she was going to do, and then come back.'

Kusanagi took a sip of his coffee and frowned. 'That's what you were doing while you sat there, eating your ice cream?'

'Watching people is a bit of a hobby of mine. It's quite fascinating, really.'

'It's good to have a hobby, but I'd rather have answers. Why are you here? And don't even try telling me this has nothing to do with my investigation.'

Yukawa twisted his body around the seat, examining the back fender.

'Not many people bother to write their names on their bicycles any more. I suppose that these days they don't want strangers knowing who they are. But it wasn't that long ago that everyone would write their names on their bicycles. It's interesting how customs change with the times.'

Now Kusanagi understood. 'This isn't the first time we've chatted about bicycles, is it.'

Yukawa nodded. 'I believe you told me that it was very unlikely that the bicycle had been left near the scene of the crime on purpose.'

'Not exactly. What I said was, there wasn't any point in deliberately leaving it there. If the killer was going to put the victim's fingerprints on the bicycle, then why go to the trouble of burning fingerprints off the corpse itself? After all, those prints on the bicycle were what led us to the man's identity.'

'Fascinating. But tell me, what if there hadn't been any fingerprints on the bicycle? Would that have kept you from being able to identify the body?'

Kusanagi had to think for a full ten seconds before answering. It was a question he hadn't considered before.

'No, it wouldn't,' he replied at last. 'We used the fingerprints to match the body to the man who disappeared from the rented room, but we didn't need the fingerprints to do that. I think I told you we did a DNA analysis as well.'

'You did. In other words, burning the victim's fingerprints off was ultimately meaningless. But, what if our murderer knew that from the start?'

'You mean, he burned off the fingerprints even though he knew doing so would be futile?'

'Oh, I'm sure he had a reason for doing what he did. Just, that reason wasn't to hide the identity of the body. What if he did it to suggest that the bicycle he planted nearby wasn't a plant at all?'

Kusanagi blinked, momentarily at a loss for words. 'So what you're trying to say is that it *was* a plant, placed there to confuse us somehow?'

'Yes. It's the *somehow* I haven't figured out yet,' Yukawa said, dismounting from the bicycle. 'I'm sure he wanted us to think that the victim got there on that bicycle by himself. Why would he want us to think that?'

'To hide the fact that the victim *couldn't* have gotten there by himself,' Kusanagi said. 'Because he was already dead when the killer carried him there. That's what the captain thinks.'

'And you disagree with that theory, yes? I assume because your lead suspect Yasuko Hanaoka doesn't have a driver's licence.'

'Well, all bets on that are off if she had an accomplice.'

'Right, but let's focus on the time that bicycle was stolen. I heard it was taken sometime between eleven in the morning and ten at night, and I wondered how you were able to pinpoint the time it was stolen so precisely.'

'Because that's what the bicycle's owner told us. It's not rocket science.'

'Indeed,' Yukawa said, gesturing emphatically with his can of coffee. 'And how were you able to find out that it was her bicycle so quickly?'

'That's not rocket science either. She reported it stolen. All we had to do was compare the registration number on the bike to the one on the police report she filed.'

Yukawa groaned at his response. Kusanagi could see his hard stare, even behind his sunglasses. 'What is it? What's bothering you now?'

'Do you know where the bicycle was when it was stolen?'

'Of course I do. I was the one who questioned the owner.'

'Then, could you take me there? It's around here, isn't it?'

Kusanagi felt the intensity of Yukawa's gaze. He was about to ask, 'Why bother?' but decided against it. The physicist's eyes had that gleam they got whenever he was close to formulating a hypothesis.

'It's over this way,' Kusanagi said, and he headed for the site.

The place was only fifty metres or so from where they had been drinking their coffee. Kusanagi stood in front of a row of bicycles.

'She said that she had it chained to the railing along the pavement, here.'

'The thief cut the chain?'

'Seems likely.'

'So he had bolt cutters with him . . .' Yukawa muttered, glancing down the road. 'There's an awful lot of bicycles here without chains. Why would he steal one that was chained?'

'How should I know? Maybe he liked that bike.'

'Liked it?' Yukawa said to himself. 'What did he like about it?'

'If you're trying to say something, why not spit it out?' Kusanagi growled.

'As you know, I came here yesterday as well. And like today, I stood here, observing. Bicycles are left here all day long – lots of them. Some are locked, and some left so blatantly unlocked I think the owners half want them to get stolen. Out of all these bicycles, why did our murderer choose that one?'

'We don't know it was the murderer who took the bike.'

'Very well. Let's stick with the original theory. Say it was the victim himself who stole it. Either way, why choose that one?'

Kusanagi shook his head. 'I'm not sure what you're getting at. It was an average bike, nothing remarkable about it at all. He probably just picked one at random.'

'Random? I think not.' Yukawa waved a finger at the detective. 'Let me guess: the bicycle was brand-new, or practically brand-new. Well? Am I right?'

Taken aback, Kusanagi reflected on his discussion with the bicycle's owner. 'Yeah, it was,' he replied after a moment. 'Now that you mention it, she did say she'd only bought it a month ago.'

Yukawa nodded, a satisfied look on his face. 'As I expected. The owner of a brand-new bicycle with an expensive chain on it is a good deal more likely to file a report with the police if it's stolen. Our thief expected this, and that's why he brought the bolt cutters.'

'You mean he went for a new bike on purpose?'

'Indeed.'

'Why?'

'There can be only one reason. The criminal wanted the bicycle owner to file a report. Somehow, having a police report on file claiming the bicycle was stolen worked in our criminal's favor. Probably because it would lead the investigation down the wrong path.'

'So you mean to say that even though we think the bicycle was stolen between eleven in the morning and ten at night, we're wrong? But how would the thief know what the bicycle's owner was going to say?'

'He might not know what they would say about the time of the theft, but he could be sure they would at least file a report that the bicycle had been stolen from Shinozaki Station.'

Kusanagi gulped and stared at the physicist. 'You're saying it was a ploy to draw our attention to Shinozaki?'

'That's one possibility.'

'We did spend a lot of time and manpower

questioning people around the station here. If your theory's right, that was all wasted time.'

'Not a waste, per se. After all, the bicycle *was* stolen from here. But I don't think this case is simple enough that knowing that fact will do you any good at all. No, our little caper was constructed far more craftily and with greater precision than that.'

Yukawa turned abruptly and began to walk away.

'Hey—' Kusanagi hurried after him. 'Where are you going now?'

'Home. Where else?'

'Wait a second.' The detective grabbed Yukawa by the shoulder. 'There is one more question I wanted to ask you. Why are you so interested in this case?'

'Was I not supposed to be interested?'

'That's not an answer.'

Yukawa shrugged Kusanagi's hand off his shoulder. 'Am I a suspect?'

'A suspect? Hardly.'

'Then I can do as I please, can't I? I'm certainly not trying to obstruct your investigation.'

'Okay, then let me be frank. You mentioned my name to the mathematician living next to Yasuko Hanaoka, didn't you? And you lied to him. You told him I wanted his help with the investigation. I think I have the right to ask what that was all about.'

Yukawa turned to face Kusanagi, his body suddenly tense, and behind his sunglasses, he stared at the detective coldly. 'You went to talk to him?'

'I did. Because *you* wouldn't tell me anything.'

'What did he say?'

'Now just hold on a minute. I'm the one asking the questions here. What was that all about? Do you think the mathematician is involved?'

Yukawa turned away and resumed walking towards the station.

'Hey, wait—' Kusanagi called to his back.

Yukawa stopped and peered back over his shoulder. 'Now it's my turn to be frank. I'm afraid I can't give you my full cooperation with this case. I'm looking into it for personal reasons. So don't expect me to be of much help.'

'Then don't expect me to give you any more information.'

Yukawa's eyes dropped to the pavement, then he nodded. 'Fair enough. We'll just each have to go it alone this time around.' He began walking again.

Kusanagi sensed a rare determination in Yukawa's gait, and he refrained from calling after him again.

After pausing for a cigarette, the detective headed for the station himself. He had decided to delay his departure so he wouldn't end up on the same train as Yukawa. For reasons Kusanagi couldn't fathom, his friend had some personal connection to this case and seemed to be determined to solve it on his own terms. Kusanagi didn't want to do anything to distract him.

What is Yukawa so worried about? Kusanagi wondered as the subway car swayed along the tracks.

Could it really be the mathematician, Ishigami? But if Ishigami was somehow connected to the case, why hadn't his name come up at all, except as the lead suspect's neighbour? What was it about him that bothered Yukawa so much?

Kusanagi thought back over what he had seen a couple of evenings before at the lunch box store. Yukawa was there with Ishigami – and Ishigami had told him it was Yukawa's idea to go there.

Yukawa wasn't the type to go out of his way to do something without a good reason. He had been after something when he went to that shop with Ishigami. But what?

And then Kudo had shown up right after that . . . But surely Yukawa would have had no way of anticipating that.

Kusanagi thought back on his discussion with Kudo, but he couldn't remember the man having said anything about Ishigami. Kudo hadn't given any names at all, for that matter. In fact, he had plainly stated that he wouldn't offer any names even if he knew them.

A thought crossed Kusanagi's mind. What had they been talking about when he said that? He pictured Kudo's face, the man suppressing his irritation as he spoke of the people who visited Benten-tei just to see Yasuko.

Kusanagi took a deep breath and straightened

211

his back. The young woman sitting in the seat across from him shot him a dubious look.

The detective glanced up at the subway map above the door. *Think I'll make a stop in Hamacho.*

It had been a while since Ishigami last sat behind the wheel of a car, but it only took him about thirty minutes to get used to driving again. Still, it took him a while to find a suitable place to park on the road near his destination. Every spot he checked seemed like it would put him in someone else's way. Finally he found a small truck that had been sloppily parked across two spaces and managed to squeeze in behind it.

It was his second time in a rental car. He'd been obliged to pick one up once while he was a university assistant in order to ferry students around on a field trip to a power plant. That time he drove a large van that seated seven, but today he was in a small economy car, which he found much easier to handle.

Ishigami's eyes went to a small building ahead of him on the right. The sign on the building read 'Hikari Graphics, Ltd'. It was Kuniaki Kudo's company.

It hadn't been difficult to track the place down. He had the name Kudo from the detective, Kusanagi, and he knew the man ran a printing company. Ishigami had gone online, found a site with links to printing companies, and checked every single one in Tokyo. Hikari Graphics was the only one with a CEO named Kudo.

Ishigami had gone to the rental car office directly after finishing up at school and picked up a car he had reserved in advance.

There was danger involved in renting a car. The transaction would leave a trail. But he had weighed the risks for a long time before deciding to act.

When the digital display on the dashboard read 5:50 P.M., several men and women emerged from the front entrance. Ishigami spotted Kudo amongst them, and his body stiffened.

Eyes fixed on the group, he reached for the digital camera in the passenger seat. Flicking it on, he looked through the viewfinder. *There*. He adjusted the focus and zoomed in as far as the lens allowed.

Kudo was dressed impeccably. Ishigami didn't even know where one would go to buy that kind of clothes. Again, it occurred to him that this man was Yasuko's type. Of course, not just Yasuko, but most women, if given a choice between him and Kudo, would have chosen Kudo.

Ishigami snapped a picture, feeling a pulse of envy course through him. He had set the camera not to flash, but even so Kudo showed up beautifully on the LCD. The sun was high enough and angled well so as to light his subject clearly.

Kudo was going around to the back of the building where, Ishigami had already ascertained, the company's private parking lot was located. The mathematician waited, watching. After a few moments a single Mercedes rolled out into the street. It was green. Spotting Kudo in the driver's seat, Ishigami hurriedly started his own engine.

He drove, eyes fixed on the Mercedes's brake lights. Driving was difficult enough, but following someone else made it even harder. The worst part was timing the traffic lights. Luckily, Kudo was a conservative driver. He drove at or under the speed limit, and always stopped at yellow lights.

Ishigami began to worry that he might be driving too close to his mark and would be noticed. Still, now that he had started, he had to keep following.

As he drove, the mathematician occasionally glanced at the car's GPS. The roads were mostly unfamiliar to him, but he could see on the map that Kudo's Mercedes was heading for Shinagawa.

The number of cars on the road increased, and it became harder and harder to keep up the chase. Ishigami let himself get too far behind, and a truck got between him and Kudo. He couldn't see the Mercedes at all, and while he was debating whether or not to switch lanes, the traffic light turned red ahead of him. It looked like the truck was at the front of the line – which meant that the Mercedes had driven on ahead.

I lost him already? Ishigami swore under his breath.

But when the light turned green and he started up again, he saw a Mercedes waiting up at the next light with its turn signal on. Without a doubt, it was Kudo. He was turning into a hotel.

Without hesitating, Ishigami followed. It might

look suspicious, but he couldn't turn back after having almost lost him once.

When the next light changed, Kudo made his turn with Ishigami right behind him. Passing through the hotel gates, the Mercedes headed down a sloping ramp into an underground parking area. Ishigami followed.

When he reached out to take a ticket for the parking lot, Kudo glanced behind him, and Ishigami had to hunch down in his seat. He couldn't tell whether the businessman had seen anything or not.

The parking lot was mostly empty. The Mercedes pulled into a spot close to the hotel entrance. Ishigami stopped some distance away. He turned the key and lifted his camera.

Kudo got out of the Mercedes. *Click.* Kudo was looking in his direction. *He suspects something!* Ishigami shrunk down even further.

But Kudo turned and went into the hotel. Once he was out of sight, Ishigami started up his car again and drove out.

I suppose two pictures will have to do for now.

He had been in the parking lot for such a short time that he didn't owe anything when he left. He turned the wheel carefully as the car climbed back up the narrow ramp.

Ishigami contemplated the note he would include with the two pictures. In his head, it went something like:

As you can tell by the enclosed pictures, I have discovered the identity of a man you see frequently.

I must ask, what is this man to you?

If you are having a relationship, that would be a serious betrayal.

Don't you understand what I've done for you?

I believe I have the right to tell you what to do in this matter. You must stop seeing this man immediately.

If you do not, my anger will be directed at him.

It would be a simple thing for me to lead this man towards the same fate Togashi suffered. I have both the resolve and the means to do this.

Let me repeat, if you are engaged in a relationship with this man, that is a betrayal I cannot forgive, and I will have my revenge.

Ishigami repeated the words of his statement to himself, considering whether it was too threatening, or perhaps not threatening enough.

Then the light changed, and he was about to drive out through the hotel gate when he saw something that made his eyes go wide.

It was Yasuko Hanaoka stepping off the pavement, into the hotel.

CHAPTER 12

Yasuko walked into the hotel tea lounge, and a man wearing a dark green jacket beckoned to her from the back. It was Kudo.

About a third of the tables in the place were filled. There were some couples, but most of the patrons were businessmen in expensive suits, leaning towards each other as they discussed their deals. Yasuko made her way across the room, her face slightly downcast.

'Sorry to call you out here so suddenly,' Kudo said. He was smiling. 'Would you like something to drink?'

The waitress came over, and Yasuko ordered a milk tea.

'Is something wrong?' she asked.

'No, nothing so serious,' he replied, lifting his coffee cup to his lips, but before drinking he said, 'A detective came to my place yesterday.'

Yasuko's eyes opened wide. 'They found you . . .'

'Did you tell them about me?'

'I'm sorry. They came right after I had dinner with you the other day, and they kept asking me questions about where I'd been and with whom.

217

I thought they'd be even more suspicious if I didn't say anything—'

Kudo waved a hand dismissively. 'No need to apologize. I don't blame you at all. If we're ever going to meet like normal people, the police should know about us. In fact, I think it's a good thing you told them.'

'Really?' Yasuko looked up at him.

He nodded. 'Just know that they'll be keeping a close watch on us, so be ready for that. You know, I was followed on my way here.'

'Followed?'

'I didn't notice it at first, but it became pretty obvious the more I drove. There was a car behind me the whole way from Hikari. They even followed me into the parking lot of this hotel. I don't think I was imagining things.'

Kudo talked as if this was nothing special, but Yasuko's eyes were frozen on him. 'And? Where'd they go?'

'Who knows?' He shrugged. 'They were too far away for me to see a face, and they were gone before I knew it. To tell the truth, I've been watching everyone in here since I arrived, but I haven't noticed anyone particularly suspicious. Of course, they could be watching in a way that I wouldn't notice. Still, I think they might have left.'

Yasuko looked around at the other people in the tea room. Everyone seemed perfectly normal.

'So you're a suspect now?'

'I think they've come up with a scenario in which

you were the leader in some plot to kill Togashi, with me your willing accomplice. The detective yesterday was very up front about wanting an alibi from me.'

The waitress arrived with the milk tea. While she was standing at the table, Yasuko cast her eyes around the room a second time.

'If they're still watching us now, won't they suspect something if they see you meeting with me like this?'

'What? No problem. Like I said, I want this – *us* – to be out in the open. Trying to hide it would make us look even more suspicious. We were never the kind to sneak around in any case.' Kudo leaned back on his sofa seat and spread his arms as if to demonstrate that he didn't care who saw him. Then he took a long sip from his coffee cup.

Yasuko reached for her own teacup. 'Well, I'm happy to hear you say that, but I don't want to be the cause of any trouble for you, Kudo. It's just not right. I think, maybe, we shouldn't meet for a while. Just until things calm down.'

'I figured you'd say something like that,' Kudo said, setting down his cup and leaning forward. 'That's why I wanted you to come here today. I knew you'd hear about the detective coming to my place sooner or later, and I didn't want you to worry about it. Frankly, I'm not worried about it at all. I told you they asked about my alibi. Luckily, I was with someone else at the time, and if they decide to pursue it, there are records to prove it. The detectives will lose their interest in me eventually.'

'Well, I hope so, for your sake.'

'Look,' Kudo said, 'what I'm more worried about is you. They'll figure out I wasn't an accomplice sooner or later. But that doesn't mean they'll stop treating you like a suspect. It makes me downright depressed to think about how pushy they're going to get with you.'

'Well, there's no helping that. After all, Togashi *was* looking for me at the time.'

'There is that, isn't there? What the hell did he want with you? Even dead, that guy is still a pain in the ass.' Kudo grimaced. Then his eyes turned back to Yasuko. 'You really didn't have anything to do with it, right? Don't get me wrong. I'm not doubting you. I'm just saying if you had any contact with Togashi at all, it's safe to tell me about it, and it might help.'

Yasuko returned Kudo's look, noticing his fine features. *So this is why he suddenly wanted to meet.* He did suspect her, if only a little.

She smiled faintly. 'Don't worry. I had nothing to do with him, really.'

'That's what I thought. Still, it's nice to hear it from your mouth.' Kudo nodded and looked at his watch. 'Well, since you're here, how about dinner? I know a great yakitori place.'

'I'm sorry. I can't tonight. I didn't tell Misato I'd be out.'

'Oh, right. Well, I don't want to make things

difficult for you, then.' Kudo grabbed the check and stood. 'Shall we?'

While he was paying, Yasuko took another look around. No one in the tea lounge looked even remotely like a detective.

She felt bad admitting it to herself, but while Kudo remained under suspicion, she felt easier about getting together with him. After all, the more the police suspected him, the further from the truth they were. But that seemed bound to change. In any case, she wasn't sure she should let her relationship with Kudo continue to progress as quickly as it had. She wasn't afraid of becoming intimate – she wanted it, in fact. But she was afraid that doing so would upset the tenuous balance of her life. Ishigami's mask-like face flitted across her mind.

'I'll give you a lift,' Kudo said after paying the bill.

'It's all right. I'll take the train.'

'No, let me give you a ride.'

'Really, it's okay. I need to do some shopping.'

'Hmph,' Kudo grumbled, but in the end he saw her off cheerily. 'All right, well, I'll see you later, then. It's all right if I give you a ring?'

'Of course, and thanks for the tea.' Yasuko returned his smile before walking away.

She was at a crosswalk making for Shinagawa Station when her mobile phone began to ring. Still walking, Yasuko pulled out her phone and looked at the display. It was Sayoko at Benten-tei.

'Yes?'

'Hey, Yasuko? It's Sayoko. Can you talk?' There was a strange tension in her voice.

'Sure, what's wrong?'

'I just wanted to tell you that the detectives dropped by again after you left today. They were asking some strange questions. I thought you should know.'

Gripping her mobile phone tightly, Yasuko closed her eyes. Those policemen were at it again, weaving a spider-web around her wherever she went.

'What do you mean, "strange"?' she asked uneasily.

'They were asking about that guy. The high school teacher? What was his name again? Ishigami?'

Yasuko almost dropped the phone. 'What about him?' Her voice was trembling.

'Well, they said they'd heard there was someone who came to buy our lunches just to see you, and they wanted to know who he was and what he did. I think they might have heard something from Kudo.'

'Kudo?'

Yasuko couldn't imagine how this had anything to do with him.

'Yasuko, I think I might've said something to him once . . . and he must've told that to the police.'

Now it made sense to Yasuko. The detectives had talked to Kudo, heard about Ishigami, then gone to Benten-tei to corroborate what he told them.

'And what did you say, Sayoko?'

'Well, I didn't want to raise any suspicions by hiding it, so I told them the truth. I told them he was a schoolteacher who lived next to you. But that we had just been guessing about his reasons for coming. It's not like he told us anything.'

Yasuko's mouth was dry. So the police had finally found Ishigami. Had it been Kudo who put them on the trail? Or was there some other reason they were watching him?

'Hello? Yasuko?'

'Yeah, sorry.'

'Anyway, that's what I told them. I hope that was okay? I didn't do anything wrong, did I?'

She had, but that was the last thing Yasuko could admit.

'No, not at all. I can't see how it would be a problem. He's certainly got nothing to do with all this.'

'That's what I thought. I just wanted you to know that the detectives had come back.'

'Right, thanks.'

Yasuko hung up. Her stomach churned; she wanted to throw up.

She felt sick and queasy all the way back to her apartment. She stopped to do some shopping at a supermarket on the way, but couldn't even remember what she had bought by the time she made it home.

Ishigami was at his computer when he heard the door of the next apartment open and close. There

223

were three photos up on his screen: two of Kudo, and one of Yasuko as she went into the hotel. He had wanted to get a shot of the two of them together, but he'd been worried that Kudo would spot him; and if Yasuko had happened to see him, too, there would have been a scene. So he had let his better judgment prevail and kept his distance.

Ishigami imagined the worst-case scenario. He'd need these photos then, for sure. He just hoped it never came to that.

He glanced at the clock on his desk before standing. It was almost eight o'clock in the evening. Yasuko and Kudo hadn't been together for very long. He couldn't help but make note of how that fact put him at ease.

Telephone card in his pocket, the mathematician left his apartment and walked down the street as usual, taking a careful look around to make sure he wasn't being watched.

He thought about the detective, Kusanagi. It was strange. Even when Kusanagi had come asking about Yasuko, Ishigami had gotten the feeling that the man was really there because he wanted to know about Manabu Yukawa. What sort of connection did they have? It was hard for Ishigami to plan his next move without knowing whether or not he was a suspect yet.

He called Yasuko's mobile from the now familiar public phone. She picked up on the third ring.

'It's me,' Ishigami said. 'Is now a good time?'

'Yes.'

'Anything happen today?' He wanted to know what she had talked about with Kudo, but couldn't find a way to ask the question. If he hadn't tailed the man, he never would have known they'd met at all.

'Er, actually . . .' she began.

'Actually what? What happened?' He imagined Kudo filling her head with all kinds of crazy ideas.

'The detectives, they came back to Benten-tei. And, well, they were asking about you.'

'About me? How?' Ishigami swallowed.

'Well, it's kind of a long story, but some of the people at the shop have been talking about you since before all this began. Sorry, I don't want to say anything to make you angry . . .'

What was making Ishigami angry was the round-about way she was giving him the information. She would be no good at mathematics, he could tell.

'I promise not to get angry. Please just tell me as bluntly as possible. What were they saying about me?' Ishigami waited, ready to hear something unflattering about his looks or demeanour.

'Well – I've denied it all along, you understand – but some of the people at the shop think that you come there to buy lunches just so you can see me.'

'What?' For a moment, Ishigami's mind went blank.

'I'm sorry. They thought it was funny, like a joke. That's how they talk about things. They really don't mean any harm by it. I don't even think they seriously believe it themselves,' Yasuko said, vainly attempting to do some damage control.

But Ishigami barely registered half of what she said. He was wondering how someone else had noticed – someone other than Yasuko.

They were right, of course. He did go to the shop every day just to see her. And he realized that unconsciously he had expected her to notice how he felt. Still, it made his entire body hot with shame to think that someone else, a third party, had noticed first. How they must have laughed to see an ugly man like him head over heels for a beautiful woman like her.

'I'm sorry. You're angry, aren't you?' Yasuko asked.

Ishigami hurriedly cleared his throat. 'No, no . . . What did the detectives do, exactly?'

'Like I said, they heard that rumour, and so they came to the shop asking who this person – *you* – were, and the person at the shop gave them your name.'

'I see,' Ishigami said, still burning. 'And where do you think the detectives heard that rumour?'

'I . . . I'm not sure.'

'Is that all they wanted to know?'

'I think so. That's all I heard.'

Receiver gripped tightly in his hand, Ishigami nodded. This was no time for indecision. He didn't know how it had happened, but it was clear the police were gradually setting their sights on him. He had to think of an appropriate response.

'Is your daughter there?' he asked.

'Misato? Yes, why?'

'Can I speak with her a moment?'

'Sure, of course.'

Ishigami closed his eyes. He focused all of his energies on divining what detective Kusanagi was planning, what action he would take, what he would do next. Yet, in the middle of his thoughts, there he found the face of Manabu Yukawa. What was the physicist's role in all this?

'Hello?' came a young girl's voice over the line.

'It's Ishigami,' he told her. 'Misato . . . you said you talked about the movie with your friend on the twelfth? Mika was her name, right?'

'Yes. And I told the detectives that, too.'

'Right, so you said. I was wondering about your other friend – Haruka, was it?'

'That's right. Haruka Tamaoka.'

'You told her about the movie, too, right? Did you talk about it more than that one time?'

'No, just the once. Well, maybe a little.'

'You didn't tell the detectives about her, right?'

'No, only about Mika. You told me I shouldn't mention Haruka, so I didn't.'

'That's right. But I think it might be time to talk to them about her now.'

Ishigami glanced around the park, making sure no one was nearby, before giving Misato detailed instructions on what she was to do.

★ ★ ★

Grey smoke was rising from an empty plot next to the university tennis courts. Kusanagi arrived to find Yukawa in a lab coat with the sleeves rolled up, using a long stick to poke at something inside an oil drum. The smoke was coming from the drum.

Yukawa heard his footsteps approaching and looked up. 'It seems I have a stalker.'

'Detectives like stalking suspicious people.'

'So I'm suspicious now, am I?' Yukawa asked, a glimmer in his eye. 'Do I detect a bold new direction from our stoic hero? It's just that kind of flexibility you'll need to rise in this world, you know.'

'Whatever you say, Galileo,' said Kusanagi sarcastically. 'Don't you want to know why I suspect you?'

'I don't need to ask. People always suspect scientists of being up to no good.' He gave the contents of the oil drum another prod.

'What are you burning there?'

'Nothing much. Some old reports and materials I no longer needed. Can't really trust a shredder to do the job.' Yukawa picked up a nearby bucket and poured water into the drum. There was a sizzling sound, and the smoke became thicker and turned white.

'I've got some questions for you. As a detective, this time.'

'You really are onto something, aren't you?' Yukawa checked to make sure that the fire was out; then, bucket in one hand, he began to walk away.

Kusanagi followed. 'I dropped by Benten-tei after talking to you yesterday. Heard something very interesting there. Don't you want to know?'

'Not really.'

'I'll tell you anyway. Seems like your friend Ishigami has a thing for Yasuko Hanaoka.'

Yukawa stopped in the middle of a loping stride. He turned his head and shot a piercing look over his shoulder at the detective. 'Someone at the shop tell you that?'

'Something like that. An interesting idea occurred to me while I was talking to you, and I wanted to check at Benten-tei to see if I was right. Theories and logic are all very well, but intuition's one of the best weapons in a detective's arsenal.'

'And?' Yukawa turned around to face him. 'How does it affect your investigation now that you know he "had a thing" for your prime suspect?'

'Don't pretend you don't know what it means. I know you've been trying to hide the fact that you have suspected Ishigami of being Yasuko's conspirator for some time now.'

'I don't recall trying to hide anything.'

'Anyway, I found out why you suspected him without your help. We're going to keep a close eye on him now. Which is why I'm here. I know we decided to part ways yesterday, but I'd like to offer you a peace treaty. In exchange for information from us, I want you to tell me what you've found. Not a bad deal, you have to agree.'

229

'You overestimate my value. I haven't found out anything. It's all conjecture.'

'Then tell me what you're conjecturing,' Kusanagi said, staring at his friend, holding his gaze.

Yukawa looked away first and then resumed walking. 'Back to the lab first.'

Back in Laboratory 13, Kusanagi sat down at a table with some mysterious scorch marks on it. Yukawa placed two mugs on the tabletop. It would have been hard to say which mug was filthier.

The physicist mixed some coffee, then followed it with an immediate question. 'If Ishigami was a conspirator, what role do you think he played?'

'What, I have to talk first?'

'You're the one who offered the peace treaty.' Yukawa sat down in a chair, absentmindedly stirring his drink.

'Fine. I haven't told my boss about Ishigami at all, so this is just my thinking – but if the murder did take place somewhere other than our crime scene, Ishigami must've carried the body.'

'Oh? But I thought you were against the whole body transportation scenario.'

'I said all bets were off if she had an accomplice. I still think it was probably Yasuko Hanaoka that did the deed. She might have had help from Ishigami, but she was definitely there.'

'You sound pretty sure of yourself.'

'Well, if Ishigami was the one who killed him *and* carried the body, he's no conspirator. That

230

would make him the murderer, probably working alone. No matter how big a crush he had on her, I can't imagine he'd go that far. Also, if he killed Togashi on his own and then Yasuko turned him in, it would all be over now. So she must have borne some of the risk, too.'

'What if Ishigami killed him, but they both helped dispose of the body?'

'I won't say that's not a possibility, but the likelihood is pretty low. Yasuko Hanaoka's cinema alibi is shaky, but her alibi after that is pretty sound. If she timed it just right, she could have committed the murder and still made her alibi, but she wouldn't have had time to do that and dispose of a body.'

'What part of her alibi exactly have you not been able to confirm?'

'The time between 7:00 and 9:10 when she says she was watching a movie. The ramen shop and the karaoke place after that all checked out. That, and she did go into the cinema at least once. We found half of a ticket stub there with her and her daughter's fingerprints.'

'So you think it was during that two hours and ten minutes that she and Ishigami murdered her ex-husband?'

'They might also have disposed of the body then. But, considering travel time, she must've left the scene before Ishigami did.'

'And where did the murder take place?'

'I don't know that. Except it was probably Yasuko who called Togashi there.'

231

Yukawa sipped his coffee without a word. He wrinkled his brow bemusedly, as if unconvinced by his friend's explanation.

'Got something to say?'

'Not particularly.'

'Well if you do, have out with it,' Kusanagi said. 'I've told you what I think, so now it's your turn.'

Yukawa sighed. 'He didn't use a car.'

'Huh?'

'I said, Ishigami didn't use a car. He would need one to carry a corpse, right? Since he doesn't have a car, he would've had to get get one from somewhere. I don't think he has the means to procure a car in such a way that he would leave no trace behind. Not many law-abiding citizens do.'

'We'll be checking all of the rental agencies, of course.'

'Good luck with that. I can guarantee you won't find anything.'

Kusanagi glared at the physicist, but Yukawa seemed unconcerned.

'All I'm saying is that if the murder happened somewhere other than the place where the body was found, then it was probably Ishigami who carried it there. There's still a good possibility that the murder did take place at our crime scene. If two of them were involved, anything is possible.'

'So,' Yukawa said, lifting the cup of coffee up to his lips, 'you think the two of them killed Togashi, caved in his face, burned off his fingerprints, stripped his clothes and burned them, and then walked away?'

'Like I said, they might have left at different times.' Kusanagi looked down at his cup of instant coffee and suppressed a small shudder. 'Yasuko would've had to reach the cinema by the time the movie ended, at least.'

'And according to your theory, the victim rode that bicycle to the crime scene?'

'I guess so, yes.'

'Which would mean that Ishigami had forgotten to wipe it for fingerprints. You really think Ishigami would have made such a simple mistake? Ishigami the Buddha?'

'Even geniuses make mistakes.'

Yukawa slowly shook his head. 'Not that one.'

'Okay, then why do you think he left those prints on the bicycle?'

'That's what I've been wondering,' Yukawa said, crossing his arms. 'I haven't come to a conclusion yet.'

'Maybe you're overthinking this. That guy might be a genius mathematician, but he's certainly a novice murderer.'

'They're the same thing,' Yukawa stated simply. 'Murder probably comes even easier to him.'

Now Kusanagi shook his head. Examining the stains on his mug, he said, 'in any case, we're keeping an eye on him. If we proceed on the assumption that there was a male conspirator, it broadens the range of our investigation considerably.'

'If this new theory of yours is correct, it means the crime was carried out in a rather slipshod manner. We have the fingerprints left on the bicycle, the half-burned clothes – all evidence of carelessness. My question is, do you think this crime was planned from the beginning? Or did it happen more spontaneously?'

'Well—' Kusanagi began. He glanced at Yukawa's calm, intent face, and hesitated for a moment before continuing. 'It could've been spontaneous, sure. For instance, what if Yasuko called Togashi up to talk with him about something, and Ishigami came along as a sort of bodyguard? The discussion got heated, and the two of them ended up killing Togashi. Something like that.'

'But that doesn't fit with the cinema story at all,' Yukawa observed. 'If they were just getting together to talk, why prepare an alibi? Even an insufficient alibi like hers?'

'So you think it was planned? That Yasuko and Ishigami told him to come someplace and then ambushed him?'

'That's hard to imagine.'

'Well, great. So what do *you* think happened, then?' Kusanagi asked sourly.

'If Ishigami planned the whole thing from the start, it wouldn't be half as full of holes as it is now.'

'Fine, but how does that help—' Kusanagi broke off abruptly as his mobile began to ring. 'Hang on a second.' He answered the phone.

A moment later he was engaged in a hurried sotto voce conversation. He pulled out a pad and scribbled a few notes before hanging up.

'That was my partner, Kishitani,' he told Kusanagi. 'I've received some very important news concerning Yasuko's daughter. It turns out one of Misato's classmates just gave a very interesting testimony.'

'What's that?'

'Apparently, at lunch on the day of the murder, this classmate of hers heard from Misato that she was going out to the movies with her mother that night.'

'Really?'

'Kishitani confirmed it. It looks solid. Which means that Yasuko had already decided to go to the movies by lunchtime that day at the latest.' Kusanagi nodded to the physicist. 'Maybe I was right to think this was premeditated.'

In response, Yukawa shook his head, his eyes dead serious. 'Impossible.'

CHAPTER 13

Club Marian was about a five-minute walk from Kinshicho Station, on the fifth floor of a building that held several other drinking establishments. The building was old, with an ancient elevator that growled dispiritedly as it carried Kusanagi and his partner upward.

The elder detective peered at his watch. It was just past seven in the evening. *Perfect time for asking a few questions*, he thought, as he stared dubiously at the peeling paint on the elevator wall. *There shouldn't be many customers around at this early hour – not that I'm an expert on this sort of place . . .*

The noise of the crowd took Kusanagi by surprise as he got off the elevator and stepped through the nightclub door. Of the more than twenty tables inside, fully a third were already occupied. Judging by their clothes, most of the patrons were salarymen, though there were a few in the crowd whose occupation he couldn't place.

'I was asking questions in a club in Ginza once,' Kishitani whispered in his ear. 'The *mama* there was wondering where all the guys who used to drink at her place during the economic bubble were drinking now – well, I think I just found out. They're all here.'

'I have a hard time believing that,' Kusanagi shot back. 'Once you get used to luxury, it's hard to lower your sights. The Ginza crowd wouldn't be caught dead in a place this seedy, hard times or no.'

He called over one of the waiters, who was dressed in a black tuxedo, and asked to speak to a manager. The young waiter's casual smile vanished, and he disappeared into the back.

A bit later, another waiter came out and showed the two detectives to seats at the bar.

'Will you be drinking something?' he asked.

'A beer for me, thanks,' Kusanagi replied.

'You sure that's okay?' Kishitani asked after the waiter had left. 'We're on duty.'

'If we don't drink anything, the other customers will get suspicious.'

'You could've had some tea then.'

'Since when do two grown men come to a bar to drink tea?'

They were still debating the ethics of drinking alcohol on the job when an elegant woman in a silver-grey suit appeared. She was about forty, and wearing a lot of makeup, with her hair done up in a neat bun on her head. *A little on the thin side*, Kusanagi thought, *but a beauty nonetheless*.

'Welcome,' she said. 'You wanted to speak to me?' The trace of a smile played across her lips.

'We're police,' Kusanagi announced in a low voice. Next to him, Kishitani reached into his breast

pocket, but Kusanagi stopped him, turning back
to the woman. 'You need proof?'

'That won't be necessary.' She took the seat next
to Kusanagi, placing her business card on the bar.
It read, 'Sonoko Sugimura.'

'You're the *mama* here?'

'You could call me that,' Sugimura replied with
a smile.

'Quite the place you've got. Business looks good,'
Kusanagi commented, glancing over his shoulder
at the tables.

'It's mostly just for show. I think the owner runs
it for the tax break. Most of the customers are
indebted to him for one thing or another.'

The detective nodded.

'This whole thing could shut down any day,
really. Sayoko was right to get out while she still
could and start that luncheon shop of hers.'

Kusanagi suspected business wasn't all that
bad – he even detected a hint of defiant pride in
the way the woman casually mentioned her prede-
cessor. This Sonoko Sugimura was a survivor.

'I believe some of our people from the department
were down here the other day?'

She nodded. 'They came a few times, asking
about Mr Togashi. Is that why you've come today?'

'We're sorry to take your time like this.'

'Well, I told the other gentlemen this, so I may
as well tell you, too. If you're trying to pin this
whole thing on Yasuko, you're barking up the
wrong tree. She has no motive, for one.'

'No,' Kusanagi said, waving a hand, 'we're not here because we suspect Yasuko. It's just that our investigation isn't going as smoothly as we'd have liked, so we're trying to make a fresh start.'

'A fresh start, hmm?' the *mama* echoed with a sigh.

'Previously, you told us that Shinji Togashi had come here on the fifth of March?'

'That's right. It was quite a surprise, seeing him after all that time. I couldn't imagine why he would be dropping by now.'

'So you knew him?'

'I'd met him once or twice. I worked together with Yasuko back in Akasaka, you know. That's where I knew him from. He was a big spender back in those days, always dressed to a T. Quite handsome, too.'

Kusanagi sensed from her tone that this description hardly applied to the Togashi she had met in March.

'And Shinji Togashi was trying to find Ms Hanaoka, is that correct?'

'I think he wanted to patch things up between them. But still, I didn't tell him anything. I knew all too well the hell that poor girl had been through on his account. I thought as long as I didn't say anything she'd be safe, but I didn't count on the girls. One of them knew about Yonazawa and Sayoko's lunch shop, and she told that smooth talker everything.'

'I see,' Kusanagi said with a nod. After working

for a long time in a business like this, which thrived on human connections, a former hostess would find it nearly impossible simply to disappear.

'Does a Mr Kuniaki Kudo come here often?' he asked next, changing his line of questioning.

'Mister Kudo? From the printing company?'

'That's right.'

'Quite often, yes. Though not so much recently.' Sugimura tilted her head. 'Has Mr Kudo done something?'

'No, no. We've just heard that he was one of Yasuko Hanaoka's regulars back when she was a hostess.'

Sugimura's lips softened and she nodded. 'He was. He thought the world of that girl.'

'Were they seeing each other outside the night-club?'

'Hmm . . .' The woman tilted her head again. 'Some of the girls thought she was, but as I see it, their relationship began and ended at the club.'

'How so?'

'Well, they were closest when Yasuko was in Akasaka. But right around then she started having trouble with Mr Togashi, and it seems Mr Kudo found out. After that, he became more like Yasuko's counsellor than her lover. I don't think things between them progressed very far at all romantically.'

'But after Ms Hanaoka got divorced, they could have started going out . . .'

Sugimura shook her head. 'Mr Kudo's not that

sort of man, detective. After he'd been giving her all this advice on how to make things right between her and her husband, he couldn't go dating Yasuko after the divorce. It would have made it look like that was his plan from the start. To be honest I think he intended to maintain a sort of platonic friendship with her after the divorce. Mr Kudo is married, after all.'

So Sonoko Sugimura didn't know that Kudo's wife had passed away. Kusanagi decided there was little to be gained by telling her, so he kept silent.

For the most part, he guessed that she was right about Yasuko and Kudo's relationship. Like other experienced detectives, he respected a hostess's intuition when it came to the affairs of men and women. Sugimura's observations were in line with his own, only confirming Kusanagi's hunch that Kudo was innocent. Which meant it was time to change the topic.

He pulled a photograph out of his pocket and showed it to the *mama*. 'Know this man?'

It was a photograph of Tetsuya Ishigami. Kishitani had snapped a shot of the teacher as he left his school one day. In the photograph, the mathematician's eyes were fixed on some faraway point. It had been taken from an angle, and at a distance, so that Ishigami wouldn't notice.

Sugimura frowned. 'Who's that?'

'So you don't know him?'

'No, sorry. I can tell you he's never come to this club.'

'His name's Ishigami. That ring any bells?'

'Mr Ishigami . . .'

'Maybe Ms Hanaoka mentioned him?'

'I'm sorry. If she did, I don't remember it.'

'He's a high school teacher. Did she ever say anything about seeing a teacher?'

'I don't know,' Sugimura replied, her frown fading. 'I talk to her now and then on the phone, but she's not said anything of the sort.'

'What about any other relationships Yasuko might be having? Has she asked you for advice with anything, or told you anything about that?'

At this question, Sugimura let slip a wry chuckle. 'The other detective who came before asked that as well, and I'll tell you what I told him: she hasn't said anything. Maybe she is seeing someone, and she didn't want me to know, but I don't think that's the case. That girl's got her hands full raising Misato. I'd imagine she hasn't the time to bother with love right now. Mind you, it's not just my opinion. Sayoko said something of the sort not too long ago.'

Kusanagi nodded quietly. He hadn't expected to hear much about a possible relationship between Ishigami and Yasuko here at the club, so he wasn't too disappointed. Still, hearing someone say that there was no man in Yasuko's life made it hard for him to feel confident about the theory that Ishigami was Yasuko's conspirator.

Another customer walked in. Sugimura glanced with interest in his direction.

'You said you kept in touch with Ms Hanaoka on the phone? I was wondering when you last talked to her.'

'The day that Mr Togashi was on the news, I think. I was so surprised I had to call her up. I'm certain that I told that to the other detective, too.'

'How did Ms Hanaoka sound at the time?'

'No different than ever, really. She told me the cops had already been by to talk to her.'

That was us, Kusanagi thought, but he didn't feel the need to mention that to Sugimura.

'And before that, you didn't tell her that Togashi had been in to the club asking after her whereabouts?'

'I didn't. Which is to say, I couldn't bring myself. I didn't want to make her upset.'

So Yasuko Hanaoka hadn't known that Togashi was looking for her. And if she didn't know he was coming, she wouldn't have had time to devise a plot to murder him.

'It did occur to me to mention it . . . but at the time, she sounded so happy, there just wasn't a good moment.'

'At the time?' Something tugged at the back of Kusanagi's mind. 'You mean the last time you talked to her on the phone, when Togashi was on the news? Or some other time?'

'Oh, that's right, I'm sorry. I was talking about a time before then. Oh, about three or four days after Mr Togashi dropped in. She'd left a message for me, so I called her back.'

'Around when was that?'

'Let me see—' Sugimura retrieved her mobile phone from the pocket of her suit. Kusanagi expected her to go into her list of calls made and received, but she pulled up her calendar instead. She studied it for a moment, then looked back up at him. 'March tenth.'

'The tenth?' Kusanagi echoed, raising his voice. He and Kishitani exchanged glances. 'Are you sure?'

'Quite sure, yes.'

The day Shinji Togashi was murdered.

'Do you remember what time you called her?'

'Well, it was after I'd gone home for the day, so I'd say around one in the morning. She'd called me before midnight, but I was still busy here at the club and in pickup.'

'How long did you talk?'

'Oh, I'd say about half an hour. We usually talk that long.'

'And you called her? Her mobile phone?'

'No, actually. I called her at home.'

'Erm, sorry to be so particular about this, but it was one o'clock in the morning, so you mean you called her on the eleventh, not the tenth, correct?'

'That's right, it would have been the eleventh, wouldn't it?'

'You mind me asking what sort of message she left on your phone?'

'She only said she wanted to talk to me, so I should call her when I was done at the club.'

244

'What did she want to talk about?'

'Nothing much, really. She wanted to know the name of this shiatsu massage place I went to for therapy. Lower back pain, you know.'

'Shiatsu? Okay. Had she called you about things like that in the past?'

'Oh, she calls about all sorts of things, none of them terribly important. I think she just wants to talk, you know. That's why I call her.'

'And always so late at night?'

'I wouldn't say always, but it's not unusual. Late nights come with the territory. I suppose mostly we talk on days I have off, but she had called me, so . . .'

Kusanagi nodded and thanked Sugimura for her time. He tapped Kishitani on the shoulder and the two of them got up to leave. But as he made his way out of the club Kusanagi found he still wasn't satisfied.

He mulled it over on the way back to Kinshicho Station. The phone call Sugimura had mentioned at the end of their conversation bothered him. Yasuko Hanaoka had been talking on the phone in the middle of the night on the tenth of March. Her home phone. Which meant she had already come back by that point.

A theory had been going around the department that the actual time of the murder was sometime after eleven o'clock on the night of the tenth. This was little more than a theory based on the assumption that Yasuko Hanaoka was the murderer. If Togashi had been killed that late, then Hanaoka could have done it even if her alibi at karaoke held up. Still, nobody gave the theory much credit – even the ones who had suggested it in the first place. If it was true, Hanaoka would've had to leave the karaoke bar and go immediately to the scene of the crime in order to get there by midnight. And if she had done the deed then, there would have been no way for her to get back to her house by public transport. Few criminals wanted to leave an obvious trail by taking a taxi. In any case, taxis hardly ever passed by the riverbank where Togashi's remains had been found.

Then there was a matter of the stolen bicycle. The bicycle had been taken after ten o'clock in the morning. If the bicycle was a plant, that meant that Yasuko had to have gone to Shinozaki Station by that time. If it wasn't a plant, and Togashi had stolen it himself, then that raised the question: what had Togashi been doing between the time that he stole the bicycle and the time that he met Yasuko near midnight?

Having worked through this line of reasoning early on, Kusanagi hadn't seen the need to establish an alibi for Yasuko after karaoke on the night of the murder. And even if he had wanted one, he now knew she could provide it: she'd been on the phone with Sonoko Sugimura.

And that was what was bothering him.

'Remember the first time we talked to Yasuko

Hanaoka?' Kusanagi asked Kishitani abruptly as they walked.

'Sure. What about it?'

'Do you remember how I asked her about her alibi? Did I ask her where she had been on the tenth?'

'I don't remember exactly how you asked, if that's what you mean, but it was something like that, yeah.'

'And what did she say? She went to work that morning, and out that night with her daughter. They went to the movie, then to eat ramen, then to karaoke. Which got them home after eleven, right?'

'Sounds about right.'

'And according to the *mama* we just talked to, Yasuko was on the phone with her after that. She left a message asking for her to call, even though it wasn't about anything serious. So the *mama* calls her a little after one o'clock, and they talk for thirty minutes.'

'So? What of it?'

'Well, when I asked her for an alibi, why do you think Yasuko didn't mention the phone call?'

'Well, I suppose she didn't think it was necessary.'

'Why not?' Kusanagi stopped and turned to the junior detective. 'If she used her home phone to call someone, that'd be proof she was at home.'

Kishitani stopped, too. He pursed his lips. 'That may be so; but from Yasuko Hanaoka's perspective, telling you about her night on the town must have seemed like enough. I bet if you'd asked her about what she did when she got home, she'd have told you about the phone call.'

'You think that's the only reason she didn't say anything?'

'Can you think of another? I mean, if she was hiding the fact that she didn't have an alibi, that would be one thing, but she had an alibi – she just didn't tell us about it. Seems a little strange to get worked up over that.'

Kusanagi turned from his partner and resumed walking, scowling faintly. The junior detective had taken Hanaoka's side even before they knocked at her door that first night. It was no use expecting anything like an objective opinion from the man now.

Kusanagi's noontime discussion with Yukawa resurfaced in his mind. The physicist had said that, had Ishigami been involved, it was unlikely the murder had been premeditated. It was too sloppy for that. He had seemed quite adamant about that point.

'If he had planned it, he never would've used the cinema for an alibi,' Yukawa had noted. 'He would've known that the movie story was unconvincing – true enough, as evidenced by your suspicion. Ishigami would have understood that. And it raises another, larger question. What possible reason would Ishigami have to assist Yasuko Hanaoka in murdering Togashi? Even if Togashi had been giving her a hard time and she had

gone to her neighbour for help, Ishigami would've thought of a different solution for the problem. Murder would have been his last choice.'

'Why, because he's not vicious enough?'

Yukawa had shaken his head, his eyes cool. 'It's not a question of temperament. Murder isn't the most logical way to escape a difficult situation. It only leads to a different difficult situation. Ishigami would never engage in something so clearly counter-productive. Of course,' he had added, 'the converse is also true. That is, he's quite capable of committing an atrocity, provided that it's the most logical course of action.'

'So how do you think Ishigami could've been involved?'

'If he was involved, then I think he was not in a position to assist with the actual murder. In other words, by the time he became aware of the situation, Togashi was already dead. So what were his options? If it had been possible to conceal what had happened, he would have tried that. If it was impossible, he would have done what he could to hinder the eventual investigation. He would have given explicit instructions to Yasuko Hanaoka and her daughter; telling them how to answer detectives' questions and what evidence to reveal at what time. A script for them to follow, in other words.'

Which meant, according to Yukawa's theory, everything Yasuko Hanaoka and Misato had told them so far wasn't their own, unsullied testimony, but one prepared by Ishigami, who had been behind them, pulling the strings the whole time.

'Of course,' the physicist had added quietly, 'this is all merely my conjecture – a theory constructed on the premise that Ishigami was somehow involved. That premise itself might be wrong. In fact, I hope it's wrong. I hope deep in my heart that he had nothing to do with it.'

Yukawa's expression when he told Kusanagi this had been unusually pained – and, the detective thought, a little lonely. Perhaps the physicist feared losing an old friend so soon after becoming re-acquainted with him.

But Yukawa had never told Kusanagi the reason why he had come to suspect Ishigami in the first place. It seemed that he had somehow come to the conclusion that Ishigami had a crush on Yasuko – but he hadn't mentioned any evidence he had to support that theory.

Still, Kusanagi trusted Yukawa's skills of observation and deduction, almost to the point that, if Yukawa thought something was so, the detective assumed it was correct unless proven otherwise. Which made what Kusanagi had heard at Club Marian all the more interesting.

Why hadn't Yasuko come to them with an alibi for the night of March 10? If she had committed murder and prepared an alibi, she would have wanted to tell them about it as soon as possible. But that might not be so if Ishigami had instructed her *not* to tell them. Maybe he had given them instructions to never say more than was absolutely necessary at any given time.

Kusanagi remembered another remark Yukawa had made, back before he had shown any real interest in the case. When Kusanagi told the physicist that Yasuko Hanaoka had retrieved her ticket stubs from the movie pamphlet, what had he said?

'If we assume that the tickets really were bought to establish an alibi, that she put them in the pamphlet expecting you to come and ask her for them, I'd say that makes her an adversary to be feared.'

It was just past six o'clock, and Yasuko was about to remove her apron, when a customer entered Benten-tei. She smiled and gave a reflexive 'Hello!' in greeting, but when she saw the man's face, she hesitated. It was a face she knew, but not well – that of Ishigami's old friend.

'Remember me?' he asked cheerily. 'I came here before, with Mr Ishigami.'

'Oh, oh yes. I remember you,' Yasuko said, regaining her poise and her smile.

'I happened to be in the area, and remembered your lunch boxes. The one I had the other day was really quite good.'

'I'm glad to hear it.'

'I'm thinking today I'll . . . let's have the special. I know that's what Ishigami always gets, but you were out of them last time. How about today?'

'No problem,' Yasuko said, giving the order to the kitchen and undoing her apron strings.

'Oh? Were you on your way home?'

'Yes. I work until six.'

'Oh, I see. So, you'll be going back to your apartment?'

'Yes.'

'Mind if I join you for a bit, then? There was something I wanted to talk with you about.'

'Talk about? With me?'

'Yes, well . . . I wanted your advice, I should say. It's about Ishigami.' The man smiled.

Yasuko grew uneasy. 'Oh, I'm sorry but I hardly know Mr Ishigami, actually.'

'I won't take much of your time at all. We can talk while we walk,' he offered, his tone soft but his words insistent.

'All right, then, for a little, I suppose,' Yasuko replied, seeing no easy way out of the situation.

The man introduced himself as Yukawa. He was an assistant professor at the university where Ishigami had studied.

After a few moments Yukawa's lunch box was ready, and the two left the shop together. Yasuko had ridden to work on her bicycle, as usual. Now as they set out down the street she pushed the bike along beside her, until Yukawa said, 'Let me take that', and began to push it for her.

'So you've never talked much to Ishigami?'

'Not much. Just a word or two when he comes to the shop.'

'I see,' he said, and then fell silent.

'You said you wanted some advice?' Yasuko asked. She felt the tension growing inside her.

But Yukawa did not reply. Yasuko's unease

became a physical pain that spread across her chest and was starting to make her shoulders ache when finally he said, 'He's a simple man.'

'What?'

'He's simple. Ishigami, I mean. I don't mean stupid – I mean he's straightforward, direct. The solutions he looks for in his work are always the simplest. He doesn't start a problem by looking for many answers at once. And he always chooses a simple approach to get where he's going. That's why he is so good at what he does. There's no indecision, and he doesn't give up over trifling obstacles. It's great for mathematics, but not so great for day-to-day life. You can't always shoot for one result, for all or nothing. And yet he's constantly doing just that, and winding up with nothing to show for all his efforts.'

'Mr Yukawa, I . . .'

'I'm sorry, I know I'm not making myself very clear.' Yukawa smiled wryly. 'Did you meet Ishigami for the first time when you moved into your current apartment?'

'Yes, when I went around to meet my neighbours.'

'And you told him you were working at the lunch shop then?'

'I did; but why do you ask?'

'I guess that's when he started frequenting Benten-tei?'

'I suppose it was, yes.'

'I know you didn't talk with him much, but did

anything he said make a lasting impression on you? Any little thing?'

Yasuko was confused. This was the last sort of question she had expected to hear.

'May I ask why you want to know? Maybe if I knew, I could give you better advice.'

'Well,' Yukawa shot her a sidelong glance as they walked, 'it's because he's my friend. He's a very important friend of mine, and I want to know how he's been lately.'

'I'm afraid we speak so little, there's really nothing much to say.'

'Yet for him, that connection to you was far more important than you make it out to be. I think you understand why.'

Yasuko caught the serious look in Yukawa's eyes, and it made her skin prickle. It suddenly occurred to her that this man knew about Ishigami's interest in her and wanted to know why it had started.

Yasuko realized for the first time that she had never given a moment's thought to that herself. She knew from years of experience that she wasn't the kind of beauty with whom men fell head over heels in love at first sight. It had to have been something else.

She shook her head. 'I'm sorry, but I can't think of anything. Really, I could count the number of times we've spoken on one hand.'

'I see,' Yukawa replied, his tone softening. 'I suppose that makes its own kind of sense, doesn't it?' Ishigami's friend was mostly talking to himself, but then he turned to her again and asked, 'What do you think of him?'

'What?'

'Surely you noticed his interest in you? What do you think about that?'

Yasuko was taken aback by the directness of the question. She wished she could just laugh it off in embarrassment, but somehow that wouldn't work in this conversation. 'I'm afraid I don't feel anything in particular – I mean, I'm sure he's a good person. And he seems quite smart.'

'Ah, so you do know him.' Yukawa stopped his feet.

'Well, I wouldn't say "know" so much as that's the impression I have of him.'

He nodded. 'Very well. Sorry to take up your time.' Yukawa handed off the bicycle. 'Say hi to Ishigami for me.'

'Oh, but I might not see him—'

But Yukawa only nodded with a smile and turned away. Yasuko watched him as he left, wondering how a man could make the simple act of walking away feel so intimidating.

CHAPTER 14

Ishigami sat staring at a line of unhappy faces. Some of them were beyond unhappy – they wore looks of outright pain. A few had gone even further, and drooped in despondant resignation. One member of the dismal class – Morioka – hadn't even glanced at the test sheet after Ishigami gave the go-ahead to start. He was staring vacantly out the window, head propped up on one hand. It was a nice day outside, with an endless expanse of blue sky stretched high over the school complex. Morioka was probably thinking about how he could be riding his motorcycle if he didn't have to be in here, wasting time.

The school and most of the students were already out on spring break. There was just this one group of students, with one final, depressing hurdle to jump. Too many kids hadn't passed even the make-up tests after finals and had been required to do remedial class work. Thirty of Ishigami's students were in these special classes – a far larger number than for any other subject. And after they were done with the extra coursework, another test awaited them: the re-make-up test.

The head teacher had stopped by while Ishigami was writing up questions for the test, to make sure he didn't make them too difficult.

'I don't like saying this, but really at this point the tests are just a formality. We can't let the students go on to the next grade with failing marks. And I know you don't like doing all these extra tests, either, do you? Besides, we've had complaints that your tests were too difficult from the beginning. Just – make sure everyone passes, okay?'

Ishigami didn't think his typical test questions were difficult. They were simple, in fact. There were no departures from the material he had covered in class. Anyone with half a brain, and a rudimentary understanding of mathematical principles, should have been able to solve them. Usually, all he did was change how the problems looked. Surely it would be too easy to use problems straight from the textbooks and practice sheets! Still, the students who simply tried to memorize answers and the ones who hadn't paid any attention at all were at a loss when faced with basic challenges.

So this time Ishigami had done as the head teacher instructed. He had used representative questions straight from the students' practice sheets. Anyone who had studied even a little should have had no problem.

Morioka gave a big yawn and looked at his watch. Then his eyes met Ishigami's. Ishigami expected him to look away, but instead Morioka grimaced and held his hands up over his head in the shape of an X, as if to predict the mark that would be on this paper.

Ishigami tried grinning at him. Morioka looked surprised, then grinned back, and resumed looking out the window.

Ishigami remembered when Morioka had asked him what good differential and integral calculus was. Ishigami had used motorbike racing as an example, but he wasn't sure if that got through to the boy. Morioka's attitude didn't annoy Ishigami. It was only natural to wonder why one had to study something. Once such questions were answered – well, then there was an objective, something to learn *towards*. And that could lead down the path towards an understanding of the true nature of mathematics.

Yet too many teachers refused to answer simple questions of relevance from their students. *No,* Ishigami thought, *they probably aren't able to answer them.* They taught without really understanding their subjects, simply following a set curriculum, thinking only of coaxing a passing grade from the students so they could send them on their way to make room for next year's flock. Questions like Morioka's would have been nothing but an irritation to them.

What am I doing here? Ishigami wondered, not for the first time. Giving students tests just so they could earn points had nothing to do with the true meaning of mathematics. It didn't mean anything. It wasn't maths, and it wasn't even education.

Ishigami stood and took a deep breath. 'Wherever you are on your test sheets, you can stop.' He looked over the classroom. 'I want you to turn your papers over and write down what you're thinking *right now* on the backs.'

Confusion washed across the faces of the students in the room. A mutter spread through the class. *'What we're thinking? What does that mean?'*

'Specifically, I want you to write down what you think about maths. No,' he amended, 'just write anything about maths at all. You'll be graded on what you write.'

Every face in the room brightened.

'What grade are you going to give us?' a male student asked.

'Depends on what you write. If you can't handle actual maths, I hope you can at least say something about it,' Ishigami said, sitting back down in his chair.

Every student turned over his or her paper. Some, including Morioka, began to write immediately.

I'll be able to pass them all now, thought Ishigami with some relief. There was no way to mark a blank answer sheet, but as long as they had each written something, he could assign grades as he saw fit. The head teacher might wonder a bit, but surely he couldn't complain about Ishigami

259

delivering the passing grades he'd specifically asked for.

The bell rang, indicating the end of the test period. A few of the students asked for a little more time, so Ishigami gave them an extra five minutes.

When it was done he collected the answer sheets and walked out of the classroom. The moment the door shut, he heard the room erupt into conversation. There were audible cries of relief.

Back at the teachers' room, a man – one of the office assistants – was standing just inside the door, waiting for him.

'Mr Ishigami? There's someone here to see you.'

'To see me?'

The assistant walked up to him and whispered in his ear. 'I think he's a police detective.'

Ishigami sighed.

'What are you going to do?' the assistant asked, peering at him intently.

'What am I going to do? He's waiting for me, isn't he?'

'Yes, but I could tell him you're occupied and send him home.'

Ishigami chuckled. 'No need for that. Where is he?'

'The parent conference room.'

'I'll be right there.' Stashing the test answer sheets in his bag, Ishigami made his way towards the conference room. He would have to grade them at home later.

The assistant started to follow him, but Ishigami waved him away, saying, 'I'll be fine on my own.' He knew well enough what the assistant was up to. The man wanted to know why the detective was there and had only suggested that they give the detective the brush-off in hopes that Ishigami would tell him what the visit was all about.

The man Ishigami had expected to see was waiting for him in the conference room: the detective named Kusanagi.

'Sorry to bother you here at school like this.' Kusanagi stood and bowed curtly.

'I'm not usually here over spring vacation. I'm surprised you found me.'

'Actually, I dropped by your apartment first, but it seemed you were out so I called the school. They said something about a make-up test? You have to give make-up tests during spring break?'

'It's worse for the students, I assure you. And today wasn't a make-up test. It was a re-make-up test.'

'You don't say. Let me guess: you like putting pretty tough questions on your tests.'

'Why do you say that?' Ishigami asked, looking the detective in the eye.

'Just a feeling.'

'They're not tough, though. I merely take advantage of the blind spots created when students assume too much. And they usually assume too much.'

'Blind spots?'

261

'For instance, I give them a question that looks like a geometry problem, but is in fact an algebra problem. If all they've done is memorize the problem sheets in their books—' Ishigami abruptly stopped talking and sat down across from the detective. 'I'm sorry. I'm guessing you didn't come here to talk about high school mathematics. So, why *are* you here?'

'Nothing much, really,' Kusanagi said, joining him at the table and pulling out his notepad. 'I just wanted to ask you about that night again.'

'By "that night", you mean . . . ?'

'The tenth of March,' Kusanagi said. 'I believe you're aware that's when the incident occurred?'

'You mean the body they found by the Arakawa River? That one?'

'Not the Arakawa, the Old Edogawa,' Kusanagi corrected him without missing a beat. 'You may remember me and my partner coming to ask you questions about Ms Hanaoka? Asking if you'd noticed anything peculiar that night?'

'Yes, I remember. And I'm pretty sure I told you I didn't recall anything out of the ordinary.'

'That's right, you did. I was just hoping you could try to remember that evening in a little more detail for me.'

'How do you mean? It's hard to remember something when nothing happened.' Ishigami let himself smile a bit.

'Right, but what I'm looking for – or what I was hoping to find – was something that maybe you didn't pay particular attention to at the time, but might actually turn out to be a valuable piece of evidence for us. Maybe you can just tell me about that evening in as much detail as possible? Don't worry if it has nothing to do with any incident.'

'All right. I suppose,' Ishigami said, scratching the back of his neck.

'I know it was a while ago now, so I brought something I thought might help you remember the day.' Kusanagi handed over a chart of Ishigami's work schedule for the week of March tenth, showing a list of the classes he'd taught along with the school events schedule. He must have procured the information from the office. 'Does anything here jog your memory?' the detective asked, smiling.

The moment he looked at the chart, Ishigami understood what the detective was up to. He wasn't here about Yasuko Hanaoka, he was here to establish Ishigami's alibi.

Though Ishigami couldn't say for certain why the police were suddenly turning their eyes in his direction, he suspected it had something to do with Manabu Yukawa's strange behaviour.

In any case, if the detective was here for an alibi, he'd better answer him. Ishigami settled himself in his chair and sat up straight. 'I went home that night after the judo team finished practice, so it would have been around seven o'clock. I think I told you that before, too.'

'Indeed you did, indeed you did. So, you were in your apartment for the whole time after that?'

'Well, I think I probably was, yes,' Ishigami said, leaving his words purposely vague. He wanted to see how Kusanagi would respond.

'Did no one visit the apartment that night? Or call on the phone?'

Ishigami lifted an eyebrow. 'Whose apartment do you mean? Ms Hanaoka's?'

'No, your apartment.'

'Mine?'

'I know you must be wondering what this has to do with our investigation. Believe me, we're not investigating you. We're simply trying to establish everything that happened in the general vicinity of Yasuko Hanaoka that night. That's all.'

A pretty frail excuse, Ishigami thought, though he expected that the detective knew he was being obvious and that the man just didn't care.

'I didn't see anyone that night. I'm pretty sure nobody called, either. I rarely have visitors.'

'I see.'

'I'm sorry I don't have more to tell you after you came all this way.'

'No, please, don't worry about me. I'm sorry for taking your time. Oh, incidentally—' Kusanagi picked up Ishigami's work schedule. 'According to this, you took the morning of the eleventh off, only coming into work that afternoon. Did something happen?'

'You mean the next day? No, nothing happened. I just wasn't feeling well, so I slept in. Third-quarter classes were almost completely over anyway, so I figured I could get away with it.'

'Did you see a doctor?'

'No, it wasn't anything so serious. Which is why I ended up going in that afternoon.'

'Just now at the office I asked the assistant there, and he said that you rarely take time off, Mr Ishigami. Just mornings sometimes. About once a month?'

'It's how I use my vacation time, yes.'

'Right. The office told me you are often up late working on mathematics, and you take off the following morning, something like that?'

'That sounds like something I would have told the office, yes.'

'And this happens about once a month or so . . .' Kusanagi's eyes dropped to the work schedule again. 'But you took the morning off on the tenth, too – in other words, the day before. The office said they weren't much surprised the first time, but when you took two mornings off in a row that got them. This was the first time that happened, was it?'

'I guess it might have been.' Ishigami put a hand to his forehead. He knew he had to answer carefully. 'I didn't have any particular reason for doing it that time, though. Like you said, I was up late the night before the tenth, and went to work in the afternoon. That night, I felt like I had a bit of a fever, and that's why I was out the next morning as well.'

'But you recovered enough to come in after lunch?'

'That's right.' Ishigami nodded.

'Right,' Kusanagi echoed, his eyes full of suspicion.

'Is something wrong?'

'No, I was just thinking, if you managed to go to school for the afternoon, you can't have been too sick that morning. But then again, if they weren't too sick, most people would have gone to work anyway. Especially if they'd missed their morning classes just the day before.' Kusanagi was openly doubting Ishigami now. He must've thought whatever information he might get out of the maths teacher would be worth annoying him.

Ishigami smiled wryly, refusing to rise to the bait. 'If you say so. I just remember having trouble getting out of bed that morning. But right before lunch I started feeling a lot better, so I decided to go in. Mostly because, as you pointed out, I had just taken the morning off the day before.'

All the while Ishigami talked, Kusanagi was staring him straight in the eye. The detective's gaze was piercing and fierce – the gaze of someone who truly believed that when a suspect wasn't telling the truth, it would show in his eyes.

'I see. Well, all that judo must keep you in good shape. Probably only takes you half a day to recover from a fever, eh? Wish I had your constitution. The fellow at the office said he'd never even heard of you calling in sick.'

'That's hardly true. I catch colds, too, you know.'

'And you just happened to catch one on the night of the tenth.'

'What do you mean by that? I know that's the night your murder took place, but it wasn't a particularly special night for me.'

'Of course.' Kusanagi closed his notepad and stood. 'Sorry for taking your time.'

'Again, I'm sorry I couldn't be of more assistance.'

'Not at all. We're just covering the bases.'

The two of them walked out of the conference room together. Ishigami saw the detective to the main entrance.

'Seen much of Yukawa lately?' Kusanagi asked as they walked.

'No, not at all,' Ishigami answered. 'How about you? You talk to him now and then, right?'

'Not recently. I've been too busy. You know, the three of us should get together sometime. I hear from Yukawa that you enjoy a drink now and then?' He motioned with his hand as if tilting a glass.

'I'd be happy to, but shouldn't that wait until you've solved this case of yours?'

'Probably, yes, but a man has to get out sometimes. I'll give you a ring.'

'All right. I'll be looking forward to it, then.'

'You do that,' the detective said, turning to walk out the door.

Ishigami returned to the hallway and watched him through a window. Kusanagi was talking on his mobile phone as he walked out to the road. His expression hadn't changed.

Ishigami thought about what his visit meant. They must have had a reason to turn their suspicions towards him. What would that be? He hadn't sensed anything of the sort the last time he'd met Kusanagi.

Based on the questions he asked, Kusanagi was a still long way from the truth. He was basically shooting in the dark. Perhaps Ishigami's lack of an alibi had given him a new direction. But if so, so be it. Ishigami had planned for this, too.

The problem was—

The image of Manabu Yukawa's face flitted across his mind. How much of the truth had the physicist been able to sniff out? And how much of that truth did he really want to expose?

Ishigami remembered something Yasuko had told him the other day on the phone. Apparently, Yukawa had asked her what she thought of him – of Ishigami. And it sounded like he had known about Ishigami's fondness for Yasuko.

The mathematician recalled his various discussions with Yukawa but couldn't remember a single careless word or gesture that might have tipped him off. So how had his old friend noticed?

Ishigami turned and began to walk towards the teachers' room. He ran into the office assistant in the hallway on the way there.

'The detective leave already?'

'Just now, yeah.'

'So aren't you going home, Mr Ishigami?'

'No, I remembered something I have to do first.'

Leaving the assistant to wonder what the detective had wanted, Ishigami returned quickly to the teachers' room. Sitting down at his desk there, he reached into a box he kept beneath it and pulled out several files. These weren't class files. They were part of the results of his work over the last several years on a particularly difficult mathematics problem.

He placed them in his bag with the test sheets and left the room.

'How many times do I have to tell you that in order to examine something you have to do more than just look at it? You can't simply say you were satisfied with an experiment because you got the results you were expecting. I don't care how you *feel* about the experiment. And not everything was really expected, was it? I want you to really look at the experiment and discover something in it that has meaning for you. Just – think a little more before you write, please?'

It was rare for Yukawa to be so obviously irritated. Shaking his head, he thrust the report back at the student who stood mute before him. The young man bowed his head and left the room.

'Don't tell me you get angry, too?' Kusanagi remarked.

'I'm not angry. He wasn't taking his work seriously, so I gave him a little direction, that's all.'

269

Yukawa stood and busied himself making a mug of instant coffee. 'So, find anything out?'

'I looked into Ishigami's alibi. Which is to say, I went and talked to him.'

'A frontal assault?' Yukawa turned from the sink, the large mug in his hand. 'And? How did he react?'

'He claims he was at home for the whole night.'

Yukawa frowned and shook his head. 'I asked you how he reacted. Not what he told you.'

'Well, he didn't seem particularly flustered, if that's what you mean. Then again, he was warned about my visit before he saw me, so he would have had a little time to get himself in order.'

'Did he seem surprised that you were asking about his alibi?'

'He didn't come out and ask me why, no. But then again, I didn't ask him all that directly, either.'

'Knowing him, he knew you'd be coming for his alibi sooner or later,' Yukawa said, half to himself. He took a sip of coffee. 'So he was home that night?'

'Yeah. Had a fever, apparently, so he skipped his classes the following morning.' Kusanagi laid the work schedule he'd received from the school office on the table.

Yukawa walked over and sat. He picked up the schedule.

'The next morning . . . hmm.'

'After the murder, he would have needed time to take care of things.'

'What about the lady from the lunch shop? You know where she was that morning?'

'Of course. Yasuko Hanaoka went to work as usual on the eleventh. And, while we're on the subject, her daughter went to school as usual, too. Neither of them was even late.'

Yukawa placed the work schedule back down on the table and crossed his arms. 'By "time to take care of things", what exactly do you think he had to do?'

'Well, dispose of the murder weapon, for one thing.'

'It wouldn't take him more than ten hours to do that.'

'Ten hours?'

'The murder took place on the night of the tenth. If he had to miss school the following morning, that means he needed more than ten hours to "take care of things", as you say.'

'Well, he would have needed time to sleep.'

'I doubt anyone could sleep if they had a murder to conceal. And if, after concealing it, they ended up without any time to sleep, they'd just go without. He'd have gone to work for sure, even if he had to prop his eyelids open to do it. Showing up on time but exhausted would raise far less suspicion than not coming in at all.'

'Then there must have been some reason he had to rest.'

'That's what I'm trying to figure out,' Yukawa said, lifting his mug.

Kusanagi carefuly folded the work schedule on the table.

'There's something I have to ask you. Why did you start to suspect Ishigami was involved? I'm just not sure how to proceed without knowing what piqued your interest.'

'That's a strange thing for you to say. Didn't you figure out, entirely on your own, that he was fond of Yasuko Hanaoka? Why should my opinion matter at all?'

'Well, it does. See, in order to report all this to my boss, I can't just say I started to watch Ishigami based on a whim.'

'Can't you say you were looking into people connected with Ms Hanaoka, and the mathematician Ishigami's name came up?'

'I did. And I looked into their relationship. The thing is, I haven't been able to find a single scrap of evidence they're closer than they are letting on.'

Mug still in hand, Yukawa began to laugh so hard his whole body shook. 'I'm not surprised!'

'What? Why? What's that supposed to mean?'

'Nothing much. It's just I wasn't expecting there to be anything between them at all. In fact, I guarantee you that no matter how hard you look, you won't find even a trace of a relationship.'

'Well, thanks for your vote of confidence. You know my division chief is already losing interest in Ishigami. Pretty soon my hands will be tied as well. That's why I need you to tell me why you've had your eye on him. Come on, Yukawa, you've had your fun. Why won't you tell me?'

A serious look came across Yukawa's face, and he set down his coffee. 'I haven't told you why because doing so would be meaningless. What I have to say wouldn't help you all.'

'Why not let me be the judge of that?'

'Okay: the reason why I started to think he might have been involved is the same sort of reason you yourself have been talking about since you got here. Somehow I got the feeling that he might have a thing for Yasuko Hanaoka, so I thought I'd see if he had anything to do with the murder. Now, I'm guessing you want to know why I "had a feeling", and all I can say is, it was a hunch. Call it intuition. I'm not sure that anyone who didn't understand Ishigami pretty well would be able to pick up on it. You're always talking about a detective's intuition, aren't you? It's something like that.'

'Well, this is unexpected. You've always made *intuition* sound like a dirty word.'

'I'm allowed to branch out now and then, aren't I?'

'All right. Then at least tell me when it was you first noticed that Ishigami had a thing for her.'

'Sorry,' Yukawa replied immediately.

'C'mon!'

'It's a matter of pride. Ishigami's pride, I mean. It's not the kind of thing I want to tell other people.'

Kusanagi sighed. Just then, there was a knock on the laboratory door, and another student stepped in tentatively and looked around.

'Over here,' Yukawa called out to him. 'Sorry for calling you up like I did, but there was something I wanted to talk to you about with regard to your report the other day.'

'What might that be?' The student froze behind his glasses.

'Your report – it was well written. Just, there was one thing I wanted to check with you. I was wondering why you used solid-state physics to describe your process.'

The student looked bewildered for moment. 'Wasn't it a solid-state experiment . . . ?'

Yukawa chuckled and shook his head. 'Actually, the experiment is, in essence, based on elementary particle physics. I was hoping you'd consider that in your approach as well. Just because the problem seems like one of solid-state physics at first doesn't mean that you shouldn't consider other theories. Tunnel vision is no way to make it as a researcher. Your assumptions are your worst enemies. Trust them too much, and you'll fail to see what's right under your nose.'

'Right.' The student nodded.

'I'm giving you this advice because you do such good work. Thanks for dropping by.'

The student thanked him and left.

Yukawa turned his attention back to Kusanagi, only to see Kusanagi staring back at him.

'What? There something on my face?'

'No, I was just thinking you science types all seem to say the same things.'

'What do you mean?'

'When I visited him, Ishigami said something a lot like what you said just now.' Kusanagi told his friend about Ishigami's mathematics test.

'Blind spots due to assumptions, eh? How like him.' Yukawa grinned. But the next moment, the physicist's expression changed. Suddenly he stood, and clutching his head in his hands, he walked over to the window. He looked out and upward, towards the sky.

'Hey, Yukawa?'

But the physicist merely held up his hand for silence. Kusanagi shrugged and sat watching his friend.

'Impossible,' Yukawa muttered. 'There's no way he could've—'

'What? Could have what?' Kusanagi asked, unable to restrain himself any longer.

'Show me that paper you had. Ishigami's work schedule.'

Kusanagi hurriedly produced the folded paper from his pocket. Yukawa took it. He stared at it for a moment, then quietly groaned. 'I don't believe it . . .'

'Don't believe what, Yukawa? What are you talking about? Tell me!'

Yukawa thrust the schedule back towards Kusanagi. 'Sorry, but I'm going to have to ask you to leave.'

'Huh? No way!' Kusanagi resisted. But when he saw the look on his friend's face, he lost the next words he was going to say.

Yukawa's expression was twisted with worry and pain. Kusanagi had never seen him look quite so miserable.

'Just go. I'm sorry,' Yukawa asked again, his voice like a moan.

Kusanagi stepped back from the table. There were a mountain of things he could have asked, but he realized the only thing he could do at that moment was leave.

CHAPTER 15

The clock showed the time as 7:30 A.M. Ishigami left his apartment, clutching his tote bag. The bag contained the thing he valued most in the world: a set of files pertaining to the mathematics problem he was currently researching. 'Currently' – or, more accurately, 'eternally'. He had written his senior thesis on it back in college, but even now his work was far from complete.

He had calculated that it would take him roughly another twenty years to complete his work on this particular theory. Possibly even longer. It was the kind of insurmountable problem worthy of an entire lifetime's devotion. And of all the mathematicians in the world, he was in the best position to crack it.

How wonderful it would be to forget everything else, all other considerations, all the time sinks of daily life, and just work on that problem! Ishigami daydreamed, as he had so often before. Whenever he considered the dreary truth that he might die before finishing, it chafed at him to do anything *but* work on it.

No matter where he went, he took his files with him. There could be no rest, no vacation while there was still progress to be made. And all he needed to work on it was paper and pencils. If only he could have been left alone to do his research, he would have required nothing else from life.

Mechanically, he walked his usual morning route past the Shin-Ohashi Bridge and down along the Sumida River, past the shacks with roofs made from blue vinyl tarps. The man with the long white hair pulled back into a long braid was once again holding a pot over a burner. Ishigami couldn't see what he was cooking. A mutt with light brown fur was tied up beside him. The dog sat, exhausted, leaning its flank towards its master.

The Can Man was crushing cans and muttering to himself as usual. He already had two plastic bags filled with flattened aluminium balanced next to him.

A little further along there was a bench. This morning it was empty. Ishigami glanced at it for a moment, then dropped his gaze to the ground before his feet, maintaining his steady pace.

He sensed someone walking towards him along the riverbank. Right about now was when he usually met the elderly woman taking her three dogs for a walk, but he could tell from the sound of the approaching footsteps that this wasn't she. Ishigami glanced up.

A surprised 'Oh' slipped from his mouth, and he stopped.

The other person kept on coming. Then with a smile he paused in front of Ishigami.

'Morning,' said Manabu Yukawa.

Ishigami hesitated for a moment, unsure of how to reply. He wet his lips and opened his mouth. 'You were waiting for me.'

'Of course I was,' Yukawa replied, still smiling. 'Well, maybe not "waiting", exactly. I've just walked here from Kiyosu Bridge. Figured I'd run into you along the way.'

'What ever it is, it must be urgent.'

'Urgent? Maybe. It could be.'

'You want to talk about it now?' Ishigami glanced at his watch. 'I haven't much time.'

'I only need ten or fifteen minutes.'

'Can we talk while we walk?'

'Suits me.' Yukawa glanced around him. 'But let's talk here a moment first. Just two or three minutes will do. How about that bench over there?' He immediately headed towards the bench without waiting for Ishigami's reply.

Ishigami sighed and followed his friend.

'We walked here once before together, didn't we?' Yukawa recalled.

'That we did.'

'I remember you saying that the homeless people here had developed routines like clockwork. You remember that?'

'I do. That's what happens when you take clocks out of people's lives – I believe that's what you said.'

Yukawa nodded, satisfied. 'Too bad it's impossible for you and me ever to be off the clock. Like it or not, we're stuck in the cogs of society. Take them away, and our clocks spin out of control. Or rather, we are the cogs in the clockworks. No matter how much we might think we are off standing on our own, we're not. It gives us a certain measure of security, to be sure, but it also means we're not entirely free. I've heard that lots of the homeless don't *want* to go back to living regular lives.'

'Keep chatting like this and you'll use up your two or three minutes in no time,' Ishigami said, looking at his watch. 'You're at one minute already.'

'Okay – the world needs its cogs, all of them; and even a cog may say how it gets used. In fact, only a cog may determine its eventual meaning in the system. That's what I wanted to tell you,' Yukawa said, staring Ishigami in the face. 'Are you going to quit your teaching job?'

Ishigami's eyes opened wide with surprise. 'Why do you ask that?'

'I just thought you might be moving in that direction. You're not planning on being the cog labelled "maths teacher" all your life, are you?' Yukawa stood. 'Shall we?'

The two stood up and began walking along the Sumida. Ishigami didn't speak, waiting for his old friend to say something.

'I heard Kusanagi paid you another visit. Checking on your alibi?'

'Yeah. Last week.'

'He suspects you.'

'Seems like it. Though I haven't the foggiest clue why.'

Yukawa suddenly smiled. 'To tell you the truth, he's a little foggy on that as well. He's only interested in you because he saw *me* taking an interest in you, that's all. I'm sure it's not my place to tell you this, but the police don't have a bit of evidence to point them in your direction.'

Ishigami stopped. 'So why *are* you telling me this?'

Yukawa stopped as well and turned towards him. 'Because I'm your friend. No other reason but that.'

'Because you're my friend you thought you needed to tell me about some murder investigation? Why? I have nothing to do with the crime. Why should I care if the police suspect me of anything?'

He heard Yukawa sigh – a long, slow sound. Then his friend shook his head. Something about the sadness in his expression made Ishigami feel nervous.

'The alibi's immaterial,' Yukawa said quietly.

'Huh?'

'Kusanagi and company are obsessed with picking apart their suspect's alibi. They think that if they keep prodding at the holes in Yasuko Hanaoka's story, they'll eventually find the truth, provided she really did kill her ex-husband. And they think that if you were her conspirator, then all they need to do is check out your alibi, too, and the fortress you've built will come crumbling down.'

'Sorry, but I haven't the faintest idea what you're talking about.' Ishigami frowned. 'Besides, what's wrong with detectives looking for holes in alibis? Isn't that what they do? Assuming there really are holes to be found, that is.'

Yukawa's mouth softened. 'Kusanagi said something interesting the other day. He was talking about the way you designed the tests you give to your students, taking advantage of the blind spots created by the students' own assumptions. Like making an algebra problem look like a geometry problem, for instance. It made sense. It's very effective for tripping up the ones who don't understand the underlying principles and just try to solve everything by the book. The student sees what they think is a geometry problem, so they attack it from that angle. But they can't solve it. They get nowhere, and end up just wasting time. Some people might call it unfair, but it's a very effective way of measuring someone's true ability.'

'What are you getting at?'

'Kusanagi and company,' Yukawa said, his face growing serious, 'think that this is a question of breaking down alibis. And why not, since their primary suspect has an alibi. Even better, her alibi feels weak. It feels like you could just keep hitting it and eventually it might break. The same thing happens all the time in our research, really. And, time and time again, we find that while we were happily swinging away at a problem, all the while we were completely off the mark. The police have fallen into that very trap. The bait was there and they took it, hook, line, and sinker.'

'If you have concerns about the direction their investigation is taking, shouldn't you be talking to Detective Kusanagi, not me?'

'Yes, eventually, I'll have to. But I wanted to talk to you first, for reasons I've just stated.'

'Because you're my friend.'

'Yes. I might also say because I don't want to lose your genius. I want to clear away all of this distraction and get you back to doing what you do best. You've got a precious brain and I don't want it being wasted like this.'

'I don't need you to tell me that. I already abhor wasted time,' Ishigami said. He turned away and began to walk again – not because he was worried about being late to his class, but because it had suddenly become too uncomfortable for him to continue standing in that spot.

Yukawa followed. 'In order to solve this case, we mustn't think that the suspect's alibi is the problem. The problem lies elsewhere. A difference greater than that between geometry and algebra.'

'So, out of curiosity, what is the problem?' Ishigami asked without looking back.

'It's not a simple thing, so it's hard to give you a simple answer; but if I had to sum it up in one word, I'd say it's a matter of camouflage. Subterfuge, even. The investigators have been fooled by the criminals' camouflage. Everything they think is a clue isn't. Every hint they uncover is merely a breadcrumb set in their path to lure them astray.'

'That sounds complicated.'

'Oh, it is. But if you simply change your way of looking at it, it becomes surprisingly simple. When an amateur attempts to conceal something, the more complex he makes his camouflage, the deeper the grave he digs for himself. But not so a genius. The genius does something far simpler, yet something no normal person would even dream of, the last thing a normal person would think of doing. And from this simplicity, immense complexity is created.'

'I thought you physicist types didn't like talking in the abstract.'

'I can be more concrete, if you like. How are we doing on time?'

'I'm still good.'

'Still have time to drop by the lunch shop?'

Ishigami glanced at his friend before returning his gaze to the path ahead. 'I don't buy lunch there every day, you know.'

'Really? I heard you did. Well, almost every day.'

'Is that your smoking gun that links me to this case?'

'Yes and no. If you were simply buying your lunch at the same shop every day, that wouldn't

284

mean anything, but if you were going to meet a particular woman every day, that's something no interested observer could overlook.'

Ishigami stopped and glared at Yukawa. 'Do you think because we are old friends, you can just say whatever you like?'

Yukawa met his gaze. Facing him straight on like this, Ishigami could sense the strength behind the physicist's eyes.

'Wait, are you really angry? I've upset you.'

'This is ridiculous,' Ishigami muttered, setting off again. He began climbing the stairs that led up towards Kiyosu Bridge.

'Clothes they think belonged to the victim were found a short distance away from the body,' Yukawa said, following a pace behind. 'They were half-burned, in an oil can. They think the murderer did it. When I heard that, I wondered why the murderer didn't do a better job and burn the clothes completely. The police seem to think it was because he wanted to leave the scene as quickly as possible, but that leads one to wonder why he wouldn't have just taken the clothes with him to burn someplace else when he had more time. Or maybe he thought they would burn more quickly than they did? Once I started thinking about it, it bothered me. So I tried burning some clothes myself.'

Ishigami stopped again. 'You burned your clothes?'

'In an oil can, yes. A jacket, a sweater, some

285

pants, shoes . . . oh, and underwear. Bought them at a used-clothes shop. I was surprised how much it cost! See, unlike mathematicians, we physicists aren't satisfied with something until we've performed the experiment ourselves.'

'And your results?'

'They burned pretty well, actually, and emitted a lot of toxic fumes,' Yukawa told him. 'There was nothing left. It didn't take long at all. Maybe five minutes, tops.'

'And so?'

'So why didn't the murderer wait those five minutes?'

Ishigami shrugged. He climbed the stairs leading back to the street and, at the top of the stairs, he turned left on Kiyosubashi Road – the opposite direction from the way to Benten-tei.

'Not buying lunch today?' Yukawa asked, as he'd expected.

'I told you I don't go there every day,' Ishigami retorted, frowning.

'I was just worried about your lunch, that's all,' Yukawa said, quickening his pace to walk beside him. 'They also found a bicycle near the body, you know. Turns out it had been stolen from Shinozaki Station. The suspected victim's fingerprints were on it.'

'What of it?'

'Kind of surprising to have a criminal who goes so far as to crush the victim's face, yet forgets to wipe his bicycle for fingerprints. Pretty stupid, really, unless he left his fingerprints on the bicycle on purpose. But why would he do that?'

'I'm sure you're about to tell me.'

'Maybe in order to link the bicycle to the victim. Clearly, it was better for the criminal for the police to draw that conclusion.'

'Why's that?'

'Because the criminal wanted the police to assume that the victim had ridden that bicycle from Shinozaki Station himself. And for that, he couldn't use just any old bicycle.'

'So there was something special about the bicycle they found?'

'I wouldn't say "special". It was your typical morning commuter bike. With one exception: it was brand-new.'

Ishigami felt every pore on his body open. It was getting more difficult for him to breathe steadily.

Someone called out, 'Good morning!' and he started at the sound. A female student was passing them on her bicycle. She nodded towards Ishigami.

'Oh, hey, morning,' he hurriedly called back.

'That's impressive. I didn't think students said hello to their teachers any more,' Yukawa commented.

'Hardly any do. So why did this bicycle have to be brand-new?'

'If you're going to steal a bicycle, why not steal a new one – that's what the police seem to think. But our thief didn't care about that. He cared about *when* the bicycle had been left at the station.'

'Because . . . ?'

'The thief had no use for a bicycle that might have been left by the station for days. And he wanted the owner to report the theft. That's why the bicycle had to be new. Owners of brand-new bicycles don't usually leave them out on the street for very long and are more likely to go to the police when their bicycle goes missing. Neither of these things was absolutely necessary for the thief to create his camouflage, but either would help, so he chose the course of action most likely to yield positive results.'

'Hmph.'

Ishigami refrained from commenting on Yukawa's conjecture. He walked on, looking only at the street in front of them. They were nearing the school. The pavement was filling up with students.

'Well, this is certainly an interesting story, and I'd like to hear more,' he said, stopping and turning to face Yukawa. 'But maybe you'll let me be for now? I don't want the students prying.'

'Absolutely. I think I've said pretty much what I had to say, in any case.'

'It was interesting,' Ishigami said. 'I recall you posing a question to me before. You asked which was more difficult, formulating an unsolvable problem, or solving that problem. Remember?'

'I do. And I have an answer for you. It's more difficult to create the problem than to solve it. All the person trying to solve the problem has to do is always respect the problem's creator.'

288

'I see. What about the P = NP problem, then? The question of whether or not it's as easy to determine the accuracy of another person's results as it is to solve the problem yourself.'

Yukawa favoured him with a suspicious look, unsure of where Ishigami was leading.

'You've given me your answer,' Ishigami went on, pointing a finger at Yukawa's chest. 'Now it's time for you to hear someone else's solution.'

'Ishigami . . .'

'Good day.' The mathematician turned his back on Yukawa and strode into the school, tote bag clutched tightly in his arms.

It's over, he thought. The physicist had seen through everything.

Misato sat in uncomfortable silence, eating her apricot pudding. Yasuko wondered once again whether it would have been better just to have left her at home.

'You get enough to eat, Misato?' Kudo was asking. He had been fretting over her all evening.

Misato nodded, mechanically sticking the spoon into her mouth, without even a glance in his direction.

You can drag a teenager to a good restaurant, but you can't make her enjoy it.

They had come to a Chinese place in Ginza for dinner. Kudo had insisted that Yasuko bring her daughter, and so she had dragged Misato along, despite the girl's protests. In the end, Yasuko had convinced her to come by telling her that it would seem unnatural for them to avoid going out – that it might make the police suspicious.

But now that she saw how worried Kudo was, she regretted it. All through dinner, he had tried a variety of approaches to get the girl to talk, but he had failed to get more than a few terse words out of her all night.

Misato finished her dessert and turned to her mother. 'I'm going to the bathroom.'

'Oh. Okay.'

Yasuko waited for Misato to leave, then turned to Kudo, clasping her hands together. 'I'm so sorry.'

'Huh? About what?' He looked genuinely surprised, though Yasuko knew it was an act.

'She's really shy, that's all. And I think she has issues with older men.'

Kudo smiled. 'Don't worry. I didn't imagine we'd be great friends by evening's end. I was just like her when I was a teenager. I'm happy just to have gotten to meet her today.'

'Thanks, you're too kind.'

Kudo nodded. He fished in the pocket of his jacket, which hung on the back of his chair, and pulled out a cigarette and lighter. He had refrained from smoking during dinner on account of Misato.

'Any developments since we last spoke?' he asked, taking a puff.

'Developments? With what?'

'That investigation.'

'Oh.' Yasuko lowered her eyes for a moment then looked back up at him. 'No, nothing. Life's been pretty normal, actually.'

'I'm glad to hear that. The detectives leaving you alone?'

'I haven't seen them in a while. They haven't been to the shop, either. How about you?'

'Nothing to report on my side. I think they've given up on me.' Kudo flicked some ashes into an ashtray. 'Though there is something bothering me. I think it might be related.'

'What's that?'

'Well . . .' Kudo mused for a moment before opening his mouth again. 'It's just, I've been getting these strange calls lately. The phone rings at my house, and I pick it up, but there's no one on the other side.'

'Really? That sounds unpleasant.' Yasuko frowned.

'Yeah. And then there's this—' After a moment's hesitation, he pulled a piece of paper out of his coat pocket. 'I found this in my mail the other day.'

Yasuko saw her name written on the paper and froze. The message read: 'Keep away from Yasuko Hanaoka. She'll never be happy with a man like you.'

The note had been written on a computer and printed out. There was nothing to indicate from whom it had come.

'Someone sent you this in the mail?'

'No, I think they put it in my mailbox by hand.'

'Do you have any idea who it might be?'

'Not a clue. I was hoping you might know.'

'I'm sorry. I can't imagine . . .' Yasuko reached down to her handbag, taking out a handkerchief. Her palms were beginning to sweat. 'That's all there was? Just this note?'

'No. There was a picture, too.'

'A photograph?'

'From the time I met you in Shinagawa. Whoever it was took a picture of me in the hotel parking lot. I had no idea.' Kudo shook his head.

Unconsciously, Yasuko's eyes swept the room. Certainly no one was watching them here?

By then, Misato had returned, so they didn't discuss the note any more. A few minutes later they left the restaurant, said goodbye to Kudo, and climbed into a taxi.

'I told you the food would be good,' Yasuko ventured, but Misato frowned and said nothing. 'I wish you hadn't made that face the whole time.'

'Then you shouldn't have taken me along. I told you I didn't want to go.'

'But he invited you specifically.'

'He would have been happy with just you, Mum. I don't care if he invites me again. I'm not going.'

Yasuko sighed. Kudo seemed to believe that, if he gave it enough time, Misato would warm to him. Yasuko doubted that was true.

'Are you going to marry him, Mum?' Misato asked suddenly.

Yasuko sat up in her seat. 'What are you talking about?'

'I'm serious. You want to marry him, right?'

'No.'

'Really?'

'Of course not. We just go to dinner every once in a while.'

'Okay. Fine then.' Misato turned and looked out the window.

'Why did you ask me that, Misato? Is there . . . something you want to say?'

'Nope.' But Misato slowly turned back towards her mother. 'I just thought maybe it's not a good idea to betray that other guy.'

'That guy? Who?'

Misato stared Yasuko in the eye and said nothing, though it was clear she meant Mr Ishigami. She wasn't saying anything because she didn't want the taxi driver to hear.

'Well, I don't think that's anything you need to be worrying about,' Yasuko said, leaning back in her seat.

'Hmph,' Misato grunted. She clearly disagreed.

Yasuko thought about Ishigami. She *was* worried about him, even without Misato's reminder. And the note and the photograph left in Kudo's mailbox disturbed her deeply.

As far as Yasuko knew, there was only one person who could have sent that message. She remembered the dark look that had appeared on Ishigami's face when he spotted Kudo dropping her off at her apartment. The image was burned vividly in her mind.

It was more than possible that Ishigami had discovered her relationship with Kudo and was jealous. She already knew his attraction to her was more serious than a passing fancy – after all, that was the only reasonable explanation for both his willingness to help them cover up Togashi's murder and his continued protection of them from the police.

It was probably Ishigami who had left the note and the photograph in Kudo's mailbox. If that was true, then what *were* his plans for her? Would he use what he knew as leverage to try and control her life? Would he never let her see – let alone marry – another man?

Thanks to Ishigami, Yasuko had, so far, avoided arrest in the hunt for Togashi's murderer. She was grateful for that. Yet what was the point if she could never live a free life? It was no better than when Togashi was alive. She was just dealing with a different man now, and this time, there truly was no escape.

The taxi arrived at their apartment. They got out and walked up the stairs. The lights were on in Ishigami's room.

Yasuko went into her apartment and began to change. Moments later, she heard the door to the next apartment open and close.

'See?' Misato said. 'He was waiting for us to get back.'

'I know that,' Yasuko shot back, her testiness showing in her voice.

A few minutes later, her mobile phone rang.

'Yes?'

'It's me,' came the familiar voice. 'Can you talk?'

'Yes.'

'Anything to report today?'

'No, nothing.'

'I see. Good.' She could hear Ishigami slowly breathe out on the other side of the line. 'Actually, there are some things I need to talk to you about. The first is, I have placed three envelopes containing letters in the mail slot on your front door. Please go get them after I hang up.'

'Letters?' Yasuko glanced towards the door.

'Please keep them safe. You'll need them shortly. All right?'

'Okay.'

'I included a memo with the letters explaining how you are to use them. I hardly need tell you to destroy the memo when you're done reading it. Understood?'

'I understand. Should I get them now?'

'No, afterwards is fine. Also, there is something else I need to say. It's very important.' Ishigami paused. Yasuko sensed reluctance in his voice.

'Yes?'

'This is . . .' he began, 'this is the last time I will call you like this. I won't be contacting you any further. Nor should you try to contact me. No matter what happens, you and your daughter are

295

to remain bystanders. Don't get involved. That's the only way you'll be safe.'

Yasuko's heart began to race as she listened to him talk. 'What are you saying, Mr Ishigami? What is this all about?'

'You'll see soon enough. I think it's better not to tell you right now. Just, don't forget what I said. All right?'

'No, it's not all right. I need you to explain.'

Misato came over, noticing her mother's consternation.

'There is no need to explain. Goodbye.'

'Wait—' she said, but he had already hung up.

Kusanagi was in the car with Kishitani when his phone began to ring. He was on the passenger side, resting, with the seat back lowered as far as it would go. He grabbed his mobile and answered it while still lying down. 'Kusanagi here.'

'It's me – Mamiya,' came the division chief's voice. 'I need you to come down to Edogawa police station immediately.'

'What, did you find something?'

'Someone found us. There's a man here who wants to talk to you.'

'Who?' Kusanagi asked, wondering if it was Yukawa.

'It's Ishigami, the maths teacher who lives next to Yasuko Hanaoka.'

'Ishigami? He wants to talk to me? Why didn't he just call?'

'Uh, I think it's more important than that,' Mamiya replied, his tone severe.

'Did he tell you what this is all about, Chief?'

'He says he won't talk about the details to anyone but you. That's why we need you here now.'

'Right, fine, I'm on my way.' Kusanagi put his hand over the receiver and tapped Kishitani on the shoulder. 'Chief wants us down at Edogawa Station.'

Mamiya's muffled voice came over the phone. 'He says he did it.'

'Huh? What was that?'

'He says he killed Togashi. Ishigami's turning himself in.'

'What the hell!?'

Kusanagi sat up so fast his seatbelt nearly left a bruise.

CHAPTER 16

Ishigami, his face expressionless, was staring at Kusanagi. *Or maybe his eyes just happen to be pointing in my direction*, the detective thought. *Maybe he's not seeing me at all.* The mathematician's face was entirely devoid of emotion; it was as if his gaze was fixed on some faraway place and Kusanagi just happened to be sitting in that blank trajectory.

'The first time I saw him was on the tenth of March,' he was saying, his tone perfectly even. 'He was loitering near her door when I returned home from school. I caught him putting his hand inside the mail slot in her doorway.'

'I'm sorry, this man – who was he, exactly?'

'Mr Togashi. Though, of course, I didn't know that at the time,' Ishigami answered.

Kusanagi and Kishitani were with him in the interrogation room. Kishitani sat off to one side, taking notes. Ishigami had asked that no one else be allowed in the room. He'd said he wouldn't be able to tell them what he needed to say if a bunch of officers were there asking questions.

'I wondered what he was up to, so I called out

298

to him. He looked surprised, and told me he had business with Yasuko Hanaoka. Said he was her estranged husband. That's when I realized who he was, and I knew he was lying, but I pretended to go along with his story so as not to alarm him.'

'Wait a second, how did you know he wasn't telling you the truth?' Kusanagi asked.

Ishigami took a short breath. 'Because I know everything there is to know about Yasuko Hanaoka. I know she's divorced, and I know she had been moving around, trying to escape her ex-husband.'

'How could you know all these things? I had heard that you hardly spoke to her, despite the fact that she's your neighbour. That you only saw her because you frequented the lunch shop where she works.'

'That's what we tell people, yes.'

'Excuse me?'

Ishigami straightened himself in his chair, puffing out his chest ever so slightly. 'I am Yasuko Hanaoka's bodyguard. It has been my duty to protect her from men with less than good intentions. And for obvious reasons, neither of us wanted people to know about it. I am a schoolteacher, too, after all.'

'But you told us you hardly talked to her at all when we first met,' Kusanagi pressed.

Ishigami sighed quietly. 'You came to my apartment to ask questions about Togashi's murder, didn't you? Of course I couldn't tell you the truth. You would have suspected something immediately.'

'Okay . . .' Kusanagi hesitated. 'So now you're telling me that you know everything about Yasuko Hanaoka . . . because you're her bodyguard?'

'That's correct.'

'So you've been close to her for some time. Since before this incident?'

'Yes. As I said before, our arrangement was a secret. We were very careful to keep our communication hidden. Not even her daughter knew about it.'

'How exactly did you do that?'

'We employed several means. Would you like me to tell you about them now?' Ishigami looked questioningly at the detective.

None of this was feeling right to Kusanagi. He had been genuinely shocked at the suggestion that the maths teacher had anything like a close relationship with his attractive neighbour, and the background the man was now giving them seemed vague at best. Still, if there was any truth to this story at all, he wanted to hear it.

'No,' Kusanagi said, 'I'll ask you about that later. I'd like to hear about your dealings with Mr Togashi first. You said that you first met him outside Yasuko Hanaoka's apartment, and that you pretended to believe he was still married to her. What happened then?'

'He asked me whether I knew where she was. So I told him she wasn't living there any more – that she'd had to move recently for work. That surprised him, as you might imagine. Then he

300

asked me if I knew where she'd moved to. I told him I did.'

'Where did you tell him she'd gone?'

Ishigami grinned. 'Shinozaki. I told him she'd moved to an apartment along the Old Edogawa River.'

I wondered when Shinozaki would come up, Kusanagi thought to himself. 'Is that all?' he prodded. 'That wouldn't be enough for him to find her. That's quite a stretch of river, and there are lots of apartment buildings along there.'

'Of course, Togashi wanted to know her new address. I told him to wait while I went back into my room, looked at a map, and wrote down an address – the address of a water treatment facility. You should've seen his smile when I handed him the paper. He told me I'd saved him a lot of trouble.'

'Why did you give him that address?'

'To get him to go where there wouldn't be many witnesses. I'm familiar with the lay of the land out there, you see.'

'Wait a second.' Kusanagi stared hard at Ishigami's face. He couldn't believe what he was hearing. 'So you're telling me that from the very moment you met Togashi, you planned to kill him?'

'Of course,' Ishigami replied, his voice matter-of-fact. 'Like I just said, it's my job to protect Ms Hanaoka. If someone showed up who I knew intended her harm, it was my responsibility to eliminate the problem.'

'And you believe that Mr Togashi intended her harm?'

'It's not a question of belief, I know he did. He had given her all kinds of trouble already by that point. She moved next door to me to get away from him, after all.'

'Ms Hanaoka told you that herself?'

'Through our usual channels of communication, yes.'

Ishigami spoke smoothly and without hesitation. *He certainly had plenty of time to get his story straight before coming in here*, Kusanagi reflected. And yet there was a lot about the story that seemed suspicious at best. For one thing, nothing he was saying matched the mental image of the stodgy high school teacher that Kusanagi had of him until now. Still, there was nothing to do about it but hear the rest of what the man had to say, whether it was true or not.

'What did he do after you gave him the address?'

'He asked if I knew where she was working now. I told him I didn't know where it was, but I'd heard she was working at a restaurant. I also told him I'd heard that she got off at eleven o'clock, and that her daughter would go to the restaurant after school and wait so they could go home together. Of course, I was making all that up.'

'And why did you fabricate this information?'

'To make it easier to predict how he would act. I couldn't have him dropping by my selected location too early. It might be out of the way, but there are still people in the area during daylight hours. I knew that if he thought Yasuko wouldn't be getting off work until that time, and that her daughter would be with her, he would have no reason to visit her apartment before then—'

'Hold on,' Kusanagi raised his hand, cutting him off. 'Are you telling me you thought of all of that right there on the spot?'

'Yes. You don't believe me?'

'No . . . it's just that I'm impressed you could come up with such a plan so quickly.'

'It's really not much,' Ishigami said, his smile fading. 'I knew he wanted desperately to see her. All I had to do was use that desire against him. It wasn't difficult.'

'Well, maybe not for you.' Kusanagi licked his lips. 'So, what happened then?'

'Before he left, I gave him my mobile phone number. I told him to call me if he couldn't find the apartment. Typically, people suspect something when strangers show them that kind of kindness, but he didn't suspect a thing. I don't think he was very smart, to tell the truth.'

'Very few people would imagine someone they'd only just met was planning to kill them.'

'If you ask me, he should have suspected something *because* it was the first time we'd met. In any case, he took the fake address, put it in his pocket, and practically skipped off down the hallway. When I saw that he had left, I went back inside my place and began making preparations.'

303

Ishigami paused and slowly reached for the teacup on the table. He took a couple long gulps of the lukewarm tea.

'What sort of preparations?'

'Nothing too elaborate. I changed into some more comfortable clothes, and waited. I also spent some time thinking about the best way to kill him. After running through several options, I chose strangulation. I reasoned that would be the most reliable method. There's no telling how much blood I might have got on me if I tried to stab or bludgeon him to death. Nor was I sure I could do it with just one blow. Also, strangulation made the choice of a murder weapon much simpler. I knew I needed something strong, so I went with the shielded electrical cord to a kotatsu.'

'Which you carried to the scene of the crime?'

Ishigami nodded. 'I left the house around ten o'clock. I had the actual cord with me, as well as a box cutter and a disposable lighter. On my way to the station, I noticed a blue plastic sheet someone had thrown out in the garbage, so I folded that and brought it with me, too. I got off the train at Mizue and took a taxi to the Old Edogawa.'

'Mizue Station? Not Shinozaki?'

'Of course not,' Ishigami replied without hesitation. 'I didn't want to run into the man by mistake. I got out of the taxi some distance away from the place I'd told him about, too. I knew that, in order to retain the element of surprise, I needed to avoid being seen until the time was right.'

'So what did you do after you got out of the taxi?'

'Taking care not to be seen by anyone, I headed towards our meeting place. Not that I needed to be too careful. There was hardly anyone on the street.' Ishigami took a sip of tea. 'Right after I arrived at the river bank, my mobile phone began to ring. It was him. He told me he'd arrived at the address I'd given him, but couldn't find the apartment building. So I asked him where he was, and he told me in some detail – all the while not realizing that I was approaching his location as we talked. I told him I would check the address again and call him back. By that time I knew exactly where he was. I could see him sitting – sprawled out, really – by a clump of grass on the riverbank. I walked up slowly, so as not to make a sound. He didn't notice me at all until I was right behind him. But by then, I already had the cord around his neck. He resisted, of course, but I had the advantage, and he went limp quickly. It was a lot easier than I'd expected, to be honest.' Ishigami's eyes fell back down to his cup. 'Might I have another cup of tea?'

Kishitani stood and poured him another cup from the pot. Ishigami nodded in thanks.

'The victim was a healthy man in his forties. I wouldn't think he'd be that easy to strangle if he resisted with all his strength,' Kusanagi ventured.

Ishigami's expression didn't change. Only his eyes narrowed slightly. 'I'm the instructor at the judo club at my school. Coming from behind, it's quite easy to overpower a man, even if he's bigger than you.'

Kusanagi nodded, his eyes going to Ishigami's ears. They were puffy, cauliflower ears – the sure sign of a judo wrestler. There were more than a few men on the police force with ears like his.

'What did you do after you killed him?' he asked.

'I knew I had to conceal the identity of the body. I thought that if you police knew who he was, you would surely suspect Yasuko Hanaoka. First, I removed his clothing with the box cutter. Then I smashed his face.' Ishigami's tone was cold and even. 'That is, I laid him on his back, put the plastic sheet over his face, and struck him several times with a large rock. I don't remember how many times I hit him, but I'd say a dozen at least. Then I used the lighter to burn off his finger-prints. After all that, I took his clothes and left the scene. A little way from the bank, I found an oil drum, so I put the clothes in there and burned them. The fire leapt a lot higher than I'd expected, and I started to worry that someone might notice, so I decided to just leave them there. I walked back to the road, caught a cab, and went to Tokyo Station, where I got in another cab for home. It was a little after midnight when I returned to my apartment.' He let out a drawn-out sigh. 'That's it. That's what I did. You can find the electrical cord, the box cutter, and the disposable lighter in my apartment.'

Kusanagi glanced at Kishitani out of the corner of his eye; his assistant was writing furiously. The detective set a cigarette to his lips. He lit it, blew out a puff of smoke, and stared at Ishigami. The man's face was expressionless once more, his eyes a total blank.

There weren't any gaping holes in the story. Everything he'd said about the body's condition and the scene of the crime matched what the police knew. Since none of the details had been released publicly, it was easier to think that he was telling the truth than to believe the alternative.

'Did you tell Yasuko Hanaoka that you killed him?' Kusanagi asked.

'Why would I?' Ishigami replied. 'I couldn't have her slipping up and telling someone else. Women are terrible at keeping secrets.'

'So you haven't talked to her at all about what happened?'

'Not at all. And once you started sniffing around, I took great pains to make as little contact with her as possible, so as not to attract suspicion.'

'You said you had a way of communicating secretly with Ms Hanaoka before. Could you tell me about that now?'

'There were several ways we communicated. For one, she would talk to me.'

'You mean, you would meet somewhere?'

'Nothing like that. People might see us. She would talk in her own apartment, and I would use a device to listen to her.'

'What sort of device?'

'By placing a sound amplifier on the wall between our apartments, I could hear her voice.'

Kishitani's pen stopped in mid-stroke and he looked up. Kusanagi knew what had stopped him.

'You mean, you were eavesdropping on her?'

Ishigami's brow furrowed with surprise and he shook his head. 'It wasn't eavesdropping. She was talking to me.'

'So Ms Hanaoka knew about this listening device?'

'She might not have known about the device, but she was facing the wall between our apartments when she spoke.'

'So that's why you say she was talking to you?'

'That's right. With her daughter there, she couldn't talk to me openly, you see. So she pretended to be talking to her daughter, when she was really sending me messages.'

The cigarette in Kusanagi's hand had burned halfway down to the filter, but he hadn't flicked it once. He dropped it in the ashtray. His eyes met Kishitani's. The junior detective was scratching his neck, perplexed.

'Did Yasuko Hanaoka tell you this – that she was only pretending to talk to her daughter, when in fact she was talking to you?'

'She didn't have to tell me. I know everything about her,' Ishigami asserted, vigorously nodding his head.

'So she *didn't* tell you that, then? Maybe this whole arrangement was just in your head?'

'Nonsense!' Ishigami's expressionless face flushed slightly. 'You see, I knew about the trouble her ex-husband had been giving her because *she told me* about it. Why would she bother telling her daughter such things? It doesn't make sense. She was giving all this information for *my* benefit. She was asking *me* to do something about it.'

Kusanagi waved one hand to calm him, squashing out the smoldering cigarette with the other. 'You were saying you had another means of communication?'

'Yes, the phone. I called her every evening.'

'You called her house?'

'Her mobile phone, to be precise. Not that we would talk. I would merely let the phone ring several times. If she had an urgent need, she was to answer. If not, she wouldn't pick up. I always let it ring five times before hanging up. That was the number we decided upon.'

'You decided? Both of you? So she knew about this?'

'Of course. We had talked it over previously.'

'So we could ask Ms Hanaoka about this?'

'Absolutely. That's the only way to be sure,' Ishigami said with an air of confidence.

Kusanagi shook his head. 'I'm afraid we're going to have to ask you to repeat this story several times. We'll be writing up a formal statement, you see.'

'Not a problem. I understand there's procedure to be followed.'

'Before we get to that, however, there's one last thing I wanted to ask you.' Kusanagi put his hands together on the table, interlocking his fingers. 'Why'd you turn yourself in?'

Ishigami took a deep breath before asking, 'Should I not have turned myself in?'

'That's not what I asked. I just wanted to know why you decided to do so, and why now.'

Ishigami snorted. 'What has that got to do with anything? Surely all you need to do your job is a confession. How about, "Wracked with guilt over what he had done, the murderer turned himself in"? I should think that would suffice.'

'Sorry, but you don't exactly look wracked with guilt.'

'If you're wondering whether I feel I did wrong, then I'd have to say I don't – well, not exactly. I do have regrets. I wish I hadn't done what I did. And if I had known how I would be betrayed, I never would've killed that man.'

'Sorry? You were betrayed?'

'Yasuko, she . . .' Ishigami dropped his eyes for a moment before continuing. 'She's seeing another man. Even though *I* was the one who dealt with her exhusband. And if she hadn't told me all those things, I never would've done it. She said it, plain and clear: "*I want to kill him.*" So I killed him for her. You might say she was my accomplice. She made me do it, after all. In fact, I don't know why you police aren't over there arresting her this minute.'

In order to corroborate Ishigami's story, the police had to search his apartment. While that was going on, Kusanagi and Kishitani went to talk to Yasuko Hanaoka. It was evening, and she and Misato were at home. The two detectives had a fellow officer take the girl outside – not to protect her from hearing anything alarming, but because they wanted to question her separately.

When she heard that Ishigami had turned himself in, Yasuko's eyes went wide; for a moment she seemed to have stopped breathing. She opened her mouth but no words came out.

'I take it this comes as a surprise?' Kusanagi asked, paying close attention to her expression.

Yasuko shook her head slowly, and finally spoke. 'I had no idea. I mean, why would he kill Togashi?'

'You can't think of any possible motive?'

Yasuko hesitated at Kusanagi's question, a look of bewilderment coming across her face. She looked as though she had something to say but was unwilling to say it.

'Ishigami says he did it for you. He says he killed your ex-husband on your behalf.'

Yasuko looked pained and let out a long sigh.

'So you *can* think of a reason.'

She nodded slightly. 'I knew he had feelings for me. I just never imagined he would go so far—'

'He told us that the two of you have been in constant contact for some time now.'

'Contact?' Yasuko frowned. 'We've barely ever spoken.'

'But there were phone calls from him? Every evening?' Kusanagi told the woman what Ishigami had said about their arrangement. Yasuko frowned again.

'So that was him calling.'

'You didn't know?'

'I thought it might be him, maybe, but I wasn't sure. He never gave his name.'

'I see. Can you tell us a little more about these calls?'

Yasuko explained that someone unknown started phoning her in the evening about three months ago. Without giving his name, the caller had suddenly started saying things about her personal life – things no one could possibly have known unless they had been spying on her. She was frightened, afraid that she had a stalker; but she'd been baffled by the question of who it might be. After that, the phone had rung every night at the same time, but she had never answered – except for once, when she'd picked up the receiver without thinking. Then the man on the other end said: 'I understand you've been too busy to answer your phone. So I have a suggestion. I will call every evening, and you only need to answer if you need me for something. I will let the phone ring five times, you just need to pick up before the fifth ring.'

Yasuko had reluctantly agreed, and since that time, the phone rang every night. Apparently, the stranger was calling her from a public phone. She never answered.

'You couldn't tell it was Ishigami from his voice?'

'Not really. We'd spoken so little. And I never picked up except for those two times, so I can't even really remember what the voice sounded like now. In any case, I can hardly imagine someone like him doing such a thing. I mean, he's a high school teacher!'

'That's no guarantee of character these days, I'm afraid,' Kishitani offered. Then, as if embarrassed by his own interruption, he quickly lowered his head.

Kusanagi reflected on how the junior detective had taken the Hanaokas' side since the very beginning. *Ishigami's turning himself in must have come as a great relief to Kishitani.*

'Was there ever anything else, besides the calls?' Kusanagi asked.

'Well . . .' Yasuko rose and retrieved three envelopes from a nearby drawer. There was no sender or return address marked on any of them; on the front of each was only the name 'Yasuko Hanaoka'.

'And these are?'

'Letters I found in the mailbox on my door. There were some others, but I threw them out. I just thought I should keep these as evidence in case there was ever a more serious problem – people are always doing that on television, you know. I didn't much like having them, but I kept these three, just in case.'

Kusanagi opened the envelopes.

Each contained a single sheet of paper with words that had clearly been typed on a computer. None of the letters was particularly long:

I notice you've been putting on more makeup recently. And wearing fancier clothes. That's not like you. Plainer attire suits you better. It also bothers me that you've been coming home late. You should come home right after work is finished.

Is something bothering you? If it is, please don't hesitate to tell me about it. That's why I call you every night, you know. There are many matters on which I could advise you. You can't trust anyone else. You shouldn't trust anyone else. Just me.

I have a feeling something terrible has happened. I fear you've betrayed me. Now, I know with all my heart that you would never do such a thing, but if you ever did, I'm not sure I would ever be able to forgive you. I am the only man for you. I am the only one who can protect you.

'Do you mind if I take these with me?'
'They're all yours.'

'Anything else like this happen recently?'

'To me? No, nothing really . . .' Yasuko's voice trailed off.

'To your daughter then?'

'Well, no. But . . . there was something with Mr Kudo.'

'Mr Kuniaki Kudo? What happened to him?'

'When I met him for dinner the other day, he said he'd received an odd letter. There was no signature or return address, but the letter told him to stay away from me. There were some photographs in the envelope, too, photos of him, taken without his knowledge.'

'So your stalker was stalking him, too?'

The detectives exchanged looks. Given all they had seen thus far, the writer of the letters would have to have been Ishigami. Kusanagi thought about Manabu Yukawa. The physicist had respected Ishigami as a fellow scientist. Kusanagi wondered if his friend would be shocked to hear that the mathematician was moonlighting as a stalker.

There was a knock at the door. Yasuko answered it, and a young detective leaned into the room. He was a member of the team that had been searching Ishigami's apartment.

'Can I have a moment with you, Detective Kusanagi?'

'Sure.' Kusanagi nodded and headed for the door.

In the next apartment, Mamiya was sitting in the chair by the desk. The PC monitor on the table next to him was glowing. Elsewhere in the room, young detectives were packing things in cardboard boxes to take back to the station as evidence.

Mamiya pointed at the wall next to the bookshelf. 'Take a look.'

Kusanagi gasped despite himself.

The wallpaper had been removed from a corner of the wall, and a square had been cut out of the drywall behind it. A thin cord dangled from the hole; on the end of the cord was a small earphone.

'Have a listen.'

Kusanagi placed the earphone into his ear and immediately could hear voices.

'If we can confirm what Ishigami is telling us, things should proceed pretty quickly. I don't think we'll be bothering you too much more after that, Ms Hanaoka.'

It was Kishitani. The sound was a little fuzzy, but perfectly audible. Kusanagi glanced back at Mamiya. He wouldn't have believed the people he was listening to were on the other side of the wall if he hadn't seen it himself. He listened again for a moment.

'. . . will Ishigami be charged with?'

'That will have to be determined by the court. But it's a pretty clear case of murder, so I should think he'll be put away for quite some time – that is, assuming he doesn't get the death sentence. In any case, he won't be bothering you any more, Ms Hanaoka.'

For a detective, he talks way too much, Kusanagi thought, removing the earphone.

'We should show this to Ms Hanaoka afterwards. Ishigami says she knew about it, but I have my doubts about that,' Mamiya said.

'You mean Yasuko Hanaoka had no idea what Ishigami was up to?'

'I heard you talking to her over that earphone,' Mamiya said with a grin. 'It's pretty cut and dried. Ishigami was a classic stalker. Delusions of sharing some kind of bond with his target, trying to get rid of every other man who gets close to her. No wonder he hated her ex-husband.'

Kusanagi grunted.

'Why the frown? Something not sitting right with you?'

'No, it's just I thought I had a good grasp on this Ishigami fellow, but everything he's been telling us lately doesn't seem to fit with my image of him. It's confusing.'

'A man has many faces. Stalkers are never the people you think there are.'

'I know that, just . . . you find anything other than the listening device?'

Mamiya nodded grandly. 'The kotatsu cord, for one. It was in a box along with his kotatsu in the closet. An insulated cord, too – the same kind as the one used to strangle the man. If we can find a trace of the victim's skin on it, we're golden.'

'Anything else?'

'Take a look.' Mamiya pushed the computer

317

mouse back and forth on the desk. His motions were jerky; he was clearly unfamiliar with using a mouse. Kusanagi guessed that someone had just taught him. 'Here.'

He had opened a wordprocessing program. A page full of writing showed on the screen. Kusanagi peered at the words.

As you can tell by the enclosed pictures, I have discovered the identity of the man you see frequently.

I must ask, what is this man to you?

If you're having a relationship, that would be a serious betrayal.

Don't you understand what I've done for you?

I believe I have the right to tell you what to do in this matter. You must stop seeing this man immediately.

If you do not, my anger will be directed at him.

It would be a simple thing for me to lead this man to the same fate Togashi suffered. I have both the resolve and the means to do this.

Let me repeat, if you're engaged in a relationship with this man, that is a betrayal I cannot forgive, and I will have my revenge.

CHAPTER 17

Yukawa stood at the laboratory window, staring intently at the outside. There was an unusual remoteness in his presence, a pained distance, as if an invisible regret weighed him down and drew him apart. It could have been shock at hearing of his old friend's crime, but Kusanagi suspected it was something else.

'So,' Yukawa was saying in a low voice, 'do you believe this testimony of Ishigami's? Do you buy his story?'

'As a detective, I see no reason to doubt it,' Kusanagi said after a beat. 'We've been able to corroborate his account from several different angles. I did some canvassing in a local park near Ishigami's apartment where there is a public phone. That's where he claims to have gone every night to call Yasuko Hanaoka. Turns out there's a grocery store near where the phone is, and the proprietor there saw someone matching Ishigami's description. He remembered him because not many people use public phones these days. He claims he saw him making calls there on several evenings.'

Yukawa slowly turned around to face Kusanagi. 'That's what you think as a detective. I asked whether you believe him. I don't care about your investigation.'

Kusanagi nodded and sighed. 'To be honest, it doesn't feel right. There are no holes in his story. It all makes sense. But I guess I'm just having trouble imagining him doing all those things. Of course, when I tried to tell the chief that, he didn't want to hear it.'

'I'm sure your superiors are happy now that they've got someone to charge with a crime. Why would they want anything else?'

'Things would be different if there were even one piece of the puzzle that didn't fit, but there's nothing. It's perfect. Take the fingerprints left on the bicycle. He claims he didn't even know the victim got there by bicycle. Nothing strange there. Ishigami's testimony supports all the facts. With that kind of momentum, there's nothing I could say to turn the train around at this point.'

'So, you don't buy it, but you have no choice but to go with the flow and accept the conclusion that Ishigami is your murderer.'

'Look, I know you're not happy about this either, but don't take it out on me. Aren't scientists supposed to shelve their doubts in the face of logical arguments? Wasn't it you who told me that? I thought you were all about facts over feelings.'

Yukawa shook his head – a barely perceptible movement – then came to sit down across from

320

Kusanagi. 'The last time I met Ishigami, he presented me with a mathematical conundrum,' he said. 'It's a famous one, the P = NP problem. Basically, it asks whether it's more difficult to think of the solution to a problem yourself or to ascertain if someone else's answer to the same problem is correct.'

Kusanagi frowned. 'That's mathematics? Sounds more like philosophy.'

'Bear with me. By turning himself in, and giving you his testimony, Ishigami's presented you with an answer that, no matter how you look at it, has to be correct. If you just nod your heads and say, "Okay, sounds good to us", you've lost. Really, what you should be doing is putting all your efforts into determining whether his answer is correct or not. It's a challenge. You're being tested.'

'And like I said, we looked into it. Everything backs up his story.'

'All you're doing is tracing the steps of his proof. What you should be doing is looking to see if there aren't any other answers that might fit what you know about this case as well. Only if you can prove that there are no legitimate answers other than the one he's offered can you say that his is the only solution to the problem.'

Yukawa's irritation was plain from his unusually hard tone. Kusanagi had rarely seen the level-headed physicist this agitated.

'So you think Ishigami's lying? He's not the murderer?'

Yukawa frowned and lowered his eyes.

'What's your basis for saying that?' the detective went on. 'If you've got a theory of your own, I'd like to hear it. Or is it just that you can't bear to think of your old friend as a killer?'

Yukawa stood and turned his back to Kusanagi.

'Yukawa?'

'It's true. I don't want to believe it,' Yukawa said. 'Like I said before, that man is made of logic. Emotion comes a distant second. He's capable of doing anything if he thinks it's an effective solution to the problem at hand. Still, it's very hard for me to imagine him going so far as to murder someone – especially someone with whom he had no personal connection.'

'And that's your basis for refuting his story?'

Yukawa spun back around and glared at the detective. But his eyes were filled with sadness, not anger.

'There are some things in life that we have to accept as truth, even though we don't want to believe them. I know that.'

'And still you think Ishigami's innocent?'

Yukawa's face twisted, and he shook his head. 'I wouldn't say that.'

'I know what you think happened. You think it was Yasuko Hanaoka who killed Togashi, and Ishigami's been trying to protect her. But the more we've looked into it, the less likely that scenario seems to be. We have several pieces of evidence pointing to Ishigami's being a stalker – so much that it would have been very hard to fake, no matter how enthusiastic he was about protecting her. Besides, how many people are there who would willingly take the blame for something like murder? Yasuko isn't Ishigami's wife or part of his family. She's not even his lover. Say he had wanted to protect her, and in fact helped conceal the murder – when all that fell apart, most people would resign themselves to their failure at that point. It's only human.'

Yukawa's eyes widened, as though from a sudden realization. 'Yes,' he muttered. 'People give up when things go bad. It would be nearly impossible to protect someone to the bitter end like he would have had to do.' He gazed off into the distance. 'Hard even for Ishigami. And he knows it. That's why—'

'What?'

'No.' Yukawa shook his head. 'Nothing.'

'As I see it, we have to accept that Ishigami did it. And unless some new facts come to light, I don't see this investigation going in a different direction.'

Yukawa rubbed his face with his hands. He breathed a long quiet sigh. 'He's chosen this,' he said at last. 'He's chosen to spend the rest of his days in prison.'

'It's not really a choice now that he's killed someone.'

'Indeed,' Yukawa whispered. He stood still for some time, his head hanging. Then, without moving, he said, 'I'm sorry, but maybe you could leave me alone for a while. I'm tired.'

Something was definitely wrong with Yukawa.

Kusanagi wanted to ask more questions, but instead he rose from his chair in silence. His friend did look terribly exhausted.

Kusanagi left Laboratory 13 and made his way down the dimly lit hallway. At the top of the stairs he ran into a student. Kusanagi recognized the young man's thin, nervous face. He was a graduate student, one of Yukawa's; his name was Tokiwa. He was the one who had told Kusanagi that Yukawa had gone to Shinozaki the last time the detective had dropped by the laboratory.

Tokiwa nodded slightly as he walked by.

'Hey there,' Kusanagi called out. Tokiwa turned around, a look of confusion on his face, and the detective smiled at him. 'Do you have a moment? There was something I wanted to ask you.'

Tokiwa checked his wristwatch and said yes, he had a little time.

They left the physics building and went to the nearest cafeteria, one frequented mostly by students in the sciences. Kusanagi bought them both coffee from a vending machine and sat down across from Tokiwa.

'This is way better than the instant stuff you guys drink in that lab,' the detective observed, taking a sip from his paper cup.

Tokiwa smiled, but his face was still tense.

So much for breaking the ice. Kusanagi inwardly debated chatting with the student for a little longer, but he decided it would only be a waste of time, so he got down to business. 'I wanted to ask you about Assistant Professor Yukawa, actually. Have you noticed anything odd about him lately?'

Tokiwa was clearly bewildered by the question. Kusanagi immediately regretted his own directness, but what was done was done. 'I mean, has he been looking into anything unrelated to his university work, or gone anywhere unusual?'

Tokiwa scratched his jaw. He seemed to be seriously considering the question, at least.

Kusanagi tried smiling at him. 'Don't worry, he's not involved in an investigation or anything. It is a little hard to explain, but I can't help getting the feeling that Yukawa is hiding something from me – because he thinks I'm better off not knowing it. I've tried asking, but you know how stubborn he can be.'

Kusanagi wasn't sure how well he was getting his point across, but the student did seem to be warming to him slightly. Perhaps mentioning his professor's stubbornness had struck a chord.

'Well,' Tokiwa began, 'I'm not sure what he was researching, but Professor Yukawa was on the phone to the library a few days ago.'

'The library? You mean the university's?'

Tokiwa nodded. 'I think he was asking them whether they had newspapers.'

'Newspapers? Don't all libraries have newspapers?'

'They do, but he wanted to know how long they kept their old newspapers.'

325

'You don't say.'

'Yeah. Not that he was looking for anything particularly old. I heard him asking whether he could read all the newspapers from this month. Something like that.'

'This month? Do you have any idea whether they had what he was looking for?'

'I'm pretty sure they did, because he went to the library straight after that.'

Kusanagi nodded, thanked Tokiwa, and stood up, his cup of coffee in his hand. The paper cup was still half full.

The Imperial University library was a substantial three-storey building. When Kusanagi was a student, he had only visited it two or three times at most. He guessed that additions had been built since he'd left, but he couldn't exactly remember what the place had looked like before. The entire edifice could have been rebuilt and he wouldn't have known the difference.

He went in now and saw a woman behind the reception counter just inside the door. He asked her if she remembered Assistant Professor Yukawa's recent visit and if she knew which newspapers he had been interested in. She hesitated, eyeing him suspiciously.

Kusanagi sighed and showed her his badge. 'Don't worry, this has very little to do with Professor Yukawa. All I want to know is which newspapers he was looking at.' He knew it was an odd-sounding question, but he couldn't think of any other way to find out what he needed to know.

'I believe he was interested in articles from March,' the woman said, choosing her words carefully.

'Do you know what sort of articles?'

'I can't say that I do.' She considered for a moment. 'Except, he did say that all he needed was to look at the Local News section.'

'The Local News? You mind showing me where the newspapers are?'

She led him to a wide, low shelf where all the newspapers were kept in stacks – one stack for every ten days.

'I'm afraid we only have newspapers for the last month here,' she informed him. 'Everything older than that we recycle. We used to keep older papers on site, but there are Internet archives where you can read past articles now.'

'But all Yukawa – Professor Yukawa – cared about was the papers from March?'

'Yes. Everything after March 10, actually.'

'March 10?'

'Yes, I believe that's what he said.'

'You mind if I look at these?'

'Not at all. Just let me know when you're finished.'

As soon as the librarian had turned away, Kusanagi pulled out the stack of newspapers and set them on a nearby table. He began with the Local sections from March 10.

March 10 was, of course, the day Shinji Togashi had been murdered. Which confirmed that Yukawa had been here to research the case. But what had he hoped to find in a newspaper?

Kusanagi looked for any articles that might have been related to the Togashi case. The first he found were in the evening editions from March 11. The next were in the morning editions from March 13, when the police had released the victim's identity. That was the last mention of the case in the news until an article from the previous day, when Ishigami had turned himself in.

So what about these articles had interested Yukawa?

Kusanagi carefully read and reread a few pertinent articles. None of them said anything he wouldn't have expected to find. Certainly, Yukawa had been privy to far more information about the case than was in the papers. Why would he have gone through the trouble of reading them?

Kusanagi crossed his arms over the stack of newspapers.

It didn't make any sense. For one thing, a man like Yukawa wouldn't normally rely on newspapers to help him investigate a case of this sort, if that indeed was what he'd been doing. With murders happening practically every day in Japan, most newspapers wouldn't continue running stories about a particular case unless there was some large development. The case of Togashi's murder wasn't a particularly unusual one, either. Yukawa knew all that.

He also wasn't the type to trek to the library for no reason, either.

Despite what he had said to the physicist, Kusanagi couldn't accept that Ishigami had done what he had claimed. Nor could the detective shake the feeling that his team had been barking up the wrong tree all along. He felt that Yukawa knew what they were doing wrong. The physicist had come to the aid of Kusanagi and the police department several times before, and maybe he had some insight this time around, too. But if he did, why wasn't he talking?

Kusanagi restacked the newspapers and went to inform the librarian that he was done.

'I hope they were of some help?' she asked uncertainly.

'Yeah, very helpful,' Kusanagi replied, without elaborating.

'You know,' the librarian said as he was signing out, 'Professor Yukawa was also interested in the local papers.'

'Huh?' Kusanagi looked up. 'Which local papers?'

'He asked about the papers from Chiba and Saitama Prefectures. Unfortunately, we don't carry those.'

'Did he ask about anything else?'

'No, I think that was all.'

'Chiba and Saitama . . . ?'

Confused, Kusanagi left the library. This time, he really had no idea what Yukawa had been thinking. Why would he be interested in local papers? Maybe he hadn't been looking into the murder case after all.

His mind churning, Kusanagi made his way back to the parking lot. He had just climbed into the driver's seat and was about to turn the ignition key when Manabu Yukawa came walking out of the university building right in front of him. He was wearing a dark navy jacket in place of his lab coat, and he was making a beeline for the front gates, a look of intense concentration on his face.

After watching as Yukawa reached the street and turned left, Kusanagi started his car and headed out onto the roadway himself. Passing through the gates, he glanced over just in time to see Yukawa climb into a cab. Kusanagi pulled onto the road just as the cab was pulling away.

Yukawa typically spent most of each day at the university. He'd always told Kusanagi that, being single, there was nothing for him to do at home, and it was easier for him to read or play the occasional game of racquetball at the university. Meals were easier there, too.

Kusanagi glanced at his watch. It wasn't even five o'clock yet. Yukawa wouldn't be headed home for the day already.

Kusanagi began tailing Yukawa's cab. As he drove he memorized the name of the cab company and the car's licence plate number, so that even if he happened to lose them along the way, he would

330

be able to call the company and find out where the cab had dropped off its passenger.

The taxi was heading east down a relatively busy street. Several other cars moved in between it and Kusanagi's car, but the detective managed to avoid losing his quarry.

He had been following them for some time when the taxi passed through the Nihonbashi area and stopped just before crossing the Sumida River, right by the Shin-Ohashi Bridge. Ishigami's apartment building lay just across the bridge.

Kusanagi pulled over to one side of the road and watched the cab from there. Yukawa got out of the cab and went down the staircase at the side of the bridge.

Doesn't look like he's headed for the apartment, at least.

Kusanagi quickly checked his surroundings, looking for a place to park. He was in luck and found a spot by a parking meter. He left his car there and quickly followed after Yukawa.

The physicist was walking slowly downstream along the Sumida River. He didn't seem to have any particular destination in mind; it appeared that he was just walking. Occasionally, he glanced at the homeless people who had set up camp there, but he never paused for long.

When he did stop, it was well past the last of the homeless camps. He rested his elbows on the fence that ran along the river's edge. Then he suddenly turned to look in Kusanagi's direction.

331

Kusanagi hesitated, but Yukawa didn't seem particularly surprised. He was even smiling, though thinly.

The detective strode forward. 'You saw me?'

'Your car kind of stands out,' Yukawa said simply. 'Hardly ever see old Skylines like that on the road these days.'

'And did you get out where you did because you knew you were being followed? Or had you planned to come here from the beginning?'

'Both, and neither. My original destination was ahead of here. When I noticed you were following me, I had the taxi driver let me off a little early, because I wanted to bring you to this place.'

'Okay, I'll bite. Why did you want to take me here?' Kusanagi asked, quickly scanning the area with his eyes.

'This is where I was when I last talked to Ishigami. I told him something then. I told him there was no such thing in this world as a useless cog, and that even a cog may decide how it is to be used.'

'Excuse me? A cog?'

'Yes. After that, I tried asking him several questions I had about the case. He was pretty much "No comment" about the whole thing, except that after we parted, he came up with his own answer. That answer was to turn himself in.'

'So you're saying that he resigned himself to his fate after hearing what you told him?'

'"Resignation" . . . I suppose you could call it

that. For him, it was more like playing his last trump card. One he had been preparing assiduously for some time.'

'So what was it you told him?'

'Just what I said, that thing about the cog.'

'No, after that. You said you asked him questions. That's what I wanted to know.'

A quiet smile came to Yukawa's face and he shook his head slowly. 'That's not the important part.'

'It's not?'

'The important part is the bit about cogs. That's when he decided to turn himself in.'

Kusanagi sighed loudly. 'You were checking out the newspapers at the university library, right? What were you looking for?'

'Did Tokiwa tell you that? I'm surprised you've taken such an interest in my daily goings-on.'

'Hey, it wasn't by choice. You wouldn't tell me anything yourself.'

'It's okay, I don't mind. It's your job, after all. Feel free to investigate me all you like.'

Kusanagi stared at Yukawa intently for a moment, then lowered his eyes. 'Yukawa, please. Stop talking in riddles. You know something. Tell me what it is. Ishigami didn't murder that man, did he? If that's true, then why would he say he did? You don't want an old friend getting locked up for a murder he didn't commit, do you?'

'Look up.'

Kusanagi looked back up. He breathed in

333

sharply. The physicist's face was twisted with grief; he pressed one hand to his forehead and squeezed his eyes closed.

'Of course I don't want him to be accused of murder. I just don't see any way out of it. I wish none of this had happened.'

'What's got you all worked up? Why don't you just tell me? C'mon, we're friends.'

Yukawa opened his eyes again, his face still severe. 'Yes. You're my friend, but you're also a detective.'

Kusanagi didn't know what to say to that. For the first time in the many years he had known Yukawa, he felt a wall between them. Here his friend was showing him pain he had never shown before, and Kusanagi was entirely unable to ask him why.

'I'm going to Yasuko Hanaoka's,' Yukawa said. 'Want to come with me?'

'Can I?'

'I don't care. Just, I'd prefer it if you kept quiet.'

'Fine.'

Yukawa spun around and began to walk back towards the bridge. Kusanagi followed after him. Apparently, Yukawa's initial destination had been the lunch shop, Benten-tei. Once again, Kusanagi found himself burning with questions he wanted to ask, yet unable to say a word. They walked in silence.

Just before Kiyosu Bridge, Yukawa climbed the steps to the road. Kusanagi followed and found Yukawa waiting for him at the top.

'See that office building?' The physicist pointed

to the building closest to them. 'See the glass doors at the entrance?'

Kusanagi looked and saw the two of them reflected in the doors. 'Yeah. What about them?'

'When I visited Ishigami right after the murder, I saw the two of us reflected like this in these doors. Actually, I didn't notice at first. It was Ishigami who brought it to my attention. Until that moment, I hadn't even considered the possibility he might be involved with the case. I was just happy to be reunited with an old competitor.'

'So you started to suspect him when you saw your two reflections?'

'It was what he said. "How have you managed to stay so young, Yukawa? You still have a full head of hair! How different we two are!" – Then he ran his fingers over his own head. It surprised me. Ishigami had never been the type to worry about physical appearances. He had always been of the opinion that a man's value was not determined by such things, and he'd never wanted to live a life where such things could be a concern. Yet here he was, worried about his thinning hair. Something about which he could do nothing. That was when I realized he was in a position where he suddenly did have to worry about his own appearance – in other words, he was in love. Yet why would he suddenly come out and reveal such a thing, here, in this place?'

Kusanagi understood. 'Because he was about to see the girl of his dreams.'

Yukawa nodded. 'My thoughts exactly. I started thinking that this woman working at the lunch shop, his neighbour, whose ex-husband had so recently been killed, was the object of his affections. Which raised an important question: what was his relationship to the case? If he was so taken with this woman, he would have to be worried about it, yet he was playing the part of a disinterested observer to a T. Or perhaps I was assuming too much and he wasn't in love at all. That's why I got together with him again and accompanied him to the lunch shop. I thought I might see something in his expression that would reveal him. And as chance would have it, we ran into someone entirely unexpected at the shop – an acquaintance of Yasuko Hanaoka.'

'Kudo,' Kusanagi said. 'He's dating her.'

'So it seems. And when I saw Ishigami's face as he watched this Kudo fellow and her talking—' Yukawa narrowed his eyes and shook his head. 'That did it. I knew at that moment that Ishigami was infatuated with her. I could see jealousy written all over his face.'

'But that raises another question, doesn't it?'

'It does. There was only one way to explain the resulting contradiction.'

'Ishigami was involved with the case – so that's why you started to suspect him.' Kusanagi glanced back at the glass doors. 'You scare me sometimes, you know. I'm sure Ishigami never suspected such a tiny imperfection in his performance would become a fatal flaw.'

'He's a unique man. And even after all those years, my memory of him as he was back then is still vivid. If it weren't, I'm sure I wouldn't have have noticed a thing.'

'His bad luck,' Kusanagi said, starting towards the road. He stopped when he noticed that Yukawa wasn't following him. 'I thought you were going to Benten-tei?'

Eyes downcast, Yukawa came towards him. 'I have to ask you to do something I normally wouldn't ask. I don't think you'll like it.'

Kusanagi chuckled. 'That depends on what it is.'

'Do you think you can forget you're a detective, just for a moment?'

'I'm not sure what you mean.'

'There's something I need to tell you, but you my friend, not you the detective. And I can't have you telling anyone else, ever. Not your police chief, not your friends, not even your family. Can you promise me this?'

Kusanagi saw a terrible urgency in the eyes behind the wire-frame glasses. He could tell that Yukawa felt forced into making a decision he wasn't ready to make.

He wanted to say, *'It depends on what you tell me.'* But Kusanagi swallowed his words. If he said that, Yukawa would never look at him as a friend again.

'Fine. I promise.'

CHAPTER 18

Yasuko passed a fried chicken meal across
the counter to the last customer in line and
glanced up at the clock. *Only a few minutes
until six.* She sighed and took off her white cap.

Kudo had called her on her mobile phone at
lunchtime. He wanted to meet her after work –
'To celebrate,' he'd said, his voice full of energy.

She'd asked what they were celebrating.

'Isn't it obvious?' he answered. 'They caught the
murderer! No more investigations. No more being
watched. Surely that rates a toast?'

Kudo had sounded so chipper and full of life
over the phone. It made sense; he didn't know
what had really happened. Still, Yasuko had been
unable to put herself in a celebratory mood. She
had told him as much.

'Why?' Kudo had wanted to know. When she
didn't answer, he had mumbled something about
understanding. 'Oh . . . I wasn't thinking about
the victim. It's surprising how deep the connections between people can run, even when they're
apart. I'm sorry. It was wrong of me to suggest a
celebration.'

He was completely off the mark, but Yasuko hadn't enlightened him.

'Actually, though . . .' he'd continued after a pause. 'There was something else I wanted to talk with you about, something very important. I'd very much like to see you tonight. Do you think that would be possible?'

Yasuko had considered refusing. She just wasn't in the mood. She felt stained by guilt, knowing Ishigami had turned himself in to save her. But she'd been at a loss for a way to turn Kudo down, and she had wondered – was still wondering – what the important thing he had to discuss might be.

In the end, they'd agreed that he would come pick her up at six thirty. Kudo had said something about wanting Misato to join them, but Yasuko had gently objected, and that was that. She didn't want Kudo seeing her daughter the way she was these days.

Yasuko had left a message on the machine at her apartment, saying she'd be home a little late that evening. It made her heart heavy just imagining what Misato would think about that.

At the stroke of six, Yasuko took off her apron. She poked her head into the kitchen. 'Looks like we're done for the day,' she called to Sayoko.

'My, that time already?' Sayoko looked up from her plate. She was eating an early dinner. 'Thanks, then. Don't worry about closing up, I'll take care of it.'

'Thanks,' Yasuko replied, folding her apron.

'You're going to meet Mr Kudo tonight, aren't you?' Sayoko asked in a quiet voice.

'What?'

'I noticed you got a phone call at lunch. He's asked you on a date, didn't he!'

Flustered, Yasuko said nothing. Sayoko took her silence for shyness. 'I'm happy for you,' she said with a suggestive wink. 'That whole unpleasant business with Togashi's murder is cleared up now, and look, there's a nice man like Mr Kudo just waiting for you in the wings. You know, I think your luck has turned.'

'Maybe . . .'

'Oh it has, I'm sure of it! You've paid your dues, now it's time for you to find a little happiness for yourself. And for Misato.'

Sayoko's words triggered an avalanche of conflicting emotions inside Yasuko. Would Sayoko be wishing her happiness if she knew she was a killer?

Yasuko took her leave and slipped out of the kitchen. She couldn't look Sayoko in the eyes.

She left Benten-tei and walked in the direction opposite her usual route home after work. She was supposed to meet Kudo at the family restaurant on the corner. Until now, she had avoided the place since that day she'd met Togashi there. But Kudo had selected it as an easy place where they could meet. She'd been unable to think of an appropriate excuse to get him to change his mind.

An expressway overpass crossed above the road to the restaurant. She was just making her way beneath it when a man's voice called out from behind her, 'Ms Hanaoka?'

She stopped and turned to see two familiar men walking towards her. One was Yukawa – the professor who was an old friend of Ishigami's. The other was the detective, Kusanagi. Yasuko couldn't imagine why they of all people would be here, walking together.

'You remember me?' Yukawa was the first to speak.

Involuntarily, Yasuko felt her gaze darting back and forth between the two men's faces. After a moment she nodded.

'I'm sorry, were you on your way somewhere?'

'Well, actually . . .' She looked down at her watch, though she was too nervous to actually read the time. 'I was supposed to meet someone.'

'I see. I was hoping that we could talk. Just for a half hour or so. It's very important.'

'I'm afraid I don't have that much time—' She shook her head.

'Then how about fifteen minutes? That's all we need. Right here, on that bench.' Yukawa pointed towards a nearby strip of green, a tiny public park that had been built beneath the expressway.

Though his tone was gentle, something in his attitude conveyed how serious he was. Yasuko understood immediately that whatever he had to say was extremely important. This university man had talked to her like that before. His tone and words were light, but the weight behind them was almost suffocating.

She felt a powerful urge to run, to flee as fast as her legs would take her. But a strange fascination held her. She was curious to hear what he had to say. Whatever it was, she knew it was about Ishigami.

'Okay, ten minutes.'

'Thank you,' Yukawa said with a smile, leading the way towards the park.

Yasuko hesitated before following, but Kusanagi waved her on. 'Go ahead,' he murmured. She nodded and followed after Yukawa. The detective's dour presence was giving her the creeps.

Yukawa sat down on the bench. It was wide enough for two, and he left space for Yasuko.

'Stand over there, if you would,' the physicist directed Kusanagi with a wave of his hand. 'I think we should talk by ourselves.'

Kusanagi looked less than pleased by this, but he stuck out his chin and strolled back to the entrance of the park, where he took out a cigarette and began to smoke.

Yasuko sat next Yukawa, glancing in Kusanagi's direction. 'Isn't he a detective? Are you sure this is all right?'

'Don't worry about him. I was originally going to come here by myself. And besides, he's here more as a friend of mine than as a detective anyway.'

'A friend?'

'Since our college days, yes.' Yukawa smiled again, showing white teeth. 'Which makes him a classmate of Ishigami, also. Though the two never met until all this happened.'

Finally Yasuko understood why Professor Yukawa had come to visit Ishigami only after the murder. Though Ishigami hadn't said anything about it, she suspected that his whole plan had fallen apart because of Yukawa's involvement. When the maths teacher was calculating how to cover up her ex-husband's murder, he certainly couldn't have counted on the detective's being an alumnus of his university or on the two of them even having a mutual friend.

But all that was done now. So what could Yukawa want to talk to her about?

'It's extremely regrettable that Ishigami decided to turn himself in,' Yukawa said, abruptly getting to the point. 'To think of a man with his talent wasting away inside a jail cell makes me, as a scientist, very sad indeed.'

Yasuko wasn't sure how to respond. She clenched her fingers into fists on her knees.

'To be honest, I'm having trouble believing it. I just can't believe he would do such a thing. To you. Spying like he says he did.'

Yukawa sensed that Yasuko was watching him out of the corners of her eyes; her body was visibly tensed.

'No, maybe *believe* isn't the right word. I'm absolutely certain he wouldn't. He . . . when he told us that story . . . Ishigami's lying. Which raises the question: why would he lie? What's the point of lying now that he's soon to be a convicted murderer? And yet he *is* lying. I can think of only one reason for it. He's not lying for himself. He's lying for someone else, to hide the truth.'

Yasuko swallowed. It was taking all of her effort just to breathe at a steady rhythm. She didn't know how, but this man had figured out the truth, even if he didn't know the exact details. *Ishigami was protecting someone – someone else was the murderer.* Now Yukawa was trying to save his friend in any way that he could. What would be the easiest way to get his friend off the hook? Why, by convincing the real murderess to turn herself in. By getting her to make a confession to the police that would sweep away everything his friend had brought upon himself.

Yasuko glanced fearfully at the man beside her and found, much to her surprise, that he was smiling.

'You think I've come to convince you, don't you?'

'No, why would I—' Yasuko jerked her head in denial. 'I don't see what – what you would be trying to convince me to do . . .'

'You're right. I'm sorry, don't mind me.' He lowered his head. 'Still, there was something I wanted you to know. That's why I'm here.'

'What might that be?'

'Well.' Yukawa paused a moment before speaking again. 'I want you to know that you know nothing of the truth.'

Yasuko's eyes widened with surprise. Yukawa wasn't smiling any more.

'Your alibi's the real deal,' he continued. 'You went to that cinema when you said you did, and your daughter went with you. I can't imagine a girl in middle school holding up under such persistent questioning from the police otherwise. Neither of you is lying.'

'That's true. I'm not lying. But why did you have to tell me that?'

'Don't you find it odd that you *haven't* had to lie? That the police have gone so easy on you? See, Ishigami put it together so you would *only* have to tell the truth. No matter how hard the detectives pushed, nothing would ever lead decisively to your doorstep. I have no doubt that, even now, you're unaware of most of what he's done. You might realize he's pulled off some nifty trick to get you out of trouble, but you're not entirely sure what that is. Am I wrong?'

'I'm sorry, I have absolutely no idea what you're talking about.' Yasuko tried smiling, but her mouth felt as if it were made of plastic.

'He has made a terrible sacrifice in order to protect you, you know. A sacrifice so great, ordinary people such as you and I couldn't even imagine doing such a thing. I'm sure that, from the night it all happened, he was prepared to take your place in a jail cell, should the situation call for that. His entire plan was constructed around that commitment. To put it another way, he knew he could do anything, as long as it didn't interfere with that trump card. Yet what a trump card

345

it is! Who could possibly follow through on such a plan? Ishigami knew it would be near impossible himself. That's why he cut off his own path of retreat – so he would never be able to turn back once things were put into motion. That's what most surprises me about all that he's done.'

Yasuko was confused. At first, she had thought she knew what the professor was driving at, but now she wasn't so sure. Whatever it was, she had a feeling that something unpleasant was waiting for her in his words.

And yet everything he had said so far was true; he had simply revealed another side of the truth, one she hadn't considered closely until this moment. Yasuko *didn't* know what Ishigami had been up to all this time – not really. And she had indeed found it strange that the detectives had been treating her with kid gloves. Not only that, but on the three occasions they had come to question her they had never even come close to guessing what had actually happened.

And Yukawa knew why—

She saw him check his watch.

'It pains me to have to tell you these things,' he said at length, his face tightening in a grimace. 'Because I know that Ishigami wouldn't want me to. I'm sure he'd rather you didn't know the truth no matter what happened. Not for his sake, but for yours. Because if you knew, you would have to live bearing even more pain than you already do. Yet I have to tell you. I feel like I would be doing

346

him a disservice as a friend if I didn't make you aware of how much love he has for you, how he has gambled his very life for you. Even if it's against his wishes, I can't bear having you not know.'

Yasuko's heart was racing. Her breathing had grown shallow; she felt as if she might faint.

'I'm not sure what you're trying to say.' She meant to speak forcefully, but her voice came out weak and trembling. 'If . . . If you have something to tell me, please do.'

'He killed that man, the one that was found by the Old Edogawa.' Yukawa took a deep breath. 'Ishigami was the killer. Not you, or your daughter. He's not turning himself in for a crime he didn't commit. He's guilty of murder.'

Yasuko gaped, not comprehending what she was hearing.

'However,' Yukawa added, 'that body did not belong to Shinji Togashi. That was not your ex-husband. He was a complete stranger made to appear to be your ex-husband.'

Yasuko knitted her brow in disbelief, but when she saw the physicist's eyes blinking with sorrow, the tears gathering on the lenses of his glasses, suddenly she understood. She gasped, darting a hand to her mouth, almost yelling in surprise. The blood drained from her face.

'Looks like you finally understand what I'm trying to tell you,' Yukawa said softly. 'Yes. In order to protect you, Ishigami committed murder – on March 10. The day after Shinji Togashi was killed.'

Yasuko felt her head spinning. She swayed dizzily, struggling to remain upright on the bench. Her hands and legs had gone cold; her skin prickled as if with a thousand thorns.

Even from a distance, it was clear to Kusanagi that Yukawa had told the woman the truth. Her face had gone completely pale. *Unsurprising*, Kusanagi thought. He didn't know anyone who wouldn't be shocked by the story, least of all someone so directly involved.

Kusanagi still didn't entirely believe it himself. He had practically scoffed when Yukawa had told him his theory on the way there. Not that he could imagine why his friend would joke about such things – it just seemed like such an unrealistic story.

'That's impossible,' Kusanagi had said. 'He killed someone else to cover up Yasuko Hanaoka's crime? Who would do something so stupid? And for that matter, who did he kill?'

Yukawa had looked even sadder at that question and had shaken his head. 'I don't know what his name was. But I know where he was from.'

'What do you mean by that?'

'There are people in this world who could disappear overnight and no one would bother looking for them, or worry where they had gone. I'll bet no one even filed a missing persons report. Whoever it was most likely had no contact with their family any more, if their family is even alive.' Yukawa had pointed back along the riverbank

348

down the path where they had just been walking. 'You saw them back there.'

Kusanagi hadn't understood what Yukawa was saying at first. But as he looked back down the riverbank, a light had flashed on in his head. 'The homeless!'

Yukawa hadn't nodded. He had only said, 'Did you notice the fellow collecting those empty cans? He knows everything about the people living in his community. I talked to him the other day, and he told me there was this guy who had joined them only a month before. Not a friend, just someone who had chosen to live there with them. He hadn't built a shack of his own yet, and still had an aversion to sleeping on cardboard. The Can Man told me that everyone was like that at first – it's hard to give up your pride – but in the end, they all broke. Anyhow, this new arrival disappeared one day, without so much as a word of parting. The Can Man wondered what had happened to him, but that was all. Some of the other people living there must've noticed, too, but no one talked about it. It's not unusual in their world for people to just go missing like that.

'Incidentally,' Yukawa had continued, 'this man disappeared on or around March 10. He was about fifty years old. He'd put on a little weight, but was otherwise of average build.'

The body on the Old Edogawa had been found on March 11.

'I'm not sure exactly how it happened, but

Ishigami must have learned of Yasuko Hanaoka's crime, and he'd decided to help her conceal it. He realized that it wouldn't be enough to simply dispose of the body. If the police should find and identify it, they would inevitably come knocking on her door. And once the questioning started, he wasn't sure how long she and her daughter could continue pretending they didn't know anything about it. So, he decided on a different plan: he would kill someone else and then make the corpse look like Shinji Togashi. Then he would slowly reveal to the police when and how the victim had been slain. The more the investigation progressed, the less suspicion would fall on Yasuko Hanaoka. Why should it? She didn't kill that man by the river. That wasn't evidence of the murder of Shinji Togashi. You were on an entirely separate case and you didn't even know it.'

It had been hard to believe that the story Yukawa was telling him could be true. Kusanagi had shaken his head the whole time he was listening to it.

'I think the solution only occurred to Ishigami because he often walked along the river here. He'd had plenty of time to consider the homeless who lived there and their lives. Why were they living at all? Were they just killing time, waiting there for the day when they would eventually die? When they died, would anyone notice? Would anyone care? That's what I imagine him thinking.'

'So because of that he thought it would be all right to kill one of them?' Kusanagi had asked.

'Certainly not "all right". But when he was putting his plan together, I'm certain he wouldn't have forgotten them or their particular circumstances. Remember what I told you. He's a man capable of doing anything as long as it makes logical sense.'

'And murder is logical?'

'A murdered body was the piece he needed to complete his puzzle.'

The story was, frankly, unbelievable. And hearing Yukawa deliver it, almost as if he was giving a lecture to his students, had made Kusanagi wonder about his friend.

'On the morning after Yasuko Hanaoka killed Shinji Togashi, Ishigami made contact with a homeless man. I'm not sure exactly what transpired between them, but it's pretty safe to say he offered the man a job. His job description was to first go to the room Shinji Togashi had been renting and hang out there until evening. Ishigami had spent the night before removing all traces of Shinji Togashi's presence from the room. The only fingerprints and hair that would be left in the room would belong to the homeless man. That night, the man was to go to a place indicated by Ishigami, wearing clothes he had given him.'

'Shinozaki Station?' Kusanagi had asked, but Yukawa had shaken his head.

'No. Probably the stop before that. Mizue.'

'Why Mizue?'

'Ishigami stole a bicycle from Shinozaki Station

351

and went to meet the man at Mizue Station. It's highly likely that Ishigami had left another bicycle there for himself. The two of them rode together to the banks along the Old Edogawa River, where Ishigami killed the man. He smashed his face to hide the fact that he wasn't Shinji Togashi. Technically, he didn't have to burn off the man's fingerprints, because he had already planted them in Togashi's rented room, which would have led the police to believe that it was Togashi's body anyway. Yet if he had crushed the man's face and not removed his fingerprints, leaving the job half done as it were, it would have raised suspicion. His hand was forced by his fear that it might take too long for the police to discover the body's identity. Which is why he left fingerprints on the bicycle. For the same reason he left the man's clothes only half burned.'

'But I don't see the reason why he had to steal a new bicycle for all that.'

'Ishigami stole a new bicycle to hedge his bets.'

'What bets?'

'Ishigami needed to make sure that the police correctly ascertained the time of the homeless man's murder. He knew the autopsy would reveal a relatively accurate time of death, but he was afraid the body might not get discovered in time, which would make an accurate time of death much harder to determine. If the span of the possible time of death extended to the evening of the day before, in other words, the evening of March 9, that would be very bad for his plan because *that* was the evening when Togashi actually was killed. Neither Yasuko Hanaoka nor her daughter had an alibi for then. To prevent that from happening, he needed proof that the bicycle had been stolen on or after the tenth. Which is why he chose the one he did – a bicycle that most likely had been left there for less than a day, so the owner would be able to determine roughly when it had been stolen.'

'So the bike came in handy in more than one way for him,' Kusanagi said, smacking himself on the forehead with his own fist.

'I heard that when the bicycle was found both tires were flat. Ishigami did that to prevent someone else from riding off with it. He did everything he could to make sure the Hanaoka's alibi would stand.'

'But why provide them with such a weak alibi, then? We still haven't found decisive evidence that they really were at that cinema.'

'Yet you haven't been able to find evidence they weren't there either, have you?' Yukawa had pointed out. 'A weak alibi that nevertheless stands up under pressure. That was the trap he laid for you, don't you see? If he had given them an iron-clad alibi, the police would have had to point their suspicions elsewhere. They might even suspect a bait and switch. Someone *might* even get the bright idea that the victim they'd found wasn't really Shinji Togashi. Ishigami was afraid of that, so he made everything point to Yasuko Hanaoka as the killer, and Shinji Togashi as the victim. Once the police took the bait, they were hooked.'

Kusanagi had groaned. It was just as Yukawa had said. Once they'd determined that the body was likely Shinji Togashi's, they started to suspect Yasuko. Why? Because her alibi was flimsy. So they continued suspecting her, which meant they'd never suspected that the body wasn't that of her ex-husband.

'What a frightening man,' Kusanagi had whispered. And Yukawa had agreed. 'It was something you said that led me to the true nature of his scheme, actually.'

'Something I said?'

'Remember what Ishigami told you about his method of designing mathematics exams? About coming at the test-taker from a blind spot created by their own assumptions? Like making an algebra problem look like a geometry problem?'

'Yeah? What about it?'

'It's the same pattern. He made a trick body look like a trick alibi.'

Kusanagi had practically yelped.

'Remember afterwards, when you showed me Ishigami's work schedule from his school? He'd taken the morning of the tenth as well as the morning of the eleventh off from work. That's what tipped me off to the fact that the incident Ishigami really wanted to hide had taken place not the night of the tenth, but the night of the ninth.'

That incident was the murder of Shinji Togashi at the hands of Yasuko Hanaoka.

Everything Yukawa had said fit the case precisely. In fact, everything the physicist had been obsessing over – from the stolen bicycle to the half-burned clothes – had turned out to be vital pieces of the puzzle. Kusanagi had to admit that he, along with every other detective that had looked into the case, had been caught in a labyrinth of Ishigami's design.

Yet it all still seemed too unreal to be true. Killing a person to hide a murder – who would think of something like that? *Of course, that's the point. He didn't want us to think of it.*

'There's another side to his setup,' Yukawa said then, as though he could read Kusanagi's thoughts. 'Ishigami planned to turn himself in in Yasuko's place should things fall apart. But if he were really taking her place of his own free will, there was always the danger that his resolve might waver. He might even break under repeated police questioning and cough up the truth. I doubt he feels any such threat to his resolve now, though. All he has to do is claim that he was the killer, which, of course, is quite true. He is a murderer, and deserves to be in prison. In exchange for paying his debt to society, he gets to protect, utterly and forever, the person whom he loves with all his heart.'

'So when did Ishigami realize the jig was up?'

'I told him as much, in a way that only he would

understand. What I told you earlier, about there being no useless cog in our society – how only a cog can determine how it is used – you know what I meant by that, don't you?'

'You're talking about our nameless victim Ishigami used as the final piece in his puzzle.'

'What Ishigami did is unforgivable. He *should* have turned himself in. And that was why I talked to him about the cogs. I just didn't guess he would go about it in quite the way he did. To protect her by making himself out to be a stalker – that was when I realized how deep his plan went.'

'So where is Shinji Togashi's body?'

'I have no idea. Ishigami must have disposed of it in some fashion. Perhaps some prefectural police department has found him already, or maybe they haven't.'

'Prefectural? You mean somewhere outside of our jurisdiction?'

'He would avoid this area, yes. He didn't want the murder of Shinji Togashi being linked to his own crime if he could possibly avoid it.'

'So that's why you were looking at newspapers in the library. You were checking to see if another unidentified body had been found.'

'And I found nothing where the corpse matched Togashi's description. Though I'm sure he'll turn up sooner or later. I doubt he was all that thorough in hiding it. There would be no danger of *that* body being identified as Shinji Togashi, after all.'

'Well, I'd better start looking then,' Kusanagi said, but Yukawa shook his head.

'You promised. Remember? I've been talking to you as a friend, not a detective. If you choose to act on this information in your official capacity, then that's all we are. A detective and his informant.'

Yukawa's eyes were dead serious. *No arguing with him.*

'I'm going to throw the ball in her court. See what she does,' Yukawa had said then, pointing towards Benten-tei. 'I seriously doubt she knows the truth of what happened. She doesn't know the sacrifice Ishigami's made. I'll tell her. Wait and see what she decides to do. I'm sure Ishigami wants her to be happily ignorant of everything. But I cannot stand for that. I think she needs to know.'

'And you think she'll turn herself in when she hears what you have to say?'

'No idea. I don't really think she should turn herself in, myself, given the circumstances. When I think of what Ishigami would want, I'm inclined to say she should go free.'

'Well, if Yasuko Hanaoka doesn't eventually turn herself in, I'm going to have to start a new investigation. Even if it means the end of our friendship.'

'I understand.'

So Kusanagi had stood there, smoking cigarette after cigarette, watching his friend talk to Yasuko Hanaoka. Now Yasuko's head was slumped forward.

She barely shifted on the bench during the whole time Yukawa spoke to her. Now the physicist's lips were moving, but his expression never changed. Still, Kusanagi could feel the tension in the air around the two of them even from where he was standing at the entrance to the park.

At last Yukawa stood up from the bench. He bowed curtly in Yasuko's direction, then walked towards the detective. Yasuko remained sitting on the bench, slumped half over, unmoving.

'Thanks for waiting,' Yukawa said.

'You tell her everything?'

'Yep.'

'She say what she's going to do?'

'No. It was pretty much just me talking. I didn't ask what she was going to do, nor did I tell her what she ought to do. It's up to her now.'

'Well, like I said before, if she doesn't turn herself in—'

'I know,' Yukawa said as he began to walk away. Kusanagi walked with him, matching his stride. 'You don't have to say it. More importantly, I have a favour to ask of you.'

'You want to see Ishigami?'

Yukawa's eyes opened a little wider at that. 'How'd you guess?'

'How long have we been friends?'

'Oh, quite some time.' Yukawa shook his head, a lonely smile on his lips. 'Quite some time.'

CHAPTER 19

Yasuko sat motionless on the bench. She felt the weight of everything she'd been told like a physical sensation, heavier than she could imagine, so heavy it shocked every inch of her body. So heavy it felt like it might crush her heart.

How could he go so far?

Ishigami had never told her what he'd done with Togashi's body. He had said she didn't need to worry about it. *I've handled everything*, he had told her over the phone in that calm voice of his.

She had wondered why the police kept wanting an alibi for the day *after* Togashi was murdered. Even before the detectives had come, Ishigami had given her explicit instructions about what she was to do on the night of the tenth. The movie, ramen, karaoke, and even the late-night telephone call. She had done everything according to his instructions, not knowing why she was doing any of it. When the detectives asked about her alibi, she had told them exactly what she had done, but in truth she had wanted to ask them: *why are you asking me about the tenth?*

Now it all made sense. Ishigami had led them into a trap. And yet, what a terrible trap it was. Even though she realized that there could be no other explanation, she still didn't believe it. No, she didn't want to believe it. She didn't want to think Ishigami had done what he had done. She didn't want to think about how he had thrown away his life for an average middle-aged woman with hardly any redeeming qualities, and certainly no great allure. Yasuko didn't think her heart was strong enough to accept such a sacrifice.

She covered her face in her hands. She wished her mind could stop working. She didn't want to think about anything. Yukawa had said he wouldn't tell the police. It was all conjecture – he didn't have any proof. It was up to her to decide what was to be done. He had given her a choice. A spitefully cruel choice.

Uncertain of what she should do, and lacking even the strength to stand, she crouched, frozen like a twisted stone, while the long minutes crawled by.

Suddenly someone tapped her on the shoulder. Her head jerked upward.

Someone was standing by the bench. Her eyes focused and she realized it was Kudo looking down at her, concern on his face.

'What's wrong?'

It took her a while to understand why Kudo was there. She stared blankly up at him for some time before she remembered that they'd planned to meet. He must have come looking for her when she wasn't at the restaurant.

'I'm sorry. I was . . . tired.' She couldn't think of a better excuse than that. And it was true. She was exhausted. Not her body, but her soul.

'Are you sick?' Kudo's voice was gentle.

Too gentle, to Yasuko's ears, and entirely out of place. Not knowing the truth could be a crime in and of itself, she realized. A crime she had been committing until only moments before.

'I'm . . . all right.' Hesitantly Yasuko stood. She wobbled, and Kudo offered his arm.

'Did something happen? You look pale.'

Yasuko shook her head. She couldn't explain what had happened. Not to him. Not to anyone.

'It's nothing. I felt a little queasy and had to rest. But I think it's passed now.' She tried to sound confident, but lacked the strength.

'My car is parked right over there. Do you want to rest a bit first before we go?'

She met his eyes. 'Go where?'

'I've made reservations at a restaurant. I told them seven, but I don't think it will matter if we're a half hour late.'

'Oh.'

The very word *restaurant* sounded like something alien. Would she have to go to a restaurant and eat now? Would she have to pretend to smile with this black lump in her chest? Smile, and nod, and daintily wield her fork and knife? Not that any of this was Kudo's fault.

'I'm sorry,' Yasuko whispered. 'I don't think I can. Not tonight. I think I need to take a rain check until I'm feeling better. Today I am . . . I'm just . . .'

'Hey, it's okay,' Kudo said, patting her arm. 'I think you're right. It's no wonder you're tired, with all you've been through. Rest today. You probably haven't had a chance to really rest for some time. I should have left you alone. It was thoughtless of me. I'm sorry.'

Yasuko looked at Kudo, marvelling at how genuinely nice he was. He truly cared for her. It made her sad to wonder why she couldn't be happy with so much love to be had.

She walked beside him, his hand resting lightly against her back. His car was parked a short distance down the road. When they reached it, he offered to drive her home. She knew she should refuse, but decided to let him do so anyway. The trip back to her apartment felt like it was an impossibly long distance to travel alone.

'Are you sure you're okay?' Kudo asked again as they got into the car. 'If something has happened, don't feel you need to hide it from me.'

It's no wonder he's worried, she thought, *with the way I must look right now*. 'No, I'm okay, really. I'm sorry.' She smiled at him, a performance that took all of her remaining strength.

She *was* sorry, in so many ways. And it reminded her that Kudo had a reason for coming to meet her today.

'Kudo – you said you had something important to discuss with me?'

'Oh, that's right.' He looked down. 'Well, maybe today isn't the best time.'

'You sure?'

'Yes.' He started the car.

Yasuko let the motion of the vehicle rock her gently in her seat as she stared out the window. The sun had set. Night had come to the city. *How easy it would be if everything went dark, and the world ended right here, right now. What a relief it would be.*

Kudo's car stopped in front of Yasuko's apartment building. 'Rest up. I'll call.'

She nodded, and laid her hand on the door handle; but as she began to open the door Kudo blurted out,

'Wait—'

Yasuko turned back to look at him. He wet his lips and slapped his hands down on the steering wheel. 'Maybe now is a good time, after all.' Kudo slid one hand into his suit pocket and pulled out a small blue jewellery case. Yasuko knew what it meant at a glance.

'They have scenes like this all the time on those television shows, so it feels kind of cheesy now, but I suppose it's the accepted ritual, so—' He opened the box in front of her. It held a ring. A large diamond caught the rays of the fading day and sent shimmers in every direction.

'Kudo . . .' Yasuko's mouth hung open; she stared amazedly into Kudo's face.

'Don't feel you have to give me an answer right away,' he said. 'There're Misato's feelings to consider, not to mention yours! I just want you to know that I'm not doing this on a whim. I know I can make you happy, both of you.' He took Yasuko's hand and placed the box in it. 'Take this, but don't let it be a burden. This is just a present. If you should decide you would like to live with me, then the ring will mean what it is intended to mean. Please, think about it.'

Feeling the weight of the small case in her hand, Yasuko's mind went blank. She only heard half of what he was saying. Still she understood – which only fuelled her confusion.

'Sorry. I know it's sudden.' Kudo grinned sheepishly. 'You really don't have to rush your response. I do want you to talk to Misato, too.' He reached out and closed the lid of the case in her hand. 'There.'

Yasuko couldn't think of what to say. Words seemed almost inaccessible. There were too many images racing through her head. Pictures of Kudo, and Togashi, and Ishigami – mostly Ishigami.

'I . . . I'll think about it,' she managed at last.

Kudo nodded, apparently satisfied. Yasuko smiled back and got out of the car.

She watched as he drove off, then went up to her apartment. As she was opening the door, her eyes were inevitably drawn to the next door down the hall. The mail slot there was overflowing with letters, but there was no newspaper. Ishigami must have cancelled his subscriptions before turning himself in. He had probably done it automatically, a common courtesy with no more significance for him then the act of waking up in the morning. She stepped inside.

Misato wasn't home yet. Yasuko sat and breathed a long ragged sigh. Then she got to her feet again and went into the back room. She took down a cookie box from a shelf there and removed the lid. The container held a collection of old letters. She lifted the entire bundle, removing one from the very bottom. Nothing was written on the envelope. It contained a single piece of ruled report paper, covered with writing.

Ishigami had put the envelope in her apartment mailbox before making his final call on that last evening. In it she had found the note it still held, as well as three letters – all of them supposed proof of how he had been a stalker. She had surrendered the three letters to the police as evidence.

The note told her how to use the letters, and what she should tell the detectives when they came to talk to her, all in Ishigami's customary detail. There were instructions not only for Yasuko, but for Misato as well. It covered everything, every situation they might find themselves in, ensuring that no matter what befell the Hanaokas, they would know what to do. It was because of his instructions that Yasuko and Misato had been able to handle the police. Yasuko knew that if she made a misstep and the detectives saw through the deception, all of

Ishigami's hard work would go up in smoke. Misato must have known that, too.

At the very end of his instructions he had added a final message:

'I believe Kuniaki Kudo to be a loyal and trustworthy man. Marrying him will certainly increase the probability that you and Misato will be happy. Please forget about me. Feel no guilt. If you are not happy, all I have done will be for nothing.'

She read the letter again and fresh tears began to flow.

She had never encountered such deep devotion. She hadn't even thought it existed. Yet Ishigami had it, hidden away beneath that expressionless mask of a face – the kind of passion unfathomable to the average person.

When she heard that he had turned himself in, she had assumed that he was simply taking their place. But now that she'd heard the truth from Yukawa, the words Ishigami had left for her stabbed even deeper into her heart.

She thought about going to the police and telling them everything. But that wouldn't save Ishigami. He was a murderer, too, after all.

Her eyes fell on the jewellery box Kudo had given her. She opened the lid and watched the ring sparkle.

Maybe she should do what Ishigami wanted her to do – seize her chance at happiness. Maybe it was like he said: if she gave up now, all of his work would be for nothing.

366

Still, it was so hard to hide the truth. Would she ever really be able to be happy, with something so dark hidden inside? She would have to live the rest of her life with this guilt, never knowing true peace. *But maybe*, Yasuko thought, *enduring that guilt is a way of doing penance.*

She tried the ring on. The diamond was beautiful. How happy she would be if she could just run to Kudo, without a cloud in her heart! Yet that was a hopeless dream. Her conscience would never be clear.

She was putting the box away when her mobile phone rang. She peered at the LCD screen. The number was unfamiliar. She opened the phone.

'Yes?'

'Hello? Is this the mother of Misato Hanaoka?' It was a man's voice that she didn't recognize.

'Yes. Is something wrong?' She felt her stomach flutter.

'My name's Sakano. I'm a teacher at Morishita Minami Middle School. Sorry for the sudden nature of my call.'

'Is something wrong? Is Misato okay?'

'Actually, she was just found behind the gymnasium. It appears that her wrists were cut with a knife or some other sharp object.'

'What . . . ?' Yasuko's heart leapt into her throat and she gasped for breath.

'She was bleeding badly, so they took her to the hospital immediately. Don't worry, she'll be fine. However, there is a chance that this was an attempted suicide. I thought you should know so you could take the necessary steps—'

The man continued talking, but Yasuko didn't hear a word he said.

A countless number of stains, scratches, and other small marks covered the wall in front of Ishigami. He chose several at random, and in his mind connected them all with straight lines. The resulting matrix was made up of triangles, squares, and hexagons. He began painting the shapes with four separate colours, not allowing any two adjacent shapes to share the same colour. All of this he did in his head.

Ishigami finished the problem in less than a minute. Wiping the image, he chose different spots and repeated the process. It was the essence of simplicity, yet he could do it over and over without losing interest. If he grew weary of the four-colour problem, he decided he would just use the spots on the wall to define an analytical geometry problem. Calculating the coordinates of every spot on the wall would take a considerable amount of time.

And that was just using the spots on the wall. Who cared if he wasn't allowed to leave his room? As long as he had paper and something to write with, he could work on his maths problems. Even if the authorities were to bind his hands and feet, he could explore new proofs in his head. They could take away his sight, or his hearing, but they could not touch his brain. Confinement was like a limitless garden of paradise for him. *How short is a lifetime*, he thought, *compared to the time it will take humankind to find all the rich veins of mathematical ore where they lie sleeping and tease them forth into the world.*

Nor, he reflected, did he need anyone to acknowledge his work. Certainly he would have liked to publish his theories, to be recognized and reviewed; but that was not the true essence of mathematics. In academia it was always a race to see who would reach the summit of which particular mountain first, but as long as *he* knew which peaks he had discovered, that would be enough.

It had taken Ishigami some time to reach this place. Not very long ago, he had been reduced to the terrible conclusion that his life had lost its meaning. If his only talent was for mathematics, he had reasoned, and yet he could make no progress along that path, what was the value of his existence? Every day, he'd contemplated death, feeling that if he died, no one would be sad, or really much inconvenienced. He doubted anyone would even notice.

He remembered a certain day, only a year ago . . .

He was standing in his apartment with a short length of thick rope in his hand. He was looking for a place on the ceiling to attach it. But he soon found that apartments lack any appropriate fixtures for hanging oneself. Finally, unable to find a better alternative, he resorted to pounding a large nail into a support post in the wall. He fixed his noose to it carefully and tested his weight on it. The post creaked alarmingly, but the nail did not bend and the rope did not break.

He had no regrets. There would be no particular meaning to his death. Just like there had been no particular meaning to his life.

He was standing on a stool, trying to fit his head through the noose, when the doorbell rang.

It had to be fate.

He only answered it because he didn't want there to be any interruptions once he got started. Not knowing who was at the door, he had to consider that it might be an emergency. He couldn't count on them just leaving him alone.

He opened his door to find two women standing there – a mother and daughter, by the looks of them.

The mother introduced herself, saying that they would be his neighbours. Her daughter bowed curtly beside her. When he laid his eyes upon them, a single realization pierced Ishigami's entire being.

How beautiful their eyes are, he thought. Until that moment, he had never been carried away by beauty of any kind. He didn't even understand art. But in that moment, he understood everything. The very same beauty he found in unravelling a mathematics problem was standing right there before him.

Ishigami didn't remember clearly what the women had said. But the way their eyes had shifted as they looked at him, every blink of their eyelids, was burned into his memory.

Ishigami's life changed after he met the Hanaokas; in that moment he was renewed. All thought of suicide faded. Joy returned to his daily rituals. It made him happy just imagining where the two of them might be, what they might be doing. He had added the coordinates of Yasuko and Misato to the matrix of his life, and to him, it seemed like a miracle had occurred.

Sunday was his happiest day. If he opened his window, he could hear the two of them talking. He couldn't make out what they said, but the faint voices that drifted to him along the wind were like the sweetest music to Ishigami's ears.

He held no aspirations of ever being anything to them. He knew he should never even attempt to make contact. It was like his relationship with mathematics: it was enough merely to be associated with something so sublime. To seek any kind of acknowledgment would sully its dignity.

Yet when trouble arrived and they needed help, it was only natural for Ishigami to go to their aid. After all, if they hadn't been there for him, he would no longer be alive. He was returning the greatest of favours. They certainly had no idea what they had done, but that was okay. Sometimes, all you had to do was exist in order to be someone's saviour.

When he saw Togashi's body, Ishigami already had a programme in his head ready to load. It would be difficult to completely dispose of the body. No matter how carefully he did so, he could never reduce the chances of discovery to a perfect zero. And even if he got lucky and succeeded in concealing what had happened, it would do nothing to ease the pain in Yasuko's heart. She and her daughter would live in constant fear of discovery. He could not bear to visit such hardship on them.

There was only one way to put Yasuko and her daughter truly at peace. He would have to detach them completely from the case. He would make it seem as though they were connected, and yet there could be no doubt that they had nothing to do with the murder.

That was when he decided to use the Engineer – the homeless man who had so recently begun living at the camp near Shin-Ohashi Bridge. It all worked quite smoothly.

In the early morning of March 10, Ishigami had approached the Engineer. He had found him sitting apart from the other homeless as usual.

'I have a job for you,' Ishigami had told the man. He explained that he wanted him to help as an observer on a riverworks project that would last several days. He had noticed that the Engineer had a background in construction.

The Engineer had been suspicious at first. 'Why me?' he had asked.

372

'Well,' Ishigami had explained, 'I'm in a bit of a tight situation.' And he'd told how the man he had previously asked to observe had been in an accident and was now unable to do the job – and, without an observer there, his firm wouldn't get permission to proceed with the work. He needed someone to stand in for the absent man.

He'd offered an advance of fifty thousand yen, and the Engineer had agreed. Ishigami had then taken the man to the rental room where Togashi had been saying. There he'd given him Togashi's clothes to put on and had told him to sit tight until that evening.

When evening came, he'd brought the Engineer out to Mizue Station. Ishigami had stolen a bicycle from Shinozaki Station in advance. He had chosen the newest bicycle he could find, to assure that the owner would promptly report the theft.

He had prepared another bicycle as well. This one he had stolen from Ichinoe, the station before Mizue. It was an old bicycle, with a broken lock.

He'd given the new bicycle to the Engineer, and the two of them had gone to the river, soon arriving at the spot along the Old Edogawa.

Remembering what happened next made Ishigami's heart fill with darkness. The Engineer never knew why he had to die.

Ishigami couldn't have anyone know about the second murder – especially not the Hanaokas. That was why he had used the very same murder weapon and had strangled the victim in the very same way.

Togashi's body he had cut into six parts in his bathtub, tossing each one separately into the Sumida River in bags weighted down with heavy rocks. He did this all under cover of darkness, in three separate locations on three separate nights. He knew that at least some of them would be found at some point, but he didn't care. The police would never be able to learn to whom the body parts belonged. According to their records, Togashi would have already been dead and his body found – and a man couldn't die twice.

He was pretty sure that only Yukawa had figured it all out. Which was why Ishigami had chosen to turn himself in to the police. This, after all, was something he had been ready to do from the very beginning, and for which he had already made the necessary preparations.

Yukawa would talk to Kusanagi. Kusanagi would then inform his superior. But the police wouldn't act. At that point, there would be no way to prove they had misidentified the body. Meanwhile, Ishigami would be charged with Togashi's murder.

There was no turning back now. Nor was there any reason to stop the plan he'd set in motion. No matter how brilliant the deductions of that genius physicist might be, they had no hope of prevailing against an actual criminal's confession in court.

I've won, he thought.

He heard a buzzer sound. It was the signal that indicated that there were visitors to the holding cell. The guard rose from his chair.

After a brief negotiation, someone entered the cell area. It was Kusanagi. He waited in front of the bars while the guard ordered Ishigami from his cell. The mathematician was searched, then handed over to Kusanagi. The detective didn't say a word while all this was happening.

Outside the holding cell, Kusanagi turned to Ishigami and asked, 'How are you feeling?'

Ishigami couldn't tell whether it was the detective's custom to be polite, or if this was part of some ploy.

'A little tired, to tell the truth. To be honest, I'd like to get through the legal proceedings as quickly as possible.'

'Don't worry, this will be the last time I'll be taking you out for questioning. There's someone here to see you.'

Ishigami frowned. *Who could it be?* Not Yasuko, he hoped.

Kusanagi led him to the interrogation room and opened the door. Manabu Yukawa sat inside. He stared at Ishigami, a pensive look on his face.

The final hurdle, Ishigami thought, bracing himself.

For a time, the two geniuses sat across the table from each other in silence. Kusanagi leaned against the wall, keeping an eye on them.

'You're looking a little thin,' Yukawa said at last.

'Oh? I've been eating fine.'

'Good to hear. I wanted to ask you,' Yukawa

licked his lips. 'Aren't you embarrassed at all to be labelled a stalker?'

'But I'm not a stalker,' Ishigami replied. 'To the contrary, I've been protecting Yasuko Hanaoka, though not openly. I've told the police this several times already.'

'I know what you told them. And I know you continue to protect her even now.'

Ishigami looked displeased and glanced up towards Kusanagi. 'How is this discussion going to help your investigation?'

Kusanagi said nothing.

'I told him what I know,' Yukawa said. 'I told him what you really did, and who you really killed.'

'I'm sure you're free to discuss your conjectures with whomever you wish.'

'I've also told her – Yasuko Hanaoka.'

The skin of Ishigami's cheeks drew taut across his face. But he soon managed a thin smile. 'Did she show some remorse, maybe? Was she thankful to me? From all I've heard, she's been going on like I did nothing for her – like I never got rid of that thorn in her side.'

Kusanagi swallowed, watching Ishigami's face twist as he played the role of spurned stalker to perfection. He hadn't realized it was possible for anyone to devote himself so utterly to another. It was as impressive as it was terrifying.

'You seem to be suffering under the belief that as long as you don't tell the truth it will never come to light, but you're not entirely correct,'

376

Yukawa said. 'A man went missing on March 10. An innocent man, guilty of nothing. If we were to find out who he was, and find his family, we could do some DNA testing. Compare those results with the results from the body thought to be Shinji Togashi, and we'll know the truth.'

'I'm not sure what you're going on about,' Ishigami said, smiling. 'But whoever this man you mentioned was, he probably didn't have a family. And even if there was some other way of finding out who he was, it would take a staggering amount of time and effort to do so. By the time you're done, I will already have been tried and convicted. Rest assured I'll plead guilty. Once the verdict is announced, the case will be closed. The murder of Shinji Togashi will have been solved. The police's hands will be tied. Or maybe—' He looked at Kusanagi. 'Maybe you'll listen to this guy's story and change your mind about charging me. Which means you'd have to let me go. But on what grounds? Because I'm not a criminal? I assure you, I am. I'm a confessed murderer.'

Kusanagi looked down at the floor. It was true. As long as they couldn't prove Ishigami's confession false, it was impossible to stop the legal proceedings. That wasn't how the system worked.

'There's one thing I need to tell you,' Yukawa said.

Ishigami looked back at him and raised an eyebrow.

'It fills me with regret to think that that brain

of yours, that wonderful brain, had to be used like this. It saddens me, truly. Like it saddens me to think that I will be losing a companion – and a competitor – like no other in this world.'

Ishigami's mouth formed a single straight line across his face, and he lowered his eyes, as if he was resisting the urge to reply.

After a moment, he looked back up at Kusanagi. 'I believe he's done talking. Can I go back to my cell now?'

Kusanagi looked at Yukawa. The physicist nodded quietly.

Kusanagi opened the door. Ishigami left first; Yukawa followed more slowly.

Once outside the room, Yukawa stood aside while Kusanagi led Ishigami back towards the holding cell. Then two figures appeared approaching down an intersecting hallway. It was Kishitani, with a woman following behind him.

Yasuko Hanaoka.

'What's this all about?' Kusanagi inquired of the junior detective.

'Sir, I . . . that is, Ms Hanaoka contacted the station and said she had something to tell us, and you won't believe what she said—'

'Wait – did she tell this to just you?'

'No, the chief was there, too.'

Kusanagi looked at Ishigami. The mathematician's face was the colour of ash. His bloodshot eyes stared at Yasuko. 'What are you doing here . . . ?' he said in a voice barely more than a whisper.

Yasuko stood frozen behind the detective. Then, gradually, her expression began to fall apart. Tears came streaming from her eyes. She stepped out in front of Ishigami and suddenly threw herself to the floor, bowing.

'I'm sorry. I'm so very sorry. What you did for us . . . that thing you did for us—' Her back shuddered as she spoke.

'What are you saying? What the hell do you think you're doing? What the hell . . .' Ishigami droned, his voice unearthly, as if he were chanting the words to some spell.

'I know you wanted us to be happy, but that's . . . that's impossible. I should pay for what I did, too. I'm to blame, too. I'll take the blame with you, Mr Ishigami. That's the only thing I can do for you. I'm sorry. I'm sorry. I'm so very, very sorry.' Yasuko crouched with both hands on the floor, her head resting against the tiles.

Ishigami stepped backward, shaking his head convulsively. His features were twisted with pain.

Then he whirled around, pressing his fists to his temples, and howled – a long, roaring howl like that of a beast. A cry of confusion and desperation. A cry that tore at the hearts of all who heard it.

Two guards ran over to restrain him.

'Leave him alone,' Yukawa barked, appearing between them and Ishigami. 'The least you can do is just let him cry.'

Yukawa turned towards Ishigami, laying his hands gently on the bigger man's shoulders.

Kusanagi watched as Ishigami screamed, and it seemed to him as if the mathematician was shouting out his very soul.